LIGHT OUT AND MODERN VIETNAMESE STORIES, 1930–1954

I0651770

A volume in the

NIU Southeast Asian Series

Edited by Kenton Clymer

For a list of books in the series, visit our website at cornellpress.cornell.edu.

LIGHT OUT AND MODERN VIETNAMESE STORIES, 1930–1954

TRANSLATED BY
QUAN MANH HA AND
PAUL CHRISTIANSEN

NORTHERN ILLINOIS UNIVERSITY PRESS

AN IMPRINT OF CORNELL UNIVERSITY PRESS
Ithaca and London

Copyright © 2024 by Quan Manh Ha and
Paul Christiansen

All rights reserved. Except for brief quotations in
a review, this book, or parts thereof, must not be
reproduced in any form without permission in
writing from the publisher. For information, address
Cornell University Press, Sage House, 512 East State
Street, Ithaca, New York 14850. Visit our website at
cornellpress.cornell.edu.

First published 2024 by Cornell University Press

Page 219 constitutes an extension of this copyright page.

Library of Congress Cataloging-in-Publication Data

Names: Ha, Quan Manh, translator. | Christiansen,
    Paul, 1986– translator. | Ngô, Tất Tố, 1892–1954.
    Tắt đèn. English.
Title: "Light out" and modern Vietnamese stories,
    1930–1954 / translated by Quan Manh Ha and Paul
    Christiansen.
Description: Ithaca : Northern Illinois University Press,
    an imprint of Cornell University Press, 2024. | Series:
    NIU series in Southeast Asian studies | Includes
    bibliographical references.
Identifiers: LCCN 2024017399 (print) | LCCN
    2024017400 (ebook) | ISBN 9781501778025
    (hardcover) | ISBN 9781501778032 (paperback) |
    ISBN 9781501778049 (epub) | ISBN
    9781501778056 (pdf)
Subjects: LCSH: Vietnamese fiction—20th century—
    Translations into English. | Vietnam—Social life and
    customs—20th century—Fiction. | LCGFT: Novellas. |
    Short stories.
Classification: LCC PL4378.82.E5 L54 2024
    (print) | LCC PL4378.82.E5 (ebook) | DDC
    895.9/223208—dc23/eng/20240627
LC record available at https://lccn.loc.gov/2024017399
LC ebook record available at https://lccn.loc.
    gov/2024017400

"Carrion Eaters" ("Thịt người chết"), by Nguyễn Công
Hoan. First published *Tạp chí Annam,* no. 23, 1931.
Copyright © 2023 by the author's grandson Lê Trung
Trực.

Contents

LIGHT OUT AND MODERN VIETNAMESE
STORIES, 1930–1954

Introduction

Quan Manh Ha and Paul Christiansen

Ngô Tất Tố's most famous novella, *Light Out* (Tắt Đèn), first published in 1939, denounces the French colonizers' draconian policies and ruthless treatment of the locals. In response, the colonial government banned the book in 1939 and inspected the author's house. Ngô was then detained for a few months in Hà Nội.[1] In the mid-1930s, floods ravaged north-central Vietnam's countryside, causing widespread poverty and famine. Peasants lived in desperation but were still forced to pay exorbitant taxes imposed by the French. Ngô wrote *Light Out* to address this historical situation and to show his empathy with the illiterate, indigent peasantry—the subalterns in colonial society. Our translation of *Light Out* came about when we realized that despite the popularity of the novella in Vietnam and the importance of Ngô Tất Tố in the country's twentieth-century literary canon, no currently in-print English version existed. Considering the insights the book offers into a period of Vietnamese history that is not often depicted in translated literature, we embarked on the project. For the second part of our book, we have included eighteen short stories

---

1. Nguyễn Việt Chiến, "Đằng sau chuyện 'thị phi' về sự ra đi của nhà văn Ngô Tất Tố," *Công An Nhân Dân Online* (Hà Nội, Vietnam), 13 May 2019, https://cand.com.vn/Tu-lieu-van-hoa/Dang-sau-chuyen-thi-phi-ve-su-ra-di-cua-nha-van-Ngo-Tat-To-i521021/.

written by Ngô Tất Tố's contemporaries to give the reader a broader picture of Vietnamese society and the literary landscape in the first half of the twentieth century, which was characterized by political turmoil, colonialism, poverty, economic depression, and revolution. These short stories thematically align with *Light Out*. They not only reinforce the themes addressed in the novella but also emphasize the role of the writer in contemporary civil society. Some of them are literary manifestos that still resonate today.

Western historians have written about major historical milestones in Vietnam during the first half of the twentieth century because they are interested in examining "how Vietnam became the vortex of intense international and domestic competitions for power," as David G. Marr states in *Vietnam 1945: The Quest for Power*.[2] Not much Vietnamese literature of the period 1930 through 1954 has been translated into English, although many prominent Vietnamese authors wrote remarkable literary works that not only vividly capture the realities of life truthfully but also reflect the literary movements and ideologies embraced and rejected by the intelligentsia at the time. It should be noted that male authors dominated Vietnamese literature in the first half of the twentieth century, primarily because not many women were literate or had the opportunity to advance their educations. The strongly patriarchal order that prevailed in Vietnamese society extended to literary production. In addition, more than 90 percent of the population was illiterate. This issue of literacy versus illiteracy is touched on numerous times in the book. Being able to read and write immediately distinguishes a character as of the upper middle class and thus becomes a stand-in for virtue, refinement, and ability. For example, in "The First Love Letter," by Tô Hoài, the character Mì is described as "by no means stuck up, but it wasn't easy to win her heart because of her beauty and literacy." Similarly, in Nam Cao's "The Eyes," Hoàng and his wife take great pride in being able to distinguish themselves from the country folks who cannot spell words correctly, expressed via the fact that they end their evenings reading from Chinese epics.

Many young Vietnamese writers were educated in France, and when they returned to Vietnam, they enthusiastically instituted significant reforms in Vietnamese literature, which had been heavily influenced by feudalistic and Confucian philosophy and traditional aesthetic modes.

---

2. David G. Marr, *Vietnam 1945: The Quest for Power* (Berkeley: University of California Press, 1997), xxiv.

As printing became easier, cheaper, and more widespread, literary journals and magazines that promoted the fiction genre, which was popular in France, proliferated. Most notably, the Self-Reliant Literary Group and the New Poetry movement liberated writers from outdated creative conventions and promoted fresher French ideas of self-liberation and individualism in the characters and plot developments in works of fiction, as well as in poetry. Martina Thucnhi Nguyen observes that the group laid out "a clear political agenda aimed at transforming and modernizing the everyday lives and experiences of the Vietnamese."[3] Various literary trends and movements coexisted and competed during this period: romanticism vied with critical realism, political literature vied with apolitical literature, and New Poetry vied with Old Poetry. Many writers were interested in depicting or satirizing the exploitive debauchery of the privileged class, while other writers drew inspiration for their fiction from the peasantry's domestic experiences and daily struggles to survive. According to the official accounts and narratives endorsed by the Vietnamese communist government, the birth of the Vietnamese Communist Party (VCP) in 1930 and the triumph of the August Revolution in 1945 had an ineffable impact on the role of the writer and the *raison d'être* of literature.[4] The literary critic Nguyễn Khắc Viện notes that the Party encouraged writers and artists to be more engaged in the country's revolution by composing texts that addressed "social and political reality" rather than texts that romanticized the lives of the common people and pastoral life.[5] For instance, in Nam Cao's "The Eyes," the Vietnamese title resonates metaphorically: the Vietnamese word implies differing points of view. The story contrasts the two main characters' perspectives about the August Revolution of 1945 against the French and the role of the Vietnamese peasantry in the revolution, and it highlights the responsibility of the artist in wartime Vietnam. The story is considered a major statement on literary aesthetics by later Vietnamese writers, especially those writing during the American War. In other words, literature must politically enlighten the masses with a revolutionary spirit, socialist agitation, and propaganda.

---

3. Martina Thucnhi Nguyen, *On Our Own Strength: The Self-Reliant Literary Group and Cosmopolitan Nationalism in Late Colonial Vietnam* (Honolulu: University of Hawai'i Press, 2020), 3.

4. Scholar Tuong Vu, in his book *Vietnam's Communist Revolution*, argues that the formation of the VCP "achieved little beyond an agreement among the groups [Đông Dương, Tân Việt, Annamese Communist Party, and Thanh Niên] to join a new organization, the VCP" (45).

5. Nguyễn Khắc Viện, "Historical Background," in *Vietnamese Literature*, ed. Nguyễn Khắc Viện and Hữu Ngọc (Hanoi: Red River, Foreign Languages Publishing House, 1986), 118.

The selected short stories demonstrate the richness and diversity of voices and perspectives in Vietnamese literature. Neither glamorized nor embellished, the depictions of hardships represent a shift away from the idealized experiences that were emerging in Vietnamese literature at the time. Many stories in this collection depict the quotidian lives of poverty-stricken peasants as well as of middle-class urbanites. Fueled by an emergent culture of literary magazines and an increase in overseas study, a focus on mundane realities was only one of the new writing styles being popularized. Nguyễn Công Hoan contrasts the plights of the Vietnamese peasants and the low-class proletarian citizens with the luxurious privileges of the upper class, while deriding corrupt local authorities and their lack of concern for the less fortunate members of society. In the chapter titled "The *Yin* of Early Modern Vietnamese Culture Challenges the *Yang* of Tradition, 1932–1939" of his book *Understanding Vietnam*, Neil L. Jamieson delineates factors that were conducive to social changes in Vietnamese society of the period, which many of the stories in this collection address. He writes, "In urban centers during the early 1930s, especially in Hanoi, there was a sudden and self-conscious rush to replace the old with the new, to Westernize, to be modern. The belief in progress was contagious, but its expression was often superficial, stressing the external trappings of change."[6] Vũ Trọng Phụng illustrates this contagion and mimicry effectively in his fiction, which often satirizes the Vietnamese who attempt to adopt and promote a Westernized lifestyle. Poverty, starvation, and illiteracy are prevalent in many of the stories as they highlight the damaging effects of French colonialism, including the exploitation of Vietnamese labor and natural resources. The characters portrayed in the stories include wealthy landowners, indigent peasants, writers, teachers, merchants, and urbanites. They come together to illustrate Vietnamese domestic realities and the larger societal circumstances that define the period in Vietnamese history. Across the stories, women bear an unequal share of burdens and household hardships. In Nam Cao's "Bright Moon," the protagonist's wife "ate very little so that her husband could have enough food. She sold her clothes to get medicine for him, but she didn't know that her sacrifices failed to make him happy." And even more drastically, in Thạch Lam's "Hunger," a woman attempts to surreptitiously prostitute herself to provide for her husband when he loses

---

6. Neil L. Jamieson, *Understanding Vietnam* (Berkeley: University of California Press, 1993), 100–101.

his job. Rather than acknowledge the sacrifice that his wife is not happy to be making, he vituperates her and wallows in self-pity. While gender inequalities certainly persist in modern-day Vietnam, the stories allow one to reflect on the progress made.

The reader will find an honest portrayal of the human condition reflected in common Vietnamese people affected physically and psychologically, as well as socially and economically, by conditions forced upon them by colonial exploitation, indigenous graft, and political abuse. Even Thạch Lam's "Moonlit Nights" and Tô Hoài's "The First Love Letter," which appear to be bittersweet romances, are to be understood within the larger context of circumstances prevailing in a country seeking to achieve a self-determined identity.

Regarding the first English translation of *Light Out*, in 1960, Phạm Như Oanh produced an English version of the novella titled *When the Light Is Out*, published by the Foreign Languages Publishing House in Hà Nội, but it has been out of print for many decades and is now difficult to find. Furthermore, this English edition has not been widely read outside Vietnam for the last sixty years. And while readable, Phạm's translation does not reflect current literary standards. We used her translation as a starting point, comparing her text with the original Vietnamese and making significantly different choices in language and format to more accurately capture the original Vietnamese while satisfying contemporary readers' expectations. Moreover, in his lifetime Ngô Tất Tố produced numerous versions of the novella, adding, changing, or removing various scenes and descriptions with each release. For our retranslation of the novella, we relied on the 2006 edition of the book in Vietnamese as promoted by the author's daughter, Ngô Thị Thanh Lịch, and her husband, Cao Đắc Điểm. They state in their introduction that, from 1937 to 2006, there were fifty-nine editions of the novella printed in Vietnam by various publishers, and their edition is closest to the author's original intent.

As with all translations from Vietnamese to English, we encountered familiar challenges as well as ones unique to this specific work. Regarding the former, there exists no perfectly satisfying way to translate Vietnamese's many gender and age-specific pronouns. We thus relied on *Mr.* and *Mrs.* when appropriate and in other circumstances replaced them with terms familiar to English readers that, regrettably, may lack the nuance of their Vietnamese counterparts. We also decided that the most accurate way to address Deputy Quế's wife was Madame Quế, as it is consistent with the characters' preference for colonial titles as a way to denote class.

As referenced by Ngô Văn Giá in his essay in our edition, Ngô Tất Tố's integration of French and Chinese influences resulted in a style that involved significant use of the passive voice. We attempted to retain this as much as possible along with his heavy use of adverbs. While neither may be as common today, we considered it essential to give readers a sense of the author's idiosyncratic style.

Readers of our translation will find numerous differences compared to that of Phạm Như Oanh's beyond variations in the versions of the Vietnamese texts used. We adhered to the author's frequent use of direct dialogue, which Phạm sometimes paraphrased and turned into indirect speech. We also incorporated more vulgarity. The Vietnamese spoken in the first half of the twentieth century did not have as many or as offensive swear words and phrases compared to English, but using euphemisms seemed disingenuous considering the characters speaking and the circumstances they were in. Phạm occasionally selected English proverbs while we preferred the original Vietnamese proverbs, even if they are unfamiliar to English readers. We also increased the number of footnotes, seeking a balance that provides necessary information but does not impede the reading experience.

Ultimately, this translation attempts to faithfully present the format, style, and content of the original while meeting the needs of contemporary readers. Our aim is to tell the story as Ngô Tất Tố intended while we remain aware that international audiences may not have the same cultural or linguistic knowledge as his target readers and some words or phrases have no perfect parallel across languages.

Light Out and Modern Vietnamese Short Stories, 1930–1954 illuminates Vietnamese history, literature, and culture of the colonial era and during the First Indochina War. They are canonical elements in Vietnam's educational system that are long overdue for broader exposure.

Bibliography

Jamieson, Neil L. *Understanding Vietnam*. Berkeley: University of California Press, 1993.

Marr, David G. *Vietnam 1945: The Quest for Power*. Berkeley: University of California Press, 1995.

Nguyễn, Chiến Việt. "Đằng sau chuyện 'thị phi' về sự ra đi của nhà văn Ngô Tất Tố." *Công An Nhân Dân Online* (Hà Nội, Vietnam), 13 May 2019. https://cand.com.vn/Tu-lieu-van-hoa/Dang-sau-chuyen-thi-phi-ve-su-ra-di-cua-nha-van-Ngo-Tat-To-i521021/.

Nguyen, Martina Thucnhi. *On Our Own Strength: The Self-Reliant Literary Group and Cosmopolitan Nationalism in Late Colonial Vietnam.* Honolulu: University of Hawai'i Press, 2020.

Nguyễn, Viện Khắc. "Historical Background." In *Vietnamese Literature*, edited by Nguyễn Khắc Viện and Hữu Ngọc, 25–191. Hanoi: Red River, Foreign Languages Publishing House, 1986.

Vu, Tuong. *Vietnam's Communist Revolution: The Power and Limits of Ideology.* Cambridge: Cambridge University Press, 2016.

PART I

Light Out

Light Out

Ngô Tất Tố

I

When the roosters started crowing, the plowmen were already lining the dirt road behind the watch station with their oxen and buffalos. By this hour, usually, the peasants and their cattle had already groped their way through the darkness and were working for their masters in the ricefields. But on this day, they had arrived to find the village gate hadn't yet been opened, and they were forced to scatter along the road-side like banner bearers waiting for some important mandarin.

The sounds of snorting buffalos, oxen flicking their tails, and men coughing rose from the dark shadows beneath a thick grove of bamboo beside the road. The flickering light from a small straw torch illuminated the interior of the watch station. Beside a row of poles and spears strewn against a wall, the village watchmen were huddled on a shabby, wrinkled mat. One man was lighting a flame; another was rolling a wad of tobacco and reaching for a pipe. Others yawned; some rubbed their eyes. One remained snoring, facing the wall with his head resting on a hunter's horn.

Five or six men passed around the pipe. After several rotations, the flame died and murmured conversation lifted into the air around the watch station.

The roosters cried repeatedly as the sky grew lighter.

The gathered oxen and buffalos stood or lay down, egg-sized balls of spit dropping from their mouths as they chewed their cud.

The peasants leaned against their plough handles and yokes, gossiping about taxes.

The drongos birds chirped from the tops of the bamboo, their onomatopoetic refrain *váy cô cô cởi* sounding like *she strips her skirt* as they imitated the songs of hoopoes at dawn.

The village gate remained locked, and the watchmen rekindled the flame and continued smoking.

"Chief watchman!" A voice rose in the darkness. "Please open the gate so that I can take my buffalo into the field. I should've plowed three *sào*[1] by now, but today I am still waiting. How will I be able to finish one *mẫu*[2] and two *sào* by noon? Please, be kind. . . ."

The chief watchman tossed the pipe down, exhaled a plume of smoke, and blinked his dull, bloodshot eyes. He spoke to the oafish peasant whose buffalo stood behind him at the end of a frayed rope.

"If you can't finish your work today, you can finish it tomorrow. The village mayor[3] says that a large percentage of the taxes are still to be collected and he won't let any oxen or buffalo into the field until they are."

"Sir, my master has a terrible temper," the peasant replied. "He told me to finish my work this morning or else he would beat me at lunch until I throw up. Besides, the mayor says he is keeping the gate locked to be able to confiscate the oxen and buffalos of those who haven't paid their taxes, but my master already paid his yesterday. So I must be allowed through."

"I'm neither a chieftain nor a tax collector, so I don't know whether your master has paid his taxes or not," the chief watchman frowned and said. "If I open the gate and the mayor scolds me, are you willing to take responsibility for that?"

The clumsy peasant shrank away from the gate, allowing another man to approach with his buffalo and harrow. "These other people own their buffalos so it's fine to not let them through, but I have to rent

---

1. 1 *sào* = 3,875 square feet.
2. 1 *mẫu* = 39,000 square feet.
3. The village mayor was not appointed by the feudal government. He was selected by the villagers and held the lowest-ranking administrative position with no monetary compensation.

this one for one piaster and twenty cents per half a day," the man said pleadingly. "I'd be very grateful if you would open the gate. It's already very late."

The chief watchman shook his head. "Then just work straight through the day until late afternoon. What do you care about the health of a hired buffalo?"

"I would, but the buffalo is worth a lot of money, and its owner won't let me have it all day. At exactly noon he will come to the field to get it back. He won't let me harrow a single furrow after then. This is prime planting season. Please consider it."

"There is nothing to consider," the chief watchman said. "Even if my father rose from the grave and asked me to open the gate, I wouldn't do it. So why would I do it for you?"

The peasant gave up and moved away from the gate. He looked dejected. The sun had risen to the top of the bamboo trees and was casting its rays into the watch station. One by one, the night watchmen left to go home, carrying their poles, mats, and hunter's horns. Only the chief watchman remained to supervise the junior watchmen who had daytime duty. He sprawled out on a mat that was filthy with tobacco ash.

A long rattling followed by an emergency pounding of a drum came from the direction of the communal house. Frightened, the buffalos and oxen that were lying down got to their feet.

With a register under his arm, one hand carrying a rattan rod and the other holding his rolled-up pants, the village mayor appeared, making his way to the watch station. "Damn it!" he shouted at the people he passed. "Their masters haven't paid their taxes yet! Whom do they try to put the blame on? If they don't pay, I'll seize their buffalos and oxen and sell them."

His tirade was so fierce that the gathered peasants stared in the direction of the communal house, shocked. Ever since the mayor of Đông Xá Village had returned from the district office five days earlier with the approved paperwork, he had been working hard to collect the taxes.

Once word of the collection efforts spread, the mayor ordered an announcer named Mới to go around to inform people of the policy. Then he sent out chieftains and tax collectors to speed up the process. He instructed his subordinates to accompany the canton chief's henchmen on their house visits. Rattles, drumbeats, and horn calls had filled the air over the past five days. From dawn to dusk chaos consumed the village, as if it were under siege. As the deadline to send the taxes to the district headquarters drew closer, the mayor became more desperate. The day before, he had requested the district's mandarin to send a chief orderly and two enforcers to punish anyone who was being stubborn. The mayor executed his power and shouted names all throughout the village.

The peasants and watchmen knew how arrogant the mayor could be and understood it was best to respond to his rebukes with silence. As the mayor passed, the buffalos and oxen wagged their ears, as if even they knew to show deference.

The mayor stormed into the watch station and threw his register onto the table. He pointed at a junior watchman and asked, "Why didn't you blow the horn? Pigheaded!"

The junior watchman immediately lifted a hunter's horn for a long, blaring call at the mayor's request. After he scraped his feet against one another to remove the dirt, the mayor took a seat on a mat. He grabbed a tobacco pipe and asked a watchman for a light.

Peasants working for masters who had already paid their taxes approached the mayor. "It's already late in the day," one of them said. "Please have the men open the gate so that we can take our cattle into the field."

"What's your rush? Stay put," the mayor said. "Is working in the field more important than paying state-owed taxes?"

The mayor packed the pipe with a wad of tobacco and took three deep draws. Two long streams of smoke blew from his nostrils like elephant tusks. After pausing, he spoke to the chief watchman: "Open the gate. Let those and the cattle that belong to people who have paid their taxes out. Everyone else—send them to the communal house to wait and I'll deal with them."

"Yes, sir," the chief watchman said.

Several junior watchmen sprang up, removed the bolt and wooden rams, and pried open the heavy ironwood door that sagged on worn hinges. The mayor rose, opened the register, and read the names of those who had paid their taxes to the chief watchman. A dozen buffalos and oxen were allowed to be led by peasants into the field. The twenty or so remaining had to follow the chief watchmen and the mayor to the communal house, where they would be punished in the place of masters who hadn't yet paid their taxes.

II

Once again, the communal house's drum and rattles sounded. A drumstick violently struck the drum hung under the purlin. The noise hit the bamboo groves in the distance and echoed back into the village. The mayor threw the drumstick into the courtyard and proclaimed, "What has Mới been doing all morning? The mats have not been laid out, so where am I supposed to sit? Such disrespect. Once tax collecting is finished, I'll send him to hell!"

From the back of the communal house, Mới's wife emerged, carrying some mats to lay on the floor.

"Mr. Mayor, yesterday you had asked my husband to go to the market early in the morning . . ."

"Spread the mats," the mayor said. "And call the village authorities. How lazy these people are! They aren't my father, and still, I need to extend an invitation to them every time. This isn't a private matter. It's an all-village concern. If the taxes aren't in by tomorrow, I'll release the names of everyone who still owes, and then they'll see who is to be thrown in jail."

"Why do you yell and worry so much, Mr. Mayor?" A voice from behind him spoke. "My wife is taking food to the plowmen, and I had to prepare the food for our sow. She has just given birth, and if she goes hungry, her milk will run dry. Then what happens to her piglets? That's why I'm a little late. I'm not lazy." It was the treasurer who offered such an explanation as he walked down the path to the communal house and up the steps, a black lacquered box carried under his right arm.

"I'm speaking of other people, of course," the mayor said, attempting to correct himself. "I know your family is small and busy. I'm not criticizing you. Look! They're coming."

The land surveyor, holding a large scroll of paper and registers, was rushing in from the central hamlet, followed by a dozen men, including the village scrivener with his headdress swinging across his arm; the deputy mayor, his black shirt flapping loosely around his neck; the chairman of the rural council, his gauze shirt hanging like a cape off his shoulders; and five or six other authorities and dignities dragging behind in their shabby wooden clogs. They took their clogs off and carried them in their hands as they jumped onto the communal house's raised floor. After placing their clogs under their mats, they sat down.

Mới's wife respectfully placed a china water pipe in a wooden bowl bound with bamboo hoops and a twisted straw torch at the foot of one of the house's support columns. Her two children carefully carried a pot of freshly brewed tea and a stack of tea-stained bowls.

The chairman of the rural council had just begun to bring up the issue of tax collection when the canton chief arrived from a nearby hamlet. In front of him, one of the mayor's servants walked in with a heavy opium tray. A chief orderly and two assistants showed them inside.

A crowd of voices arose from among the people gathered.

"You've come, Mr. Canton Chief!"

"Good morning, sir!"

"Please, take a seat on the highest floor!"

The canton chief slowly removed his shoes and walked across the rows of mats, leaving dirty footprints with each step until he took an exaggerated seat on the highest mat. The mayor's servant passed the opium tray to the chief orderly, who then placed it beside the canton chief as if it were a court subject.

For breakfast that morning the canton chief had taken a few scores of opium at the mayor's office and thus felt quite lively. Solemnly and with great power, he spoke. "This village's authorities are very lazy. Until now a large portion of the taxes remain unpaid. What's been collected doesn't even cover half of what is owed according to the record book. I'm officially ordering that by this evening all the taxes must be in, or tomorrow morning I'll report this village to the district mandarin."

"You're right," the mayor said, making use of the opportunity. "Make it difficult for them. They're lazy! No one has anything to say? How are we going to get people to pay their taxes?"

The room sat in complete silence. It wasn't that the authorities were afraid of the canton chief's or the mayor's threat. Their eyes were fixed on the village gate.

Mới, the announcer, was walking toward them with a heavy rod across his shoulders. From one side hung a pan filled with pig offal and coagulated blood inside a basket of chitterlings and, on the other, a basket of pork. He slowly entered the courtyard and lowered the items onto the ground for the mayor to inspect.

"Mr. Mayor, today meat is expensive. I had to pay 6.5 piasters for this."

The chairman of the rural council, the treasurer, and the other officials rushed out to see while remarking that the price was too high. Without getting up, the canton chief simply said, "It doesn't matter whether it's cheap or expensive. It's plowmen from other villages that will have to pay, not you. Well? Go prepare lunch. It's nearly noon."

Feeling pleased, Mới picked up the load and continued walking. As he headed into the distance, the mayor reminded him to prepare a bowl of coagulated blood for each person's tray. The men then returned to the communal house and began their work.

Throwing the land register onto the mat, the mayor said to the village scrivener, "You read, and the others count. Determine how much each taxpayer owes and write it down on a slip of paper. Only record the names of those who haven't paid."

The treasurer opened his box, took out a pencil and a sheet of paper for himself and an abacus for the former mayor. "You count by our traditional Oriental method, and I'll count by the French method. We'll compare at the end, and if our numbers match, we will know we're correct."

A woman slipped into the communal house holding a string of copper coins.

"Good morning, sirs," she said.

Beside the opium tray, a young district guard craned his neck out and shouted, "Why did you wait until today to pay? And what are these? Khải Định[4] coins? Who is going to accept these?"

"She is a relative of mine," the mayor intervened. "Let's see how much ricefield she owns."

The village scrivener opened the register and read, "Nguyễn Thị Quí's ricefields are as follows: one patch in the east is seven *sào* nine *thước*,[5] and one in Đồng Cá Plain is six *sào* three *thước* two *thốn*."[6]

The former mayor slid the beads of the abacus, whispering, "Once five is five, twice five is ten, three times five is fifteen . . ."

The treasurer busied his pencil on his slip of paper. Some time passed. The former mayor finished and asked, "Her ricefields cover three *mẫu* four *sào* five *thước* and three *thốn*, correct?"

"I don't know yet; I'm still counting. The French method is always slower," the treasurer replied.

"Mr. Treasurer, please check carefully," Quí requested. "I don't think I have anywhere near three *mẫu* of ricefields."

---

4. King Khải Định (1885–1925): the twelfth emperor of the Nguyễn dynasty.

5. 1 *thước* = 24 square meters.

6. 1 *thốn* = 2.4 square meters.

More time went by. The treasurer finally finished scrawling, lifted his head, and scolded her, "Ridiculous! Your ricefields total four *mẫu* and two *sào*. How dare you say they don't even cover three?"

"If I cheat, Heaven will not bless me," Quí swore. "All I can say is that my ricefields only cover two *mẫu* and seven *sào*."

The former mayor and the treasurer both disagreed, but she remained adamant. The abacus and pencil went back to work.

The canton chief had grown impatient. "Let them fiddle with their calculations. Go and tell the others to hurry with receiving the payments," he said, rushing the mayor. "If everyone stands around here, they'll never finish collecting."

The mayor agreed. He sent some of his men to accompany the district orderlies and the canton chief's men on their visits to all the homes of the poor and gave a final order: "Round up everyone who hasn't paid their poll or property taxes and bring them here. I'll deal with them myself."

The rattles, drums, and horns again sounded. The sun fell onto the communal house's courtyard. The cattle were still lying beneath the flamboyant and banyan trees, gasping for breath.

III

Hidden behind a yellow bamboo grove along the wall of a hamlet located at the end in Đông Xá Village stood a quiet thatched hut. Seen from afar, it could be mistaken for a pigsty or ash storehouse. This was Mr. Dậu's home.

Its veranda was so low that those not paying attention always hit their heads as they passed through. A yard as wide as a harrow track and covered with moss, sparse crabgrass, and dead bamboo leaves served as both a footpath and a means to drain the water away from the house during a heavy rain that would otherwise eat away at the mud wall, cover the foundation, and block the door.

The household kept all the necessities inside. Conventionally built, the house consisted of nothing but two sections and a lean-to. Behind a loosely hanging torn blind stood a room at the front of the house. A bamboo partition had been erected to provide some sense of privacy. However, the cracks near the door and the slits at the bottom of the partition made clear that besides the worn bamboo bed adjacent to the partition, there was nothing but an array of chipped clay water vessels and mended jars cluttering the ground between walls scarred with rat holes.

Across from the chamber was an even more dilapidated, untidy kitchen. Outside, shafts of light made their way through the many cracks in the low and narrow lean-to and did their best to dry the puddle left by last night's rain.

Near the piles of wet firewood, battered lids lay upside down on bamboo pot pads as if to laugh at the empty earthen pots that were strewn around the ground.

In a heap of cold paddy husk ash, a triangle of broken bricks sat waiting for a cooking pot.

The pantry cabinet was empty. The bent bamboo casing tried its best to support the mud wall, and the torn bamboo blind was about to fall apart.

Behind the ancestral altar on the wall that separated the bedchamber from the kitchen, a sheet of blue paper had recently been put up as a sign of mourning. Intricately spun cobwebs stretched between the spent incense sticks, revealing how the owner of the home had not given offerings to the dead for some time.

In the center of the house, a torn mat covered the rickety bamboo bed.

Under the plank bed, some hungry puppies barked constantly.

Bamboo poles for carrying things across one's shoulders, scythes, and sickles hung haphazardly beside clothes on a horizontal pole that ran along the veranda.

Holding her two-year-old daughter in her arms, Mrs. Dậu, a twenty-four-year-old woman, lounged on the ramshackle bed. Her quick, sharp eyes, alluring crimson lips, smooth, suntanned skin, and overall beauty were at odds with the sorrows in her mind. She dolorously gazed down at her two well-behaved children, quietly watching their sweet gestures.

Tý and her little brother Dần were busy looking for the biggest sweet potatoes remaining in the heap of sweet potato roots. They shouted with joy when they found an undamaged one and uttered disappointed words when they found nothing.

The sun was at its peak. Sunrays traversed bamboo clumps and poured on the bumpy dirt floor.

Roosters crowed in the back of the house.

A column of smoke rose from the roof of a nearby kitchen.

Dần sulked away from the heap of sweet potato roots and muttered to his mother, "Since morning I've only found a few tatters of sweet potato. I don't want to go on shifting through them anymore. Mom, hurry up and go buy some rice. The neighbors are preparing their lunch while we haven't even had our breakfast. We are hungry!"

Heartbroken, Mrs. Dậu looked at her children and tenderly told her son, "Keep trying. You'll find some more sweet potatoes, and your sister will cook them. I have no money to buy rice."

"Yesterday and two days ago you sold a few baskets of sweet potatoes and earned five dimes, but you haven't spent that money," the little boy complained. He'd barely finished speaking when he sprinted toward her, attempting to get at her purse.

"The money from the sale of sweet potatoes is to pay off Dad's poll tax, not for us to buy rice," Tý gently reminded her brother. "If you're hungry, help yourself to some raw sweet potatoes."

Such sensible words coming from her seven-year-old daughter moved Mrs. Dậu to tears. Sluggishly, she picked up little Tỉu and walked listlessly to the front door, waiting for her husband to come home.

Mr. Dậu, despite being only twenty-six, had already been plowing the fields for seventeen years. With their strength, frugality, and diligence, the couple had once been able to make ends meet easily as farmhands, despite it being just the two of them. However, in the last few years, they had earned barely enough to scrape by because of the exorbitant price of rice and poor crops, and because the young wife had to spend her time tending to the children.

The prior August, Mr. Dậu's mother had passed away from an illness, and last January, his brother caught a serious fever and lost his life. Mr. Dậu was very thrifty, but the cost of two funerals—eight piasters for two coffins and six piasters for funeral expenses—was enough to overwhelm them. He searched everywhere to try and find more money as the two misfortunes had completely bankrupted them. Making matters worse, as of last March, malaria had forced him to stay home. So for nearly three months, the entire needs of the family of five had fallen on his wife's shoulders alone.

His heart ached when he witnessed his children's starving, shabby lives and his wife's misery. Moreover, during the last few days, the mayor's tax demands were making him feel like an ant crawling in a frying pan. He didn't know what to do. So when his fever finally subsided, leaning on a cane, he went out to try and borrow money to pay his taxes. But he had no idea where to go or when he would return.

Waiting in vain for her husband, Mrs. Dậu carried her baby, Tỉu, back inside and threw herself down on the bed. Her oldest daughter, Tý, was still busy searching in the heap of sweet potato roots while her son, Dần, sat chewing a raw sweet potato voraciously.

The clinking of bowls on a tray could be heard from a nearby house. The neighbor children called to each other to come and eat. The succulent scent of pickled vegetable soup and braised fish wafted on the breeze.

Dần gulped down a sweet potato and quickly put on his tattered brown jacket. He rushed toward his mother and tapped her on the shoulder. "Mom, I'm going to play at the neighbor's house. Okay?"

Tý glared at him. "They are about to have lunch," she said. "Don't go now, or their mother will chase you away like she did the other day. Forget your hunger and try to find some more sweet potatoes. I'm going to heat the pot."

Dần furiously threw his jacket onto the bed and turned around, a miserable expression on his face. "I am so mad! Mom has sorted out all the good sweet potatoes to sell. Only their roots are left. How can I find any edible ones?" he asked.

"If Mom didn't sell them, how could she get the money to pay Dad's poll tax?" Tý explained gently. "Now come here and help me. There are still some big sweet potatoes left."

"I'm so starving that my eyes have turned yellow," Dần said. At that, he sulked toward the basket of sweet potatoes, carefully dusted one off, and popped it in his mouth.

Mrs. Dậu sat without speaking, tears rolling down her cheeks. She turned toward the wall to hide her sorrow from her children.

IV

Beneath a wooden bed, a female dog began wagging its tail joyously. Mr. Dậu entered through the gate languorously. He was very pale and looked disheartened. Tý and Dần clapped their hands and shouted as he approached, "Daddy is home. Daddy is home."

Paying them no attention, the feeble, skinny man leaned his walking stick against a bamboo panel and struggled to mount the steps into the house, his hands on his knees. He staggered toward the bed and collapsed onto the torn mat. In the distance, drumbeats and horn calls came from the communal house like frogs croaking.

Holding her baby against her chest, Mrs. Dậu felt her husband's forehead and gently asked, "What's wrong, dear? Are you exhausted? Why are you home so late? Your forehead is hot."

Mr. Dậu was mute and motionless. She tried again. "You must be very tired, huh? Where have you been since this morning? Whom did you ask to lend us money?"

Laying his hand across his forehead, he let out a long sigh and faintly replied, "I only visited the village councilor, Mr. Ích."

"Did you get anything?" she asked.

"Nothing. I knew that old, disgusting miser would never lend us anything while we already owe him. But we are so pinched for money; I was bold enough to try. I had barely opened my mouth when he started berating and threatening me, reminding me about the three piasters we borrowed against our mortgage last January and how it will come due in June at the rate of 12 percent a month, which will mean we owe five piasters and sixteen cents. If we don't pay, he will seize our home and land to build an outhouse."

"For Heaven's sake!" Mrs. Dậu cried and furrowed her eyebrows. "He'll take our land and house to build an outhouse? Will Heaven smile upon him for that? Why didn't you go to our uncle to borrow one piaster?"

"I've already asked our uncle, but nothing came of the visit. He railed at me, chastising us for both being able-bodied but unable to pay a few piasters of poll tax . . ."

Mrs. Dậu stomped the floor. "Such a bastard! He's your uncle, a wealthy uncle living in clover. If he nags his own nephew the first time he dares to try and borrow money, what can we expect from anyone else?" She continued, "Have you thought of trying to get the money another way, my dear?"

Her husband remained silent for a while and let out another labored sigh. "I've talked to Deputy Quế in Đoài Hamlet. I think it's better to sell . . ." Mr. Dậu stammered and grumbled and left the sentence unfinished, a lump in his throat.

"What do you intend to sell? Speak up! There is no one else here to hear you."

"I plan to sell our daughter Tý to the deputy," he responded, misery quivering in his voice.

Tears streamed down Mrs. Dậu's cheeks, and she bowed her head, not knowing what to say. Having overheard, Tý dropped the sweet potato she was holding in her hand and begged her parents to let her stay at home to play with her siblings, not to sell her.

Dần dropped the sweet potato from his mouth and cried, "No, no! I don't want you to sell Tý. I'd rather you sell Tiu."

Mr. Dậu and his wife wiped their eyes and pretended the matter was done. Tý continued begging her parents to take pity and not sell her. Unable to resist the earnest, sad words of such an innocent daughter, Mrs. Dậu patted Tiu on the head affectionately and comforted Tý.

"Dad is joking," she said. "If he sells you, who will look after Tíu for me while I go to work?"

Relieved, Tý returned to the heap of sweet potato roots and resumed her sorting enthusiastically. A tedious silence hung over the house; each heartbeat of the poor couple practically echoed off the walls. Just then, outside, the dogs began barking and someone rapped on the wall.

"Is the yokel Dậu at home?" someone rose his voice loudly.

Mrs. Dậu ran to the gate, with Tíu in her arms, and chased the dogs away. Her husband sat up and looked into the courtyard.

Swinging a wooden stick and rope, two of the mayor's servants had stomped in with the chief orderly, who held a rattan whip in his hand. They threatened the dogs away and stood on the veranda. Pointing the whip at Mr. Dậu's face, the chief orderly shouted, "Give us your tax money! We're here to collect, and yet you seem unconcerned."

Mr. Dậu stood up, quivering. His sallow face turned even more pallid. He raised a trembling hand to scratch his ear.

"Sir, I have no money," he said.

The chief orderly glared at Mr. Dậu.

"Your annual taxes are only two piasters and seventy cents, and you haven't paid any yet. When do you expect to?"

"I'm sick and have had no time to attend to it," Mr. Dậu pleaded. His breath was coming in gasps. "I'll pay tomorrow. There are still five days until the collection has to be sent to the district headquarters."

"So you plan on using those five days to delay payment, huh?" the chief orderly responded.

Without giving him a moment to answer, the chief orderly shifted the rattan whip to his left hand, and balling up his right into a fist, rained a series of whip cracks down on Mr. Dậu's chest. The professional punch of an authority figure hurt more than an amateur one from an ordinary civilian. Mr. Dậu could only emit faint cries. The chief orderly then seized Mr. Dậu by his jacket collar, turned his head toward the mayor's servants, and said, "Take your rope and tie him up. He can't pay, and now he starts arguing."

The servants grabbed Mr. Dậu's arms, twisted them behind his back, and tied them with a rope. He was bound like a pig ready for slaughter. Dần began weeping. Tý rushed toward the chief orderly sobbing, clasped her hands, and bowed at his feet repeatedly, begging him to pardon her father and untie him.

The chief orderly raised the whip that was still in his hand and gave her a blow across the buttocks.

"Get out of here!" he shouted.

In agony, the little girl fell down and wriggled like a scalded hen. Dần bawled loudly.

His anger not yet satiated, the chief orderly was about to whip the little boy when Mrs. Dậu, her baby in her arms, intervened.

"Sir, please don't beat my son," she pleaded. "He's just a little boy."

The pleading of such a beautiful woman had some effect on the chief orderly, and the innocent young boy was spared.

She turned her head and saw her husband's face, furrowed with pain. Mrs. Dậu humbly asked the chief orderly, "Please have mercy on my husband and loosen the knots because he is ill."

This time, her charms didn't work.

"This won't kill your husband," the chief orderly curtly answered, "and if it did, he'd be free of his debt."

"The rope hurts so much," Mr. Dậu interrupted. "Please loosen it a little bit. I won't be able to escape anyway."

In a rage, the chief orderly gave Mr. Dậu a few slaps in the face and threatened, "You stubborn scoundrel! You are bound because you are guilty."

Mrs. Dậu gazed at the chief orderly with her bloodshot eyes.

"The tax will be paid tomorrow," she said. "There is no reason to persecute my husband. Beat me instead. I can bear any harsh punishment. My husband is ill. He has committed no crime."

"Are you challenging me?" the chief orderly shouted. "Because I showed you kindness once, now you go too far. I'll show you what I can do. How dare you challenge me?! How dare you?!"

Each time he roared, "How dare you?!" the chief orderly struck Mrs. Dậu several times in the chest. She staggered back and collapsed onto the ground. Her little daughter Tỉu, still clutched to her chest, began bawling. Tý and Dần, hidden in a corner and helplessly watching their parents being beaten, wept loudly.

One of the mayor's servants pointed his stick at Mrs. Dậu's face and said, "I've never met anyone with so much to say. If every family were as stubborn as yours, perhaps the entire tax collection would have to be abandoned. Now, stand up! Don't just lie there. Find a way to pay your husband's poll tax."

The servants solemnly grabbed the end of the rope and dragged Mr. Dậu down the steps. At the gate, he turned his head and said to his wife, "Leave Tỉu at home! Go to see Deputy Quế right now."

V

Deputy Quế's property could be seen from the entrance of Đoài Hamlet. Behind its gates, the cone-shaped roofs of a group of barns and granaries pointed to the sky, boasting about the four or five years of crops he had harvested. Mountains of hay standing near the jackfruit and cluster fig trees indicated that the owner of the house owned several hundred *mẫu* of land.

A one-story brick house that defied elementary principles of fine art was built in the middle of the compound. It featured garish doors and windows, thick columns, and gaudy dragons and phoenixes gracing yellow lacquered panels. Its ostentatious tile roof was put up according to traditional architecture styles with upward-curving corners studded with square Chinese ornaments in relief. A mosaic of broken chinaware representing open-mouthed carp ran along its walls.

The property covered nearly three hundred *mẫu* and was surrounded by four brick walls topped with sharp shards of broken bottles. The jumbled collections of items and structures on the property made it feel like a market amid a barracks filled with all sorts of valuable and worthless items, new and old. Deputy Quế's father bequeathed the property to him, and he then greatly enlarged it.

Deputy Quế was neither a merchant nor a contractor. He was a landlord and loan shark. He lent at a minimum rate of 10 percent a month. Loans of one piaster or more were only offered against a home or land mortgage or some other type of deposit as security. If the debt went unpaid after the due date, the mortgage was foreclosed upon. Most of his property, including the land he lived on and his ricefields, as well as all his knickknacks and objects of worship, had been obtained from generations of insolvent debtors.

Deputy Quế came from a line of petty dignitaries. He began with the position of village mayor, and then rose to deputy canton chief, followed by canton chief. Through flattery and bribery, he obtained his current position as deputy with the help of the district and provincial mandarins.

Unlike men with "the hearts of animals," who took advantage of their positions representing the people to peddle stories to the authorities in order to win favors, Deputy Quế entered politics simply to purchase a "modern" social rank, guzzle booze, and hobnob with the region's dignitaries. He was far less literate than his fellow deputies, even though they were simple pig dealers and coolie overseers. Like most of them, he avoided debates and refused to listen to people's opinions on various matters. He occasionally yawned during official sessions, but he never fell asleep because he was afraid that if he did, his habit of putting his feet up on a chair would result in his leather shoes being stolen.

Because he was a deputy, his name was known throughout Trung Sơn Province. Still, as was the case before he received his position, he never invited anyone for a meal, except on the anniversaries of the deaths of his father and his mother. He was, of course, a stingy man who permitted only the tiniest expenses. However, on a few occasions, he spent lavishly—especially during the New Year festival when he sent chickens, pigeons, and baskets of fragrant rice to dignitaries in the region as gifts.

Mr. Dậu and his wife had neither blood ties nor relations with the deputy. They knew him and his property only because they had worked for him for a long time.

After Mr. Dậu was led away to the communal house by the chief orderly and the mayor's servants, his wife, on her husband's advice, left Tiu with Tý, took her battered conical hat and went out, pretending to be deaf and ignoring Dần's cries for food.

The summer sun pummeled her face. Mist lifted from the ricefields like steam off a boiling pot. Pregnant crabs and water snakes, unable to survive in the hot water in the rice paddy, scurried onto land and hid in the grass.

Đông Xá and Đoài Hamlets were about two miles apart in the same village. The hot sun made the distance between them feel like an endless desert. But it didn't affect Mrs. Dậu, as she was accustomed to toiling under the sun. Under the protection of her tattered conical hat, she soon reached Deputy Quế's house.

The sun was at its peak.

The peasants and their cattle had returned home.

Mrs. Dậu wiped sweat off her brow with a front panel of her brown blouse. She then opened her blurry eyes widely and looked inside the gate.

A shadeless, paved brick courtyard as big as a soccer field.

A flock of pigeons was pecking at a bamboo tray of beans.

A broody hen clucked and jumped from the chicken coop onto the ground. Then she pooped into a pot of orchids.

A sow and her piglets circled a slop pail.

There wasn't a soul in sight.

Boldly, Mrs. Dậu entered the courtyard. All of a sudden, a pack of fierce dogs lunged at her. Frightened, she crouched down and swung her hat to scare away the savage animals. "Is the cook here? Please call the dogs off," she cried.

A woman's shrill voice came from inside the house. "Who is making so much noise? Every house has dogs, so why don't you carry a stick with you? The cook is busy and has no time for you."

It seemed that the deputy and his wife were eating in the living room. Mrs. Dậu's voice annoyed Madame Quế, so she scolded the uninvited guest without standing up to see who was out there. She never bothered with keeping the dogs off debtors or farmhands.

The dogs, loyal to the wishes of their masters, surrounded Mrs. Dậu. They bared their teeth, stuck out their tongues, and attempted to bite her legs. They tore the hat she was using as a shield to pieces. Not knowing what else to do, she fought them with her bare hands.

A female farmhand ran out from the kitchen swinging a stick, and the dogs ran off in all directions. Injured, Mrs. Dậu got off the ground and walked to the open area in front of the living room. She didn't know her right hand had been bitten until she saw blood coming from the wound. She tore a strip of fabric from her clothes and bandaged the wound. Hesitatingly, she mounted the steps and bowed to Deputy Quế and his wife.

"Your right hand is bitten quite badly," Madame Quế said coldly. "Why do you come during our meal? What do you want?"

"This morning her husband came and told me that he wanted to sell his daughter to us," Deputy Quế put his rice bowl down on the tray and said while chewing. "I guess she's here to discuss that matter."

"Yes, it's true, sir," Mrs. Dậu answered. "I have come about that."

"No rush," Madame Quế winked at her husband and then said to Mrs. Dậu. "Sit down and wait until we have finished our meal. Don't disturb us."

Deputy Quế took his wife's hint and continued eating without saying another word. Mrs. Dậu sat on the brick floor. In all her time working for Deputy Quế, Mrs. Dậu was only familiar with the kitchen, which was in a different building. The actual residence was foreign territory for her. This was the first time she had ever laid eyes on the living room. It seemed very luxurious to her.

Next to a panel inlaid with mother-of-pearl hung a picture that depicted several smiling maidens showing their bare breasts and knees.

Between red and gold wooden panels with parallel verses written in Chinese script, a picture showed two plump children carrying milk tins as big as their bodies.

Beside a large red porcelain vase rested a water pipe with a bamboo stem as long as a fishing rod.

Inside a cupboard carved with grapevines, a basket full of eggs stood on a shelf above a perfectly white tea set.

In front of the polished plank bed, four marble-backed chairs circled a blue woven-rattan table.

At the head of the modern varnished bed, black pants and blue shawls hung in disarray.

There were more valuable items than Mrs. Dậu could even lay her eyes on.

There was a clattering at the dining table. Deputy Quế placed his chopsticks down on the tray, grabbed a bowl of soup and emptied it in one gulp. Still chewing and swallowing, he asked a servant to bring him a toothpick. His wife held up a plate of leftover pork, poured it into a pot, and told the cook to hang it from a pole.

"There are fourteen slices of pork left," she said. "I counted them, so you are responsible if any is gone."

The cook took the tray of food away. A little servant boy, with great care, brought in a washbasin. Deputy Quế and his wife dipped their fingers in and rubbed their lips clean. They sipped tea and picked their teeth with toothpicks. Two servants stood fanning them. Madame Quế opened a lacquered box and took out some betel leaves and areca nuts to chew with tobacco. Deputy Quế brought the water pipe down from the cupboard, rolled a pinch of tobacco, and lit the pipe before taking a bubbling hit.

"Now you," Deputy Quế said, addressing Mrs. Dậu. "What about the business of selling your daughter? Tell me."

Timidly, Mrs. Dậu entered the room and stood respectfully beside the door. Stammering, she said, "We are desperate for money. Please help us."

"It's not a matter of helping or saving you," Madame Quế, with a frown, said, after she spat out the betel in her mouth. "If you want to sell your daughter, I'm willing to buy her."

"Yes, I want to sell her," Mrs. Dậu affirmed.

"This morning, your husband said that your daughter is seven years old and asked for three piasters. The deputy took his word for her age and offered two piasters. Now we've been told that she is only six years old, so I will offer you only half the price—one piaster. If you agree, bring her here."

Mrs. Dậu was confused. "It's true that my daughter is seven years old. She was born in the first month during the Year of the Rat. We would never dare lie to you."

"I believe neither you nor your husband," Madame Quế said. "Other people have told me her true age. I know nothing of her year of birth."

Mrs. Dậu was speechless.

"My daughter *cái* Hai . . ." Madame Quế continued.

"Watch your mouth! Why do you call our daughter that?" Deputy Quế frowned and interrupted. "I've told you to call her *mợ* as the mandarins call their daughters. I'm a deputy at least and I often socialize with mandarins and dignitaries. My social status is certainly not below that of a mandarin. It's not an exaggeration to refer to your daughter as *mợ*."

"You're wrong." His wife burst into laughter. "They call their daughters-in-law *mợ*. They call their own daughters *cô*. And not just the mandarins. Clerks and traders in Hà Nội do so as well."

"*Mợ* or *cô*—either honorific is fine, but don't use the discourteous term *cái* like the common folks use," he insisted.

"OK, fine," Madame Quế retorted. Then she turned to Mrs. Dậu and said, "My *cô* Hai has no child. The fortunetellers advised she would need to adopt a son or daughter if she wants to change her luck. That is why we are seeking one to improve her fate. As you can see, we surely don't need more house servants. Besides, your daughter is only six, so what type of work could she possibly do? With *cô* Hai, your daughter will be well taken care of, and she will be far happier living with *cô* Hai than living with you. You should really be giving your daughter to us for free. One piaster is already too much. Don't bargain for more."

Mrs. Dậu suddenly hit the floor and sat motionlessly like a piece of wood, not sure how to respond.

VI

Madame Quế pointed her finger at the servant boy and ordered him to bring her some tea. While sipping it, she asked Mrs. Dậu, "What do you think of my suggestion?"

"I know it would be very fortunate if my daughter can find shelter in your house or *cô* Hai's," Mrs. Dậu replied with tears in her eyes. "But we owe more than two piasters in taxes and have come to you for that reason. If you only give us one piaster, where can we find the rest? Please take pity on us . . ."

"I don't give a damn about your taxes." Deputy Quế roared into the conversation. "Don't spin me a sad story. Are you making us responsible for your taxes?"

Mrs. Dậu grew shy. She dabbed at her eye with her camisole.

"Why don't you look around your house for something worth selling that can make up the difference?" Madame Quế suggested in a comforting voice. "Your daughter is only six years old; she should be given to us for nothing. No one would be so foolish as to pay you more."

"There is nothing in my home worth even twenty cents," Mrs. Dậu responded.

"I'm told you have a very smart dog. Isn't that so?" Madame Quế spoke, with a knowing smile.

"Oh yes! She just gave birth to such cute young puppies. But I'm afraid no one wants to buy them. If we could find someone who did, we wouldn't have to sell our daughter."

"How many puppies does she have? Have they opened their eyes yet?"

"Four. They began eating two days ago. So better yet, lend me two piasters please, at any interest rate you'd like, and within two market days, when they are strong enough, I'll sell them and repay the money."

"My money isn't clamshells." Madame Quế curled her lips. "Do you think such small interest is so enticing? How about this? The dogs are too young, but I'm willing to buy them. Bring them here, mother and puppies together. I'll pay you one piaster. That, combined with the sale of your daughter, will make two piasters . . . you'll have enough money to pay your husband's poll tax. And you'll no longer have to bother with breeding dogs or raising your child. How lucky for you!"

Madame Quế smiled at her husband. "Taking pity on people is just in my nature. If anyone else were in my position, they would care less about her. She would be left alone with her misfortunes."

Mrs. Dậu once again began crying. She sat down on the doorstep, looked up and said, "Yes! I know that you are doing us a great favor. Who else would want to buy a dog with young puppies? Still, I beg you to realize that the dogs aren't worth so little. At the market, the mother would fetch one piaster and fifty cents alone, and on lucky days the puppies would bring fifty cents each. That would be three piasters and fifty cents total. Selling them for only one piaster would be a great loss for me. Please reconsider."

Deputy Quế banged his fist on the wooden bed. "Go to the market and sell them, then. Don't waste my time trying to argue. In this 'French era,' time is precious, and I don't have any of it to sit here bargaining with you. You just said no one would buy the dogs, so we are offering to buy them out of pity. And now you complain the price is too low! If it's such a bad deal, go sell them at the market. Go ahead!"

Mrs. Dậu was rising to her feet when Madame Quế spoke in a soft voice. "You've a habit of bargaining; that's why nobody else will take pity on you. Taxes are weighing down on everyone right now, so borrowing one piaster comes at 5 percent interest per day. We are doing you a favor already by purchasing puppies whose eyes have just opened. Do you think we can't find dogs somewhere else? Are your dogs made of gold? Fine, I'll pay you ten cents more. So all together, your daughter and the dogs will bring you two piasters and ten cents cash. Is that all right?"

Mrs. Dậu hesitated and sat down again.

"For you, a few dimes are nothing, but to us, it matters a great deal. Please give me fifty cents more."

Madame Quế's temper flared. "You *really* know how to bargain, huh! We're being kind, and you keep asking for more. Well, I'll pay you ten cents more, making it two piasters and twenty cents. If you agree, go tell the teacher, and he will write you a receipt. But don't forget to pay him the twenty-cent receipt fee, understand?"

Unable to hide her disappointment Mrs. Dậu asked, "So I get only two piasters?"

"How much more do you want? Twenty piasters?" Deputy Quế fumed. "We are already offering you too much. If you agree, sign the receipt. If not, get out right now."

Mrs. Dậu could hear a voice inside her head: *If I go home empty-handed, how long will my husband remain tied up? My fate is already doomed. I must now follow it blindly . . .*

Tears ran down her face as Mrs. Dậu again got up. Dejectedly, she agreed and asked Madame Quế to tell the teacher to prepare the receipt.

Madame Quế called in the direction of the back house. "Is anybody there? Go to the study room and invite the teacher to come here."

The chimes of the clock atop the cabinet slowly counted to eleven. Madame Quế smiled and said to her husband, "Why is it only eleven o'clock? Something must be wrong with the clock."

Deputy Quế shook his thighs and stroked his curved mustache, and with a toothpick in his mouth, spoke. "You are so ignorant, dear.

French-made clocks are never wrong. Eleven o'clock is correct, so we must have had our lunch a little too early today."

The sun savaged the paved yard. In the distance, the one o'clock train whistled. The teacher emerged from the altar room, dragging his worn shoes and carrying a pen, inkstand, paper, and notepad. The chignon on his head made him look like an old-fashioned tutor rather than a modern teacher, which was fitting as his knowledge of the common *Quốc ngữ* alphabet[7] paled in comparison to his already-poor knowledge of the traditional Chinese writing system. Deputy Quế and his wife upgraded his title from "tutor" to "teacher." He was hired to teach their children the *Three Character Classic* as well as *Quốc ngữ*, in addition to his work writing IOUs to mortgagers and debtors.

In the living room, the teacher slowly pushed aside the basket of sticky rice on the wooden bed and sat down respectfully. After listening to Deputy Quế's lengthy and specific instructions, he began writing. His face looked serious. The room was completely silent save for the scratching of his pen.

Five minutes, ten minutes, half an hour passed. The teacher finally looked up at Mrs. Dậu and said, "Come hear what I have written, and place your fingerprint."

Mrs. Dậu tiptoed toward the bed. The teacher cleared his throat three times, and in the slow, steady voice used when teaching his students, he read: "I, Nguyễn Văn Dậu, twenty-six-years old, of Đông Xá Village, and my wife, Lê Thị Đào, twenty-four years old, living in the same village, declare that we have borrowed from Mrs. Hoàng Thị Sẹo, fifty-eight-years old, first wife of Deputy Trần Đức Quế, of Đoài Thôn Village, a pair of gold earrings weighing eleven grams, at the value of twenty piasters, payable within five years. If payment is overdue, we shall be responsible for the breach of trust. We deliver this as our act and deed in Đoài Thôn Village on the tenth of March, 1936."

"You must be mistaken!" Mrs. Dậu stammered. "I'm selling my child and my dogs, not borrowing any earrings from Madame Quế."

Deputy Quế removed the toothpick from his mouth, laid it across his cup of tea, and said, "We haven't written it like this to cheat you. The new law simply forbids parents from selling their children and thus the IOU can mention neither her nor the dogs. It must be this way. If your

---

7. Vietnam's Latin-based writing script, developed by the Portuguese missionary Francisco de Pina in the seventeenth century, which the French instituted to replace the centuries-old Chinese-based *chữ Nôm*.

daughter ends up living with *cô* Hai permanently, I will consider the paper null and void. If you change your mind and want your daughter back, we will use this document to have both you and your husband thrown in jail. It is to prevent you from cheating us. But we will never cheat you. We simply need to hold the handle of the knife, not the blade, understand?"

Deputy Quế finished speaking, emptied his tea in a big swig to clean his mouth, and spat on the floor.

"It's up to you to decide. If you trust us, put your fingerprint on the paper and then take it home for your husband to sign before the mayor certifies it. Then, come back here with the certified paper, and I'll give you the money. And if you don't trust us, so be it. I'm not pressuring you at all."

Mrs. Dậu stared downward as her face grew wet with tears and sweat. Finally, she agreed, saying, "I'll do what you just told me."

She held out her bandaged hand. The teacher inked two of her fingers and pressed them against the receipt. Finished, she folded the paper and put it in her waistband. She walked down the steps, picked up her hat that the dogs had torn apart, and bowed to Deputy Quế, his wife, and the teacher. As she left, Madame Quế reminded her, "Don't forget to keep the puppies out of the sun."

VII

The sun shone through the banyan and *gạo* trees, casting a shadow near the communal house's front railing.

Oxen and buffalos, kept as collateral, were lying in the sun, idly chewing on the sweet potato roots and wilted grass that their masters had left for them.

A group of women who were waiting to pay their taxes sat around the veranda.

Below the communal house, dogs were barking and scrapping over scattered bones.

The meal inside the communal house was nearly finished. With a toothpick still in his mouth, the canton chief dozed off beside the opium set.

The chief orderly was squatting on his heels. His dark lips stretched all the way to his ears.

A district guard was trying to grind the remaining opium off a chipped cup. His face was red and veiny.

The nobles, chieftains, and the chief orderly circled a clay water pipe and kettle, smoking or blowing on bowls of hot tea. The village mayor, leaning against a banister, offered the chairman and the vice-chairman of the rural council the meal's remaining Melissa leaves and minced banana flowers.

Pointing their chopsticks, the village scrivener and the land surveyor politely invited each other to take slices of dried pork.

The former mayor, the deputy mayor, and the treasurer held cups of rice wine and bent their heads over the bowls, dishes, and blue bottles of alcohol.

The canton chief's and the mayor's lackeys as well as the watchmen on daytime duty sat around a basket of cold rice and a pot of soup covered in flies and ate loudly.

The noisy commotion made the room hotter, and people couldn't hear themselves speak.

Arriving at the gate, Mrs. Dậu heard the former mayor scolding someone inside the communal house. "Mới, go to the market and get some more bottles of rice wine. We're still drinking. We don't care about anyone who wants to stop."

"Hold on!" the chairman then spoke loudly. "There's still plenty of wine here. Have him go buy a few ounces of opium. The canton chief has been craving it for a long time."

"Don't go to get the opium yet," the hamlet chief said to Mới. "I haven't rinsed my mouth. Go to the well and get me some water."

"Bring us some fish sauce first before you bring the water," the treasurer snapped at Mới.

"Give me some respect!" the former mayor interrupted, speaking to the others. "I asked Mới to go buy alcohol, and now you are ordering him to serve you instead."

Mrs. Dậu boldly entered the communal house, took off her tattered hat, and bowed to the men inside.

"Good morning, sirs," she greeted them.

Everyone stared at her. The mayor's servant pointed at her with his chopsticks and asked, "Do you have your husband's taxes ready?"

The district guard stopped scraping at the opium, raised his head and asked, "Is she married to the man who lives at the edge of the village? She is a stubborn, nagging woman. If I hadn't been busy looking for people to arrest, I would have given her a few more blows to her face."

"Yes—she is Mr. Dậu's wife," the deputy mayor intervened. "Why don't you give her another lashing? That is why the mayor asked you to be here."

"Excuse me, Mr. Chairman, chief orderly, and everyone else here," the village mayor shook his thighs and said, "but I must remind you that I have been tough in my duties related to collecting taxes. I beat those who disobey because all year long we have a lot of trouble doing our work, and it is only when there is a flood or it's time to collect taxes that we are given some authority. Then we are allowed to beat people, tie them up, even whip the stubborn ones to death with no consequences."

Mrs. Dậu remained silent. She moved her eyes around the room.

In the far corner of the communal house, ten or so young men were sprawled out behind a messy heap of bowls and trays. Each of their arms was tied up to a wooden railing with big ropes.

Women were not allowed to enter where people were eating. Mrs. Dậu exited through the back door to where her husband was tied up.

Mr. Dậu leaned his head against the railing. His eyes were shut, his mouth open, and he was gasping for breath. His fingers were swollen up like bananas.

Mrs. Dậu was shocked at the horrible state of her husband. The men tied up like Mr. Dậu around him shared the same fate.

"Since midday he has been suffering a fever," one of them said. "He has been shaking and groaning and then fainted. It breaks our hearts to see him suffer."

"Try to get the money he owes by any way possible and take him home," another man urged Mrs. Dậu. "We're healthy, but being tied up like this causes us great pain. But for a man as sick as him . . ."

"Damn it!" Mrs. Dậu said, with tears in her eyes. "I would stop at nothing to save my husband. It's agonizing to see him like this. But I have nowhere to borrow the money and nothing to sell."

She sat next to her husband and patted him on his shoulder. "Dear! Wake up, dear!"

But Mr. Dậu remained unconscious.

From the center of the communal house, the deputy mayor threatened to slap Mrs. Dậu if she did not keep quiet. "The communal house is not your private room for you two to chitchat. What kind of woman are you? You only have a single head tax to pay for your husband for the entire year, and yet you cannot come up with even that. Now you are crying and cooing 'Dear, dear,' and it's getting on our nerves!"

Mrs. Dậu ignored his threats and continued to shake her husband, attempting to rouse him. After a long while, Mr. Dậu wearily opened his bloodshot eyes and groaned.

"What is the matter, dear?" Mrs. Dậu, sobbing, asked him. "Do you have a fever, or is it the rope causing you pain?"

"Go and bring me some water," Mr. Dậu mumbled. "I'm thirsty and my throat has been dry since this morning."

Mrs. Dậu cleared the tears from her eyes and stood up. She asked Mới for a cheap clay bowl and filled it with water from the well. Mr. Dậu bent his head and drank it in a single gulp. He then leaned his head back against the railing as he struggled to breathe. His stomach boiled like a cauldron.

The authorities continued to booze, smoke, and argue with one another while fanning themselves.

Mrs. Dậu touched her husband's forehead, feet, and wrists and tried to loosen the rope's knot. But it was fastened too tightly so she gave up. A short time later, Mr. Dậu returned to consciousness. He looked at his wife, half-consciously, and asked, "So, have you gone to see Deputy Quế?"

"Yes, I have."

"Did he agree?"

"Yes, he did. But he made me sign a bill of sale that involved another provision . . ."

She could hardly find the courage to finish the sentence. With some hesitance, she took out the slip of paper from her waistband and handed it to her husband. "The bill was written by the teacher at Deputy Quế's. Please look at it," she said.

Mr. Dậu took the paper in his hand but couldn't hold it close to his eyes to read because his arms were bound so tightly. Mrs. Dậu held it in front of his face to see. Spelling out the words to himself, Mr. Dậu read it.

The mayor caught sight of the paper and seethed with rage. "What kind of paper is that? Is it a complaint to sue? All right, go ahead and lodge it right now. I'll give you another beating, and you can sue me next!" he said sarcastically.

The mayor got to his feet and started to walk. But he stumbled and had to grab a column so as not to fall down. He threw himself down onto the floor and sat on the mat.

A district guard stood up and said, "Sir, stay still and don't trouble yourself. Let me deal with these people. If they want to sue anyone, they'll get a chance soon enough."

VIII

With those words, the young district guard raced toward Mr. Dậu and gave him a stiff slap across the face. Roaring with rage, he clenched his teeth and challenged Mr. Dậu to lodge the complaint. "Go ahead and sue. You haven't paid your tax yet. How dare you provoke me?"

Mr. Dậu was utterly dumbfounded. Tears covered his face like rain. He knocked his head against the rails and screamed, "Oh Heaven! Oh Father, oh Mother! How miserable I am! I have no intention to sue anyone."

A lump formed in Mrs. Dậu's throat, but she couldn't cry. The other bound men around them were in tears.

The district guard was not pacified, and he threatened Mr. Dậu with his fist. "Are you trying to make a false accusation against me?"

Scared, Mrs. Dậu stood up immediately. She showed him the bill of sale with one hand and placed the other on the guard's wrist.

"Sir," she said softly. "My husband is ill. Please spare him. This is not a complaint to sue. It's a bill for the sale of my daughter so I can get the money to pay my husband's tax."

To prove his literacy, the guard took the letter and silently read it, top to bottom. He was satisfied that it wasn't a complaint to sue but continued to berate her. "You liar! This note is for borrowing a pair of gold earrings. It's no bill of sale."

"It really is a bill of sale!" Mrs. Dậu said respectfully. "Just now at the deputy's house, when the teacher who wrote it read it to me, I was shocked and had the same reaction as you. The deputy explained to me, however, that the new law forbids parents from selling their children so the paper must be written this way. Earrings have nothing to do with it. Who would risk lending us earrings when we are in such a desperate situation?"

Her gentle voice seemed to have some effect on the guard, who was compelled to pause and listen to her speak without interruption. He returned the paper, winked slyly, and leered at her.

"Your husband has not signed it yet?" he asked. "Why don't you tell him to sign it so you can get the money and this whole tax matter can be resolved? Why drag things out like this?"

Naively, Mrs. Dậu didn't grasp what the guard was suggesting. She continued in a sad tone, "I just showed the bill of sale to my husband, but the authorities thought it was a complaint to sue and told you to beat him."

"So, your dear husband has been unfairly beaten." The young guard grinned. "He can sign it now. It's not too late."

"My husband is bound too tightly and cannot hold a pen. I would be so grateful if you would untie the rope for him," Mrs. Dậu begged him.

The guard continued smiling. "I would happily do that for you . . . but it is up to the mayor . . ."

Upon hearing his name, the mayor spoke in a loud slur, "Who wants me?"

The guard ran toward him and said, "That woman wants to ask you to loosen her husband's ropes so that he can sign a bill of sale."

"Oh! So she is no longer lodging a complaint and now asks us to untie her husband? Tell her that it's impossible. The rope will be removed once the tax has been paid. Without paying the tax, not even Heaven could remove it. I'm the one that had him tied up. Let them sue me if they dare."

The former mayor lifted a bowl of alcohol to his lips and said, nodding, "I don't give a damn about all this. Tie people up, untie them, let them sue. I've paid my tax and want to continue drinking. Mới, where are you? I asked you for more alcohol, where is it? I'll chop you into pieces if you are disobedient."

The chairman of the rural council threw his chopsticks down onto the tray and said, "Mr. former Mayor, this is no concern of yours. Why are you putting your spoke in the wheel? Keep on drinking, and let them continue speaking. You tend to jump into everybody's throat and get in the way of the discussion."

The former mayor put down his alcohol, pounded his fist on the ground, and cried, "You can't stop me from speaking! What right do you have?"

With a cocky look on his face, the chairman replied, "Yes, I can. I have the right. The mandarin told me to help the mayor speed up the tax collection. Anyone who is stubborn and gets in the way will be chained up."

The former mayor was enraged. "I'm free to speak and to sit in the communal house. I dare anyone to try and touch me."

The chairman made an attempt to get up but staggered and flopped to the ground. "Watchmen," he shouted, "come and chain up the former mayor. I will accept all responsibility."

The watchmen remained silent. The former mayor rolled up his jacket sleeves and dared anyone to try and restrain him.

The chairman grabbed a bottle of alcohol from the tray and was about to throw it at the former mayor when the vice-chairman was able to diffuse the situation. "All right! Don't be hot-tempered! The former mayor is drunk."

The former mayor protested, "Mr. Vice-Chairman! You say I'm drunk, and maybe I am, but what is the point of alcohol if it doesn't get you drunk? Is it to pour down a rat's hole? But anyway, I'm not drunk. Don't speak nonsense. Let me tell you, the village collects two piasters per *mẫu* of ricefield from migrant tenants. You, the authorities, collect three piasters and fifty cents. What do you have to say about that? You invite me here for something to drink, and now you provoke me? Never mind. I'm drinking the migrants' alcohol and no one else's."

Startled, the mayor spoke, "The female tenants are still sitting on the veranda, money tucked into the waists of their skirts. Go and get it as payment for your drink. This round is on me. I'm free to invite anyone I please. I don't have to answer to anyone. True, I do collect 'extra money,' and what can anyone do to me about it?"

The former mayor went on a tirade like a maniac. "Hey! You say I'm to suck the blood from these female tenants, huh?"

As soon as he had asked this question, the former mayor hurled a bowl at the current mayor. Meanwhile, a pot flew in the opposite direction and hit a column near where the former mayor was sitting. Soup and fish sauce splashed all across the floor. The surrounding men tried to get up and out of the way, but too drunk to stand, they sat back down. The watchmen and the mayor's and canton chief's servants crept in to gather the trays, bowls, bottles, and cups to take out to the courtyard.

The chief district guard carefully moved the cup of opium and the opium set to the opposite side of the room.

The treasurer made an attempt to slip out with his box, but he was also too drunk to stand.

The canton chief had come down from his opium ecstasy and asked briskly, "What is going on? Drinking and talking nonsense! Who is fighting with whom?

Many voices rose from the crowd:

"The former mayor and the chairman of the rural council."

"The former mayor and the current mayor."

With authority, the canton chief spoke, "Watchmen! Take the former mayor to the courtyard. Is he trying to steal money from the mayor? I'll inform the mandarin."

The former mayor grabbed a sharp piece of the broken pot from near the column and was about to slash his own forehead, but the chief orderly rushed in, grabbed it, and threw the shard away. He propped the former mayor up by his armpit and helped him into the courtyard.

Once outside, the former mayor threw up violently.

IX

Hamlet chiefs, chieftains, and those not involved in the matter got up one by one and attempted to help the former mayor to his home. Only a few authorities remained to attend to the tax collecting.

Mrs. Dậu waited until the fight ended to approach the mayor. "Sir, please untie my husband just long enough so he can sign the paper," she begged.

The mayor remained angry. "Stop nagging! He can sign it while still tied up. There is no need to free him."

"Sir, kindly take pity on us. My husband is bound too tightly. He can't sign with his arms twisted behind his back. I wouldn't beg you if he were able to sign."

"Let me see the bill of sale."

Mrs. Dậu handed him the paper and waited near the railing.

Sunrays were angling into the back of the communal house through the rails and shining on Mr. Dậu's face.

Mới swept the floor to clean the scattered food and pieces of the broken bowl and pot. In the courtyard, his wife was washing the bowls and trays and gathering the meal's leftovers.

The female tenants from other villages came one by one to the communal house and asked the treasurer to open his book to calculate their taxes.

After reading the bill of sale, with alcohol on his breath, the mayor asked Mrs. Dậu, "Do you only need your husband's signature? Nothing else?"

"The deputy told me to ask for your seal, but I don't want to bother you, so I don't dare ask."

With a mischievous laugh, the mayor responded, "My seal is not a sweet potato. Do you think I place it free of charge?"

"Take pity on me," Mrs. Dậu begged. "The deputy will not give me the money without your seal."

"A fee of one piaster. You hear me? I am being kind to you. Others would charge five piasters."

"Please, be considerate of my situation. I'm selling my child and dog and only getting two piasters for them."

"I don't know anything about that. Give me one piaster, and I'll place my seal."

"If you don't take mercy on us, I won't have the money to pay the tax," Mrs. Dậu said while crying.

"If the tax is not paid, your husband will be thrown in jail."

Dejected, Mrs. Dậu said nothing. Her husband came to her rescue.

"This is beyond our control," he said to the mayor. "Heaven doesn't bless me but instead condemns me with illness. Think about our predicament. We can agree to pay for your seal, but please delay it until tomorrow. Once the tax is paid, my wife will plant rice seedlings to cover the charge."

The canton chief burst out laughing. "Hilarious! How does that work? A seal mark in exchange for planting rice? That's even better. Mr. Mayor, accept it and don't let them get on your nerves."

The mayor gave a perfunctory pause and agreed to the offer. He turned to Mrs. Dậu and asked, "How much do you plan to plant?"

"One *mẫu*, sir," she said.

The mayor calculated, "One piaster for one *mẫu*, or ten cents for one *sào*. No, I'll only agree to one *mẫu* and a half."

"I accept your proposal," Mr. Dậu said.

Thus, the affair was over. Mr. Dậu was untied long enough to sign the bill of sale. But he had been bound for so long that his arm was swollen and stiff. His fingertips were numb, so a long time passed before he was able to write.

X

When Dần saw his mother appear at the gate, he leaped for joy. "Where have you been all afternoon?" he asked her. "Did you buy any rice? Why are you coming home empty-handed?"

From the kitchen, Tý scolded him. "I've told you that Mother has no money left for rice and you are just causing her stress. Do you think people will sell her rice on credit? Okay, the sweet potatoes are ready. I will bring them to you to eat. Stop bothering Mother."

With her little sister dangling on her hip, Tý rushed to the veranda to greet her mother. "You're back!" she said, grinning. "Has the mayor released Father? Why is your hat torn to shreds and your hand bandaged?"

Mrs. Dậu gave no answer. She listlessly embraced Tỉu and sat down on a corner of the bamboo bed.

Tý affectionately patted little Tỉu's head and chatted with her mother about her sister, "Today this little one has been very naughty. She hasn't stopped crying since you left. I tried to comfort her, but she wouldn't shut up. When I put her down on the bed, she clung on to me and tried to stand up. I had to wash the sweet potatoes, put them in a pot, and start the fire with her attached to my side. The wood was too damp to burn. But the sweet potatoes are cooked. I am a good girl, aren't I?"

Mrs. Dậu remained silent. She wore a downcast expression as she pulled her camisole aside and began breastfeeding little Tỉu. Her nipple looked pale and veiny. She squeezed it really hard; a few drops of sour milk fell on the floor. Dần stood beside her and looked attentively at the wasted milk with regret. Tỉu was sucking her mother's nipple while bawling continuously. The milk didn't come out fast enough for Tỉu to swallow. The girl's mouth and hand moved back and forth between her mother's nipples like a cat playing with a flat balloon.

A few wrinkles appeared on Mrs. Dậu's nose. She uttered, "Shhh, baby," and was heartbroken by Tỉu's voracity. She nearly cried out in pain as she pressed on her breast and massaged in a circular motion to encourage milk to flow toward her nipple. Next to the bamboo bed a strand of smoke rose.

Tý brought a basket of steaming sweet potatoes in and put it against a column near the wooden bed. "The sweet potatoes are piping hot," she said to Dần. "Don't touch them now, or you'll burn yourself."

Tý then cheerfully hurried to another basket to collect two large bowls and a pair of long chopsticks. She picked through the potatoes to find the biggest roots to fill the bowls. In a jovial mood, she gently laid one bowl on the bamboo bed and invited her mother to eat. She then walked across the room, craned her neck, and placed the other bowl on the altar. Turning around to Dần she said, "This is for Father to eat when he comes home. Anyone who touches it won't be allowed to play with me."

The young boy ignored her. He sat close to the basket of potatoes, his mouth watering. Tý ran off to find a fan to cool the potatoes.

As soon as the potatoes had cooled, the two children sat on the ground beside the basket. They each picked up a root and without waiting to peel them, chewed greedily, occasionally blowing on them. Tý and Dần were like two tigers in a zoo that voraciously swallowed fresh meat. They only spat out the bitter potatoes with mildew or stringy roots.

Mrs. Dậu's heart ached at the spontaneous sight of her two docile children acting so calm and loving. Watching their innocent behavior was like a dagger slicing her flesh. The more she watched, the harder she cried.

Astonished to see her mother cry, Tý softly urged her to have some sweet potatoes because she hadn't eaten anything since that morning. "Mother, eat some so you can have milk to feed Tĩu."

Mrs. Dậu was heartbroken. Her tears fell even faster.

Tý felt uneasy. She lifted the bowl of sweet potatoes to her mother. "Take some," she said. "Why don't you want to eat? I will only eat if you do."

To make her happy, Mrs. Dậu took a sweet potato but immediately placed it down on the bed.

Hesitating, the little girl asked her mother earnestly, "Did the beating this morning hurt much?"

"No," Mrs. Dậu said after drying her eyes.

"Why are you crying and not eating? Do you feel sorry for us because we are hungry?" Tý asked. "But we are not hungry. If we eat all these sweet potatoes, our stomachs will be too full. Eat, Mother! Eat all the sweet potatoes in the bowl. If you don't eat, how will you have enough milk to feed the baby?"

With tears again forming in her eyes, Mrs. Dậu replied, "No, I won't eat. The sweet potatoes are for you. This is the last time you will eat at home. I don't want to take your food, darling. Eat all you can, and don't worry about me."

Not quite understanding what her mother just said, Tý turned pale and asked hastily, "Where will I eat then, mother?"

After a long, piercing wail, Mrs. Dậu looked at her daughter and explained that she would live and eat in the deputy's house in Đoài Hamlet.

The news was a thunderbolt to Tý's ears. She threw her sweet potato into the basket and burst into tears.

"So you're selling me," Tý said. "Please, Mother, don't. I'm so young. Have mercy on me. Let me stay at home to play with my brother and sister."

Dần cried loudly. He abandoned the basket of sweet potatoes and stood up, his butt quivering, and repeated what he had said that morning: "I won't allow you to sell Tý. Sell Tĩu instead."

Mrs. Dậu could do nothing but weep. Her face looked miserable. Despondent, she stretched out on the bed and turned her face toward her baby.

Wisps of hair fell over Mrs. Dậu's arched eyebrows and fluttered like tenuous strands of smoke in the wind. A few drops of tears ran down her rosy cheeks like drops of glittering dew on rose petals.

XI

The wind shook the bamboo leaves, scattering them thinly across the ground. The setting sun shone onto the veranda. Dần and Tý stopped eating and could do nothing but beg and wail. Little Tỉu had been fed enough milk, so she turned her face away and began to play cheerfully.

Mrs. Dậu became even more depressed. Burying her head in her hands, she let her thoughts drift. She then stood up, with determination and said, "May Heaven punish me for my sin. We're so poor, and I've no choice but to let them separate you from me." She wiped her eyes and began to perform the painful task.

Tỉu still dangled on Tý's hip.

The mother dog bowed her head to allow Mrs. Dậu to chain her to a column. She placed the puppies carefully in a basket with a string fastening the lid.

Everything was ready. Mrs. Dậu fed Tỉu again. She then took the torn mat from the bed, spread it out on the ground, and laid her baby down. She told Dần to look after his little sister while she gathered Tý's clothes and wrapped them in a bundle. She picked up the basket with the puppies with one hand and put it on her head while grabbing the chain with the other, ready to lead the dog away.

"Take an old hat to protect yourself from the sun and get your bundle of clothes and follow me to Deputy Quế's house," she said to her daughter.

Tý had been experiencing a moment of comfort, thinking that the dogs were being prepared to send away as a substitute for her. But on hearing her mother tell her it was time to go, she could not help but cry. She asked her mother, "If you sell me, who will I play and live with tomorrow? Why is my fate so cursed?"

With tears running down her cheeks, Mrs. Dậu begged her, "Take pity on me and your father. Please stop crying. Come with me. I'm completely heartbroken. By selling you, all the care, the loving care I gave you these past seven years, is lost. But try to understand. The tax has not been paid, and your father is being punished despite his illness. His arms are all swollen. If I do not sell you, how can I manage to pay his poll tax? How much suffering can your father endure? If you love me, if you love your father, follow me."

Tý continued sobbing bitterly. Mrs. Dậu, the basket of puppies on her head, tried to find the words to comfort her daughter as she too was crying.

After a long while, Tý seemed to understand her mother's grief and stopped sobbing. She wiped her face and ran toward Tỉu. She bent her head and kissed her sister's cheeks. But she could not refrain from tears when she told Tỉu, "Stay home with Dần. I have to go live at the deputy's house. From now on, I won't have a chance to hold you in my arms. When you grow up, come and see me."

She then embraced Dần and kissed him on the cheeks. "Do you love me? Will you miss me?" she asked her brother, tears in her eyes. She then continued sadly, "Mother has sold me, so you will play with Tỉu at home. When she cries, comfort her, and don't beat her. When she grows older, bring her to the deputy's house to see me. I'm going away forever. Goodbye, Dần."

Dần grasped her blouse and screamed, "You must stay home with me. I won't let you live at the deputy's house. Who am I going to play with after you're gone?"

Tý sobbed and clung to him. Turning to Mrs. Dậu, she begged, "I'll miss my brother and sister a lot. May I stay here tonight and spend some more time with them? I'll leave early tomorrow morning."

Mrs. Dậu was heartbroken. "Forgive me," she said. "If you love me and your father, come now. Without you, the deputy will not give us the money to pay the tax. If you stay here tonight, the mayor will detain your father for another night. Your father could die in the communal house. I beg you."

She spoke gently to Dần. "Darling, be a good boy and loosen your hold on your sister. Let her come with me, please, so that I can get the money to pay the tax; then Daddy can return home and be with you. This morning your father was beaten. Don't you feel sorry for him? If you don't let go of your sister, the mayor will tie both of us up when he comes here."

Dần was as afraid of the mayor as other children were of the bogeyman, and the mere mention of him gave him goose bumps. He immediately let go of the flap of Tý's blouse and spoke tenderly to his mother. "I will only let Tý go away for a short while. When you have the money, bring her back to me."

Mrs. Dậu offered a reluctant "yes." But she felt guilty for lying and attempted to fix it by saying, "Yes, if the deputy agrees to let her come home for a few days, I'll bring her back to you."

Tearfully, Tý kissed her brother and sister once more, dejectedly put on her tattered hat, and gathered her bundle of clothes under her arm.

Mrs. Dậu told Dần to watch little Tỉu. She then unfastened the dog's chain from the column and led her away.

In Mrs. Dậu's home, the dog had not played the role of a guard in the same way dogs of wealthy families did but was reliable in case of emergency. As a "faithful" animal, she was fully devoted and obedient to her masters. Her entire life, she was always eager to "work" for them and never hoped for a "retirement pension," though she was merely an appreciated animal. Thus, when Mrs. Dậu placed the chain around her neck, dragged her, and treated her so strangely, the dog didn't quite understand what her master wanted to do—probably sending her to a place where she would be treated with great cruelty. The dog resisted and refused to go. With a pleading expression, she resisted Mrs. Dậu's efforts to drag her away. If an animal psychologist had been standing there, he would have surmised that she was begging her master to grant her more time to serve them.

But the dog's supplications were of no use. Mrs. Dậu used all of her "masterful authority" to yank the canine away. Yet the dog remained confident that her master would again act kindly toward her. That is why, after exiting through the gate, she frisked and rolled about on the ground, her tail wagging. She barked as soon as she heard the puppies in the basket.

The sun was sinking. People's shadows became as long as the slim stems of areca trees that had been thrown across the ricefields.

Oxen and buffalos, finished with their afternoon work, lumbered behind their caretakers to the ricefield terraces to graze.

Her heart aching and with tears covering her face, Mrs. Dậu led her child and dog to Deputy Quế's house. Ignoring her daughter's wailing and the barking of the dogs, she walked through the summer heat, wanting nothing but to reach her destination as quickly as possible.

XII

The setting sun cast soft rays across the tops of the bamboo trees.

Water ouzels chirped in star fruit and areca trees.

In the courtyard, Deputy Quế jerked his head up, his mustache bristling, and stared at a group of pigeons cooing outside their coop. When he saw Mrs. Dậu and her daughter peering in through the door, he said mockingly, "Why are you so late? We've been waiting for you for hours.

Dealing with you is always a nuisance. Punctuality is a foreign concept to you."

Mrs. Dậu and her daughter bowed respectfully.

"Sir, my husband is tied up in the communal house," she said. "It took a great deal of time to have the authorities untie him so he could sign the bill of sale. Besides, it's a long walk from our home to yours. Please forgive me!"

"My wife is in the living room. The two of you go and have a talk with her," Deputy Quế said. "Will somebody come and manage the dogs for these people?" he shouted into the yard.

With a clownish, exaggerated voice, the cook said he would. Armed with a stick, he drove the dogs away. He then showed Mrs. Dậu and her dogs to the room where she had earlier spoken to the deputy and his wife.

Madame Quế was furious. "I warned you to use something to shelter the puppies from the sun, but you've offered them such paltry cover."

Embarrassed, Mrs. Dậu mumbled an apology. She asked the cook to chain the mother dog to a column and gently put the basket of puppies on the ground.

Madame Quế glanced at little Tý and in a shrill voice scolded Mrs. Dậu, "So this is your daughter. Why did you and your husband dare say she was seven years old? If so, why is she such a runt? You liar! You never tell the truth."

"I wouldn't dare lie," Mrs. Dậu replied. "She is seven. Her brother is five, and her little sister is two. I have three children in all."

Arriving from the courtyard, Deputy Quế pointed his finger at Mrs. Dậu and yelled, "Hold your tongue! Don't babble. We don't care how many children you have. The more children you birth, the more you have to sell. That's all! Uncover the basket and let me see the puppies."

Madame Quế continued, talking to her husband, "Listen to her! I can't believe a word she says." Then she turned toward Mrs. Dậu and threatened, "Behave, or I'll cancel this purchase and dismiss you all. Do you think you're my equal? I barely finish speaking and you start objecting. How insolent! That very small girl—how dare you say she is seven? Only a dog would believe it."

Standing behind a column, Tý appeared despondent, feeling as if a whole year of her life had just been thrown away. Mrs. Dậu was silent. Tears filled her eyes. The veins on Deputy Quế's temples swelled, foreshadowing his wrath. He scolded Mrs. Dậu, "Why is it taking you so long to uncover the puppies? If you are regretting selling them, take them back."

Mrs. Dậu's tears fell on the floor. She loosened the strings, removed the lid, and laid it on the floor. Deputy Quế sat down beside the basket. One by one, he lifted the puppies by the scruffs of their necks and inspected their eyes, ears, tongues, legs, bellies, and tails, scrutinizing their fur. Then he examined their mother. His anger dissipated. He got up and walked over to the carved wooden bed, sat down cross-legged, and asked Mrs. Dậu, "Where's the bill of sale? Give it to me."

She unknotted her cummerbund and obediently placed the paper on the bed.

Deputy Quế held the paper in his hands and only looked at the mayor's seal. Some time passed, and he told a servant boy, "Fetch a full bowl of rice for the dogs. I want to see how they eat."

"Yes, sir." The boy ran in a full sprint to the kitchen.

Mrs. Dậu and her daughter sat beside a column, occasionally glancing at one another, their faces wet with tears.

The four puppies wandered out to the veranda where their mother lay and sucked at her nipples.

Now in a better mood, Deputy Quế said to his wife, "Go see if any of the puppies have tails that curl onto their spine."[8]

"I'm checking," his wife answered. "It seems none do."

XIII

The servant emerged from the kitchen with a basket filled with cold rice. Deputy Quế told Mrs. Dậu and Tý to take the puppies to the other side of the veranda. The servant quickly followed and gave a bowlful of rice to each dog. Mrs. Dậu didn't lie—the puppies were able to eat rice. However, their mother was loath to eat. She paused frequently, seemingly tired and nervous.

With a satisfied grin, Deputy Quế stared at Mrs. Dậu. "Where did you buy this dog?" he asked.

"My mother bought it in Lầu Cai," she answered.

"I see—perhaps it is a Mongtseu[9] breed. It's impossible to find this type of dog in the countryside."

---

8. A dog whose tail curls back onto its spine is believed to be lazy.

9. The French spelling of Mengzi, a city in southern China that was an important trading port for the colonial government.

Madame Quế immediately began praising herself. "It was great of me to find these dogs. Many people have said she has a smart dog. That's why I tried my best to buy it and its puppies. Otherwise, I wouldn't have been so foolish to buy the puppies when they are so young. How do you like them?"

Nodding his head, Deputy Quế muttered, "Fine indeed. Each puppy has its own character: the first one has an extra claw, the second has tiger-like fur, the third is completely black, and the fourth has white spots on its legs. Each has lopped ears, short noses, speckled tongues, and slanted eyes. Very fine."

He happily returned to the wooden bed. Sitting cross-legged, he brought his pipe's curved bamboo stem to his mouth and took a draw. Rocking on his thighs with a satisfied air, he said, "The more things you know, the more trouble you get. Mandarin Đặng, Deputy Bùi, Secretary Tiên, and Noble Xung, who all live in town, know I am knowledge-able about dog breeding. They have requested that I buy dogs on their behalf. I have decided to give them these puppies when they've grown up. However, I would regret giving away the black one and prefer to keep it for myself as having such a dog brings prosperity to a household . . ."

His wife interrupted him, saying half-seriously, half-jocularly, "You're not giving away any of these dogs. Anyone who wants to have such well-bred dogs has to give me cash. Otherwise, I'm keeping them."

"We already have a pack of fourteen. Why do you want to raise more? Where will we get enough rice to feed them?"

"I'm raising them to guard the house. Raising dogs is better than hiring servants. Our property is large, so a dozen dogs are not so many." Then sneering and pointing a finger at Mrs. Dậu, she scoffed, "The rice for my dogs costs me much more than the rice for your family does."

Feeling sorry for herself, Mrs. Dậu bent her head and wiped off her tears, not knowing what to say in response.

The puppies finished eating and returned to their mother, leaving behind some rice.

Deputy Quế told the boy servant to scoop up the rice that the dogs left behind and give it to Tý. With affected generosity, he, a representa-tive of the people, said to the poor little girl, "Take this and eat. Don't waste precious food. Eat with your fingers. There's no need for chop-sticks and a bowl."

With tears welling in her eyes, Tý looked at the basket of cold rice but hesitated in holding out her hand. Deputy Quế was enraged. "Don't you want to eat the dogs' leftovers?"

Madame Quế also fumed, "Is that the way your mother has raised you? If you continue this attitude here, I'll break your bones. You don't deserve to eat my dogs' food. They are worth a lot of money while you have been bought for a single piaster. Don't you dare be picky with me."

"Bitch! Don't just sit there and stare at me like that," Deputy Quế berated Mrs. Dậu. "Why don't you talk to her? Or are you ashamed for your daughter to eat dogs' food?"

Tý felt sorry for her mother. She quickly picked up the basket, put some rice in her mouth and begrudgingly chewed like a cow chewing hay.

Madame Quế ground her teeth and pointed at the poor little girl, "By tomorrow you must finish all the rice in that basket if you want to receive any more food."

Mrs. Dậu could only lean her head against a column and sob quietly.

"Do you want the money, or do you regret selling your daughter and dogs?" Deputy Quế asked her.

She wiped away her years and stood up. "Sir and Madame . . ."

But Deputy Quế interrupted, urging his wife, "Pay her. I can't tolerate her presence any longer."

Madame Quế opened a trunk, took out two strings of copper and threw them down onto the veranda. "Here's your money."

Mrs. Dậu stooped down and collected the coins. As she was about to untie the strings to count them, Madame Quế shouted, "I'm not so cruel as to short you. No need to count."

Mrs. Dậu tied the strings around her waist and, between sobs, said to her daughter, "Stay here to serve the deputy and Madame Quế. I'm going home."

Tý clung to her mother and cried bitterly, "Don't go home right now, Mother. Stay with me for a while."

With a menacing look in his eyes, Deputy Quế stood up and with his chubby hand gave the child a violent blow. Like a general on a stage, he roared, "Boy, take her to the kitchen."

Tý had to let go of her mother. The little servant dragged her down the steps. She looked back at her mother and wailed, "Tomorrow bring my brother here. I miss him greatly."

XIV

Mrs. Dậu's breasts were round and firm. She found her camisole was suddenly wet with milk, and this made her worry about her baby at home because nursing mothers believe that when their milk flows unexpectedly, their absent babies are hungry and crying for milk. Mrs. Dậu did not dare think of Tý any longer and quickly collected her basket and torn hat. She hurriedly made for Đoài Hamlet's gate.

The sun was sinking behind the horizon. White-necked ravens hovered over the cemetery. Buffalo boys whistled, calling their grazing buffalos home.

When Mrs. Dậu arrived at Đông Xá Village, it was already getting dark. The communal house was empty save for some bats flying around in search of mosquitoes. An oil lamp on the altar cast a dim light on a few incense sticks burning on the pediment below.

The communal house was completely dark, giving it a foreboding air. The mayor's house now held all the noise.

Mrs. Dậu went in the direction of the sound of conches.

Beneath the bright light of a hanging lamp, the mayor's house offered a scene similar to that of the communal house earlier in the day. Mr. Dậu and the other men who hadn't paid their poll taxes had their elbows tied to a column. Men and women filled the doorway, waiting for their turn to pay.

The district guards and the chief orderly were still attending to the canton chief beside the opium tray. The rural council treasurer, scrivener, chairman and vice-chairman, and various other authorities were sitting among books and registers.

When Mrs. Dậu appeared on the steps, her face was soaked with sweat and tears. The authorities immediately asked her, "Have you sold your daughter? Hurry up and pay the tax!"

"I have, sirs," she said.

With those words, she removed the strings of copper along with eighty cents in silver coins—the proceeds of the sale of the potatoes—that she had carefully wrapped in a corner of her camisole. She kept ten cents and timidly presented the two piasters and seventy cents to the mayor. "Sir, I haven't had time to change the coins into paper money. Kindly accept these, please," she said.

The mayor handed the strings of coins to the treasurer to count and told her, "Pay three cents more for each piaster paid in coins. Give them to me. And look! Why are there only two piasters and seventy cents?"

Mrs. Dậu was confused. She gave the mayor the ten cents for the exchange fee and replied, "Sir, I think that is the correct sum for this year's head tax."

"True! This year's tax amounts to two piasters and seventy cents. But you have to pay two head taxes. One for your husband and one for Hợi, understand?"

"My brother-in-law died last January of the lunar calendar. Didn't my husband make a declaration of death for him?"

The mayor became angry. "Even if he did, his tax must be paid. He should have died last October."

Mrs. Dậu grew even more confused, her face revealing that she didn't understand. She wondered if this wasn't some act of trickery.

"My brother-in-law died nearly five months ago. Why should I pay his poll tax?" she asked.

"Go ask the French," the mayor shouted. "I don't know!"

Slowly, the village scrivener gave her an explanation: "Even if your brother-in-law is dead, his tax must still be paid to the government. He died last January of the Annamese[10] lunar calendar, but the tax rolls are tabulated at the beginning of the Western calendar, which was January of the Annamese lunar calendar. Thus, Hợi, who was alive then, is on the list. When the rolls were submitted to the provincial authorities, the French Residency drafted a list of taxpayers according to that list and sent it to the Public Treasury for collection purposes during the next tax campaign. Even if your brother-in-law hadn't died in January of the lunar calendar, but last month instead, it would be just the same, because the list of taxpayers was already determined, and no changes can be made. A declaration of death makes no difference. That's why we cannot strike Hợi's tax from this year's rolls. Because he didn't leave behind a wife or children, the mayor must pass the tax burden on to his relatives. Who is more responsible for the payment than you and your husband?"

Mrs. Dậu wailed and said, "I'm a woman and know nothing about public proceedings. What will happen to us? With the death of my brother-in-law, we've lost our right hand. If he were still alive, we would not be so poor. Now that he has passed away, we must pay for him, but may I request that you be so kind as to delay the payment until tomorrow? Today I am giving you one head tax and ask that you release my

---

10. The French divided Vietnam into three regions: Tonkin (the northern region), Annam (the central region), and Cochinchine (the southern region). Because the Nguyễn dynasty was retained in Huế, a province in central Vietnam, the French called all the Vietnamese people *l'Annamite*.

husband because he is sick and will certainly die if he remains tied up all day."

The mayor stared at her fiercely. "I'll bury him if he dies. Do you think that the threat of his death scares me? If you want to free your husband, bring two piasters and seventy cents to pay Hợi's tax. He will remain tied up until the money arrives."

The situation had become unbearable. Mrs. Dậu sat down beside her husband and groaned, "I've sold my daughter, my dogs, and my sweet potatoes for only two piasters and seventy cents. I believed that it would be enough to pay my husband's poll tax and save him from being punished tonight. I didn't know I also had to pay the tax of a dead man. With Heaven as my witness, my brother-in-law is dead, yet his tax must still be paid. Where can I find so much money now?"

"Don't cry here," the chief orderly shouted at the top of his voice. "If you want to live, shut up, or I'll beat you again."

In a trembling voice, Mr. Dậu advised his wife, "Go home to the children. Perhaps they are crying. Leave me alone here. I won't die if I remain tied up for another night. Don't complain anymore, or you'll be beaten."

Mrs. Dậu remained bitter about the situation.

When the treasurer finished counting, he told Mrs. Dậu, "Stop wailing. Come and look here. There are four coins missing from each string, so another eight cents will be taken from the ten cents you paid as an exchange fee, so you still owe four cents more."

Mrs. Dậu sobbed. "Damn it! I thought that there would be ten cents left to buy rice for my children. Now I don't even have money to cover the tax. What sort of woman is that Madame Quế? So rich, but so dishonest."

Mrs. Dậu cried desperately. Her husband urged her, "Stop crying. Listen to me. If you love me, go home to our children. Don't stay here crying. It will only make me feel worse."

The other detained men were also moved. "Now that your eldest daughter has been sold, who will take care of your two children at home?" one asked.

"They will look after each other," she replied, sobbing.

The men were quite affected. "What misfortune!" they exclaimed. "A five-year-old boy has to take care of a two-year-old girl!"

"As the authorities have said," another chimed in, "even the dead must pay their taxes. If you have no cash for your late brother's tax, your presence here will do nothing to convince them to release your husband. They won't listen to your cries. You'd better go home to your children."

"My friend is right," another man added. "Leave your husband here and go home. Your being here only intensifies his suffering. And if you don't stop talking, they'll beat him."

As kind as the advice was, it was of little use to Mrs. Dậu, who had already been thinking the same thing. She whispered to her husband, "Can I bring you the plate of sweet potatoes Tý has saved for you?"

Mr. Dậu shook his head. "My tongue is bitter. I can eat nothing. Go home to the children. Don't worry about my appetite."

Tearfully, Mrs. Dậu said goodbye to her husband and went home with her empty basket, bamboo tray, and tattered hat.

XV

The moon was poised above the tops of the bamboo trees. Water in the pools glistened like melting gold in a pot. Intermittent cries of black grouse came from a thicket alongside the chirping of crickets in abandoned gardens.

Dusk had just begun to fall, but already the doors were shut and the lights turned out. The peasants, who had been toiling and sweating all day long, needed a good night's sleep to regain their vitality for the next day's work. Except for the mayor's hamlet, all the hamlets were completely quiet, save for the dogs that barked at the arrival of tax collectors and the sound of grinding and pouring coming from some rice dealers' homes.

Mrs. Dậu heard her children's hoarse crying as she arrived at her house.

She ran through the gate, threw her things down in the courtyard, and rushed inside.

Dần was sitting next to his little sister. His eyes were swollen, and his face had the panicked expression of a child who had just escaped a near-drowning. He showed no signs of joy at his mother's arrival. On the contrary, he felt sorry for himself and burst into tears as if wanting to draw attention to the miseries he had been put through. However, while his mother was gone, he had cried so much that he was completely out of breath and could only muster a few faint tears.

Mrs. Dậu had no time to speak to him and quickly gathered Tiu in her arms. The little girl's eyes were red and swollen. Her body and clothes were covered with shit, urine, and dirt. She was crying but not making a single sound, her mouth wide-open like a carp's. Mrs. Dậu picked her baby up and took her over to the water jar. She washed the dirt off perfunctorily and, removing her camisole, offered Tỉu her breast. Still holding Tỉu in her arms, she hurriedly went inside to fetch her son, to take him outside to wash him.

The little boy tottered out to the veranda, crying. He was as filthy as a statue that had just been unearthed during an excavation.

Mrs. Dậu took him to the water jar. She held Tỉu in one arm and poured water over her son and scrubbed him with her other hand. She then carried them back into the house and laid them down on the wobbly wooden bed. The mat that she had spread out on the floor earlier in the afternoon was stained with Tỉu's waste and urine, so Dần had to stand on the floor while his mother took Tỉu into her chamber to get another mat.

Since early that morning she had been racing back and forth without a chance to eat. Hungry and tired, she wearily stretched out on the bed, her children's heads resting on her arms.

Tỉu became livelier. She was sucking her mother's nipple and playing with it at the same time. Every once in a while, she would let out faint sobs. Dần cried from hunger and repeatedly urged his mother to go and buy some rice. Mrs. Dậu thought of the bowl of sweet potatoes that Tý had placed on the altar. She got up to get them for Dần, but mice had eaten all but three or four small bites.

Dần waved his hand, saying, "I won't eat it. The food is for Daddy. Tý has told me, if I have a bite, she will scold me and won't play with me."

After saying that, Dần suddenly asked his mother, "Where is my sister? Why don't you bring her home to me?"

Tears filled Mrs. Dậu's eyes as she heard his innocent words. Putting down the remains of the potatoes, she hugged and caressed her son. "Tý is now at the deputy's house. I've sold her and cannot bring her home."

Dần cried loudly. "This afternoon I asked you to bring her home when you'd received the money. Why did you leave her there?"

"The deputy won't allow her to come back home," Mrs. Dậu said. "Eat the sweet potatoes and go to bed. I'll take you to see her tomorrow."

"Not tomorrow. Bring her home to me tonight. I want to sleep next to her."

Mrs. Dậu comforted her son while wiping off her tears, "Be a good boy. Tonight, sleep by my side."

But Dần was adamant. "No! I won't sleep by your side. When Daddy comes home, I'll tell him you have sold my sister." He seemed quite bold.

Mrs. Dậu tried everything to quiet him: sweet words, threats and scolding, but nothing worked. She gave in and wept as well. This made him cry even louder. He threw himself on the bed, stamped his feet, and called wildly for his sister to come home. After a long while, he grew tired, his cries grew softer and softer, and he shut his eyes and slept.

Tỉu stopped nursing. She released her mother's breast and fell asleep. Mrs. Dậu lay down quietly on the bed.

Mosquitos buzzed around and stung her feet. She waved her hand slowly to drive them away, afraid to wake her children.

Tỉu was sound asleep.

All of a sudden, Dần laughed deliriously and said, "Here you come, Tý! Come and eat with us. The rice is ready."

After a pause, his dream continued, "Now you must stay at home. Don't go to the deputy's house anymore. I miss you."

Then he awoke with a startle and sat up. "Where is Tý? Mom, where is my sister?"

Blinking, it all seemed to come back to him. He cried out while gazing at his mother's face, "Why don't you bring Tý home, Mother? Get up, go and get her. I won't let you sleep."

Mrs. Dậu gently withdrew her arm from around Tỉu and laid her head on the bed. She picked up Dần and held him in her lap. The moonlight was bright enough for Mrs. Dậu to see his sulking face.

"Stop crying. Let your sister sleep. We'll go out for a walk," she said, trying to comfort him.

But Dần cried more loudly. Mrs. Dậu picked up the sweet potatoes in the bowl and took her son out onto the veranda.

Outside it was as bright as daytime.

XVI

The moon shone overhead. The sky was as clear as crystal. A south wind blew softly, and shadows of bamboo leaves that landed like silhouettes on the moss-clad courtyard undulated like duckweed floating on a current.

Dần hid against his mother's breast and wailed. Now and then he nagged Mrs. Dậu about bringing his sister back. The sight of her son hungry and unable to sleep troubled her. She carefully peeled a sweet potato and coaxed him to eat it, but he curtly refused, saying that the food was for his father.

Dần grew sleepy. Mrs. Dậu carried him back into the house, took a fan to chase the mosquitoes off her daughter, and then carried her son back to the courtyard. She paced back and forth in the moonlight and sang a lullaby to put him to sleep.

The moonlight filling her teary eyes brought her back to her youth. At the age of six or seven, her mother and father had tenderly cared for her. Back then she had done nothing but play. She didn't have to watch her younger brothers or sisters, sweep the house, or work in the kitchen like Tý had to. When it was nice out and the moon was bright like tonight, she was free to run around and play with the neighborhood children. How many games they had enjoyed together: hopscotch, hide-and-seek, and skipping.

Such merriments were still fresh in her mind. When she was fourteen or fifteen, she had enough food to eat and not much work to do; she never experienced real poverty. She didn't know the source of this present misfortune, but her family's situation had gone from bad to worse since her marriage. Year after year, the couple toiled endlessly from dawn to dusk but could never make ends meet.

She thought: *How many struggles I've had to endure, how much medical attention I have had to give to my daughter so she could reach the age of seven. Now, because of an unpaid tax, she has been sold along with two loads of sweet potatoes and five dogs, and there still isn't enough money to cover the debt. My husband is still tied up and experiencing great physical pain throughout the night. Can he survive until tomorrow? Where can I find the additional money needed to have him released? If I fail, what will happen to him? Even if my husband is bailed out, my daughter is no longer with me. When can I hope to bring her home? Has she eaten yet? Who does she sleep next to?*

Mrs. Dậu returned to the veranda. She leaned against a column and sobbed.

The moonlight slanted down onto the yard. An owl screeched from within a bamboo grove in front of the house, announcing the start of his nightly hunt. The cry was like a demon's wail. A few sleepy storks woke up, flapped their heavy wings and flew out from their shelters. Roosters crowed throughout the neighborhood. Three drumbeats signaled the start of the night watch.

Tiu stirred and began to cry. Mrs. Dậu stood up slowly. She went inside to lull her baby back to sleep, but Dần awoke, still in her arms.

He opened his eyes and uttered a phrase he spoke every night, "Tý, take me out to pee."

Mrs. Dậu carried him outside. When they reached the gate, he said, "I don't want you. I called for Tý, not you."

He then shouted as loud as he could and struggled in her arms. Inside, Tỉu continued to cry loudly. Troubled, Mrs. Dậu put down her son on the ground and hurriedly went inside to pick up her daughter. Just then, the little girl crawled to the edge of the bed and was about to fall to the ground. Mrs. Dậu raced to grab her and bring her into the courtyard, where Dần was lying. She carried her children in her arms and brought them both through the veranda and sat down on the bamboo bed. Tỉu stopped crying when Mrs. Dậu offered her breast again. Dần, however, continued to sob, demanding, "Take me to find Tý. Hurry up!"

Mrs. Dậu was very concerned. "It's late at night. The roosters are crowing. If you go out, the bogeyman will eat you," she threatened.

"I'm not afraid of the bogeyman," Dần replied. "I'm going to find my sister. I want her to sleep next to me. Go with me to find her."

Mrs. Dậu didn't know what to say. Dần thrust his hand into his mother's camisole, snatched the suckling's mouth from her nipple, and scolded Tỉu, "No more nursing! I want Mother to take me to find Tý."

Tỉu cried loudly. Dần tried everything he could think of to convince his mother to go out with him. He pulled her hair, ears, and collar, urging her to stand up and go with him immediately.

Mrs. Dậu finally had to give in because his insistence was a sign of his love for his sister. Dần missed Tý because she had always been by his side. She lulled him to sleep every night. He longed to see her immediately. He shouldn't be blamed for the way he nagged his mother. It was she who had sold Tý.

The moon began to slip behind the bamboo grove. Dim light and shadows streaked and speckled the village path, making it resemble a Chinese pastoral painting.

Everyone in the homes along the path was fast asleep.

With Tỉu on one hip and Dần on the other, Mrs. Dậu shuffled along the path. The children were silent. Tỉu was busy with nursing, and Dần was consumed with the hope of seeing his sister soon.

It was a long, quiet night. Mother and children ambled along the deserted path. Mrs. Dậu realized she was being foolish. Many times she decided to turn around and go back, but Dần was stubborn and demanded they continue ahead.

Her wandering caused some movement in the hedge outside a house and set dogs to barking. Other dogs responded in kind. Everyone woke up and wondered what was going on. From the communal house and the watch stations, horns and conches blared loudly.

Dogs barking, men shouting, horns blasting. The mingling of the noises set the hamlets in an uproar.

XVII

Noises and people's shouts abated.

The villagers realized it was Mrs. Dậu probing around in the darkness that was causing all the commotion. But nobody thought of having her arrested because she was known for her honesty; she never took so much as a needle from anyone. Moreover, she was carrying two children—one crying, one nursing—and not even her worst enemy could accuse her of attempting any theft.

It was cloudy out.

The stars gradually disappeared from the sky.

Fog filled the air.

The moon sank down as low as the top of the wall.

Roosters crowed from house to house.

Beneath the roof of their tiny hut, Mrs. Dậu stared at the waning moon as if she had something to confide in it.

Tỉu had been fed enough and was now lying in her mother's arms, playing with Dần's shadow on the wall.

Frightened by all the earlier commotion, Dần sobbed silently and no longer dared to ask his mother to go out and fetch his sister.

Mrs. Dậu started to worry about Tý.

Usually, when the first roosters crowed and Mrs. Dậu had to get up to cook rice, Tý would take care of Tỉu. She would rock her sister to sleep or sing and talk tenderly to her. Now that she was away, the house felt as desolate as if it were in mourning. It wasn't her fault. Tý had been separated from her family and sold for one piaster because of her father's head tax. Poor thing, she had to work as a servant for wealthy Deputy Quế's arrogant family. Never would she receive a gentle word from her masters. That night she would have no one to keep her company except the dog and her four puppies.

Thinking of her daughter made Mrs. Dậu's eyes fill with tears and her heart burn.

Dogs barked in the distance. They howled most loudly in the center of the hamlet and continued their commotion in the lane near Mrs. Dậu's home.

Someone was shouting at Mrs. Dậu's door, "Dậu, are you sleeping or awake?"

Mrs. Dậu sprang up and stared toward the gate, dismayed to see a crowd had gathered in the dark shadows cast by a bamboo thicket.

But they had not come to apprehend her for having caused a disturbance. Rather, they were bringing a lifeless body carried on the back of one of the mayor's servants. Two other men supported the body's shoulders, his dangling arms like two long calabashes.

Mrs. Dậu and her children stood up, shocked. She asked, "Sirs, what is wrong with that man?"

Out of breath, they couldn't answer right away because they had been taking turns to carry the heavy body there. They dragged their feet into the house and laid the body on the wooden bed. One of them made an effort to speak, "Your husband has caught a fever. See if any of your neighbors have some peppermint camphor to give him. Perhaps it will revive him."

At that, the men turned and quickly left the house, not daring to look back.

Aghast, Mrs. Dậu placed her children on the ground and rushed toward her husband.

Mr. Dậu lay motionless on the bed. The waning moon's dim light revealed his half-closed eyes.

She touched his forehead, face, and limbs and found them cold. He was breathing faintly. Mrs. Dậu bent her head and spoke to her husband, "Wake up, dear, wake up!"

But Mr. Dậu was as still as a log while his two kids were bawling on the floor.

She raced out to the gate and called loudly, "Mr. Dậu! Where are your three souls and seven *vía*?[11] Come home to your wife and children!"

She ran up and down the lane. After calling out for the sixth time, she could yell no more, her tongue tied, and she staggered back to the wooden bed. She did not know how to revive her husband. She placed her hand on his forehead and shook him while repeating, "Wake up, dear."

---

11. See Ngô Văn Giá's explanation in his essay.

But Mr. Dậu did not return to consciousness. Their two children cried loudly.

XVIII

Drumbeats announced the end of the night watch.

Roosters were crowing.

Dawn was arriving.

Her heart aching, Mrs. Dậu looked at her husband's pale face. Thinking there was no way to save him, she slammed her fist on the bed's wooden planks and sobbed, calling to Heaven and Earth. She then went to the water jar and came back with a china basin of water. She removed the shawl from her head, dipped it in the water, and washed her husband's face, legs, and arms so that if he were to join his ancestors, he would be clean and presentable.

The neighbors flocked in. They watched after the children, touched Mr. Dậu's body and shouted into his ears. Some went out to the fork in the road and summoned his soul once more.

The house was filled with people who had come to check on Mr. Dậu. They comforted Mrs. Dậu, telling her not to cry and reassuring her that nothing would happen to her husband. Then they helped her with whatever they could. A woman told Dần to pee into the basin. A man put a comb between Mr. Dậu's teeth.[12] Another man poured Dần's urine into his father's mouth. Another woman held the basin and rubbed urine on Mr. Dậu's face, neck, nape, and temples. A young woman ran home to get some burnt locusts for him to sniff. A neighbor burned a broom in the middle of Mr. Dậu's house.[13]

After a long while, Mr. Dậu began to breathe more forcefully and started to open his eyes. Everyone cheered as he came to.

He hadn't caught a fever, but rather he had been bound so tightly that his circulation had been restricted, which made him faint. Thanks to the cold water that Mrs. Dậu had applied to his face and the urine that someone had poured into his mouth, he regained consciousness.

Conversations became lively.

The neighbors asked about Tý, as she was nowhere to be seen. Mrs. Dậu explained that she had been sold to Deputy Quế in Đoài Hamlet along with their five dogs for two piasters to pay the poll tax.

---

12. So that he wouldn't bite his tongue.
13. Most of these are folkloric remedies.

Everyone felt sorry for Mrs. Dậu. They advised her to continue nursing her husband instead of worrying about her daughter because when Tý grew up, she would return home. She was not lost.

Mr. Dậu was still very tired, and Dần cried for food.

Having heard that the little boy had only been given some pieces of sweet potato and that Mrs. Dậu and her husband had nothing to eat, a female neighbor generously gave her a pint of rice and told her to prepare porridge for the family.

Very moved, Mrs. Dậu thanked the woman, her eyes drenched with tears. She began to cook porridge while breastfeeding Tỉu.

The sun rose high in the sky and shone into the house through a crack in the door.

Mr. Dậu began to speak to his neighbors in a feeble voice. The young women were the first to leave the house, followed by the elderly folk. The hut again took on an air of desolation.

Mrs. Dậu held Tỉu in her arms and sat beside her husband. She massaged his limbs, comforting Dần while occasionally getting up to feed the fire.

Drumbeats, rattles, and horn blasts resounded from the communal house once more.

From the lane behind Mr. Dậu's house, Mới was calling for the junior watchmen to go to the communal house and prepare banners and drums to welcome the mandarin.

Mr. Dậu sighed and groaned, "How can I find money for another tax by the time the mandarin comes? I might be tortured to death."

Tearfully, he turned to face the bamboo partition, mumbled the names of Tý and his late brother Hợi, and felt sorry for his own poor fate.

From the kitchen, Mrs. Dậu ran in and sat next to him. "Don't cry, dear, don't cry!" she comforted him. "Brother Hợi is dead, and you can't bring him back to life. Tý has been sold, but she is probably being well taken care of. When we have enough money, we can have her back. As for the tax, although it's desperately needed, we can ask for a delay. After all, they cannot eat us, because human flesh smells disgusting. Rest now, darling. Don't worry. What will I do if you fall sick and faint again?"

Mr. Dậu loved his wife. He dried his eyes with his hand and turned to Tỉu, pretending to talk as if nothing had happened.

The pot of porridge boiled over and doused the flames. Mrs. Dậu laid her baby next to her husband and ran to the kitchen to rekindle the fire. Dần followed his mother and urged her to take the pot off the fire, saying the porridge was ready to eat.

Outside, someone knocked on the wall, and the mayor's servant called, "Is Mr. Dậu still alive? Silence means that he is not dead. Pay the tax, Mr. Dậu! The mandarin is coming."

From the kitchen, Mrs. Dậu replied meekly, "Sir, since early this morning I have been very busy taking care of my husband and have had no free time. Tell the mayor that I will pay the tax tomorrow afternoon."

"Tomorrow afternoon? That's easy enough to say! Do you think you can treat the state tax as a mere nothing?" he replied.

Mrs. Dậu insisted, "I know, but I have no money on me. You and I are both people in need, so you can tell the mayor for me."

"I'm not like you. I have no smooth tongue and I'm not authorized to accept your proposal. You can tell the chief orderly directly," he said and took out his cudgel, leaving irritated.

Mrs. Dậu sat by the fire. She stirred the pot with a long chopstick to prevent the porridge from overflowing. Through a slit in the roof, the hot sun shone down onto her sweat-streaked face.

It was about mid-morning, and Dần cried for food. Sitting next to his mother, he greedily stared into the pot of porridge.

XIX

A car horn blared at the entrance to the village. Horns sounded hastily and drums beat slowly.

An elderly female neighbor hurried in and asked Mrs. Dậu, "Have you paid the tax?"

"We have paid only one tax, and there is one more that we haven't paid."

"Why do you have to pay two taxes?" the old neighbor inquired.

"My husband's and my brother-in-law Hợi's."

"But Hợi is dead; why do you have to pay his?"

"Well," Mrs. Dậu replied, "they told me that because my brother-in-law died in the middle of last year according to the Western calendar, his poll tax has to be paid for the entire current year. If he had died a year ago, he would have been exempt."

"Damn it!" the old woman exclaimed. "Hợi died nearly a year ago and yet his relatives must still pay his tax. What a strange custom! What can you do if you don't have the money? I've heard that the mandarin has arrived."

"You're right. The mandarin has arrived. But if I have no money, I'll ask for an extension. What else can I do?"

The elderly neighbor felt sorry for Mrs. Dậu's situation and left.

The porridge was ready. Mrs. Dậu brought the pot into the middle of the house and poured it into several bowls that she cooled with a fan.

Drumbeats and horn blasts echoed from the entrance to the village all the way to the communal house. Dogs barked loudly everywhere.

The elderly neighbor came again and inquired about Mr. Dậu's health, "How's your husband doing?"

"Thank you for asking. He's regained consciousness, but he's very tired."

"Tell him to find somewhere to hide. If he remains lying in bed, when they come here to collect the tax and he has no money to pay, they'll beat or tie him up. You don't want that to happen to him. He is sick and in pain, and if they beat him again, it will take months for him to recover."

"Yes, I was thinking the same thing. He is waiting for the porridge to cool before he can eat some. He has had nothing to eat since yesterday morning," Mrs. Dậu said.

"You should tell him to eat quickly. The tax collectors will be here soon." Then the elderly neighbor left for her home with an anxious look on her face.

The porridge had cooled. Dần bent his head and ate voraciously. Mrs. Dậu, with great care, brought a large bowl for her husband and said, "Try to sit up and eat some."

She gathered Tỉu into her arms and sat beside her husband, anxious to see if he had an appetite.

Mr. Dậu stretched his arms and yawned. Weakly, he leaned his arms against the bed and looked up, groaning. With a trembling hand, he took the bowl of porridge and was about to take a spoonful just as the mayor's servant and the chief orderly broke into the house, carrying a rattan whip, a cudgel, and a rope.

With the husky voice of a degenerate opium addict, the chief orderly yelled, whipping the ground, "So you're alive, are you? I thought you died yesterday! Hurry up and pay your taxes now."

Frightened, Mr. Dậu hastily laid down his bowl and threw himself back on the bed without uttering a word. The mayor's servant laughed contemptuously. "He will probably catch a chill like last night," he said and pointed a finger at Mrs. Dậu. "If you want to postpone the payment, ask the chief orderly. He'll go to the communal house and ask the mandarin to consider your situation. The mayor is not authorized to grant you any further delays."

Mrs. Dậu answered with a trembling voice, "We are destitute, and we have to pay my brother-in-law's tax. That's why we're asking for an extension. We dare not disrespect the law. Please kindly request the mayor to grant me an extension."

Rolling his eyes menacingly, the chief orderly interrupted, "Listen! I am not your father. How dare you ask to postpone payment of the state tax!"

Mrs. Dậu made another attempt to convince him to consider their situation: "We're so miserable! We have no money, so even if you berate us, there's nothing we can do. Please reconsider our situation."

The chief orderly was not appeased. "If the tax is not paid immediately, I'll dismantle your house." Turning to the mayor's servant, he said, "Let us not waste our time negotiating with her. Tie up her husband and take him to the communal house."

But the mayor's servant did not dare manhandle a sick man for fear of something going wrong. While the mayor's servant was hesitating, the chief orderly wrenched the rope from him and rushed toward Mr. Dậu.

Mrs. Dậu grew pale. She put her baby down and rushed up to grab his hand. "I beg you. My husband has just regained consciousness. Please spare him."

"Spare? Spare indeed!" The chief orderly rained down a volley of blows onto Mrs. Dậu's chest and moved toward her husband.

Mrs. Dậu, unable to control her anger, retorted boldly, "My husband is sick. You've no right to abuse him!"

The chief orderly gave her a stinging slap across the face and bounded over to Mr. Dậu. Gnashing her teeth, Mrs. Dậu grabbed him by his neck and hurled him against the door. She challenged him, "Go ahead and tie him up. And I'll show you what I can do."

The weak opium addict could not withstand the assault of a strong female field hand and collapsed onto the ground. But he didn't stop shouting to the others to tie up the poor couple.

Furiously, the mayor's servant rushed in and attempted to cudgel Mrs. Dậu. Quickly, she grasped the cudgel. A fight broke out. Abandoning the cudgel, they began to wrestle. Weaker than the young woman, the mayor's servant was hurled out onto the veranda.

Mr. Dậu was appalled at the scene but could not rise to his feet to stop his wife. He could only shout with a trembling voice, "Don't do that! They face no risk by beating us, but if we beat them, we'll be sent to jail."

But Mrs. Dậu did not calm down, saying, "I'd rather be jailed than constantly persecuted."

When the incident finally ended, the mayor's servant got up from his crouched position and shouted abuses at Mrs. Dậu but didn't dare touch her. She took little Tiu in her arms and returned the mayor's servant's verbal abuse.

Not knowing what to do, Mr. Dậu berated his wife and apologized to the mayor's servant.

All of a sudden, a long conch blast sounded from the communal house. The mayor and the chief orderly—followed by some watchmen armed with sticks, cudgels, and whips—swarmed down on the Dậus' house. During the melee between Mrs. Dậu and the mayor's servant, the chief orderly had been able to slip away and ran to report the incident to the mayor. They came to arrest the Dậus: a sobbing, sick man, a belligerent woman, and their crying children. They were all brought to the communal house to wait for the mandarin's judgment.

XX

The communal house looked quite different from the previous day. A pair of blue parasols had been placed at either side of the main entrance. A big drum lay with its carrying pole near the banister. About ten banners had been planted on the veranda and in the adjacent buildings. An array of spears and spikes had been erected; their heads pointed toward the roofs of the two buildings with parallel façades located on the sides of the communal house.

The mandarin arrived. The deputy mayor and the chieftains, as well as the watchmen and their chief, were busy running around, despite not having any direct responsibilities in the affair. The vice-chairman and the treasurer stood leaning their backs against a column waiting with folded arms, faced by the scrivener and the land surveyor. They all looked intimidated.

Behind the banister, the canton chief let out the occasional yawn, not even bothering to shoo away the flies that landed near his mouth. The chairman flipped through the pages of the tax books, looking around absentmindedly.

Mr. Dậu, his wife, and their son Dần were afraid. Glancing toward the center of the communal house, the sight of the mandarin's bristling mustache frightened them.

How strange was that mustache! It looked like a smear of asphalt. It curved like a sickle, ending in points like drills or chisels. It surrounded his lips like bat wings. It sprang up toward his ears like water caltrop roots and appeared to penetrate his nostrils. It made his shameless face more arrogant and his complaining mouth even more authoritative.

If one did not know that he had begun his career as a government clerk, one could assume he had been promoted to the position of mandarin on account of that mustache alone.

And for anyone who did not know he was a mandarin, he could be mistaken for a rickshaw supervisor or a contractor.

Placing his hands on a table covered with a piece of red cloth typically used for religious services, the mandarin sat down pompously on the smooth varnished chair covered with a luxurious mat edged with red cloth. From beneath his black gauze turban, his plump face gazed at everything disapprovingly.

A short distance away, a stout watchman cooled the mandarin with a feather fan.

In front of him, his stenographer, Thừa, and his clerk, Nho, were busy checking the mayor's receipt books.

The chief orderly was the first to lodge his complaint. "Your Honor," he said to the mandarin, "on your order, the mayor's servant and I proceeded to Nguyễn Văn Dậu's residence and summoned him to pay his poll tax. In an attempt to aid him in avoiding it, his wife beat the mayor's servant and me. The mayor and the watchmen witnessed it. May I request that . . ."

Before the chief orderly finished his sentence, the mayor, standing behind him, intervened, "Your Honor! Her real name is Thị Đào—the most stubborn person in our village. During the past few days, I've sent my men to urge Mr. Nguyễn Văn Dậu to pay his tax, but she told her husband not to pay. We told her that the taxes must be sent to the district office and that if she refused to pay, we must report the matter to you. But she said that she couldn't care less. Today, on your authority, the chief orderly and one of my servants went to expedite her payment, and she beat us. Many people, myself included, witnessed the assault with our own eyes. We beg you, 'Light of Heaven,' to examine this case and send her to jail. We shall be so grateful."

The mandarin held up his head vaingloriously and slammed his fist on the table. "They refuse to pay the tax, and they even beat the orderly? Are they trying to be rebellious? Bring them here!"

The mayor dragged Mr. Dậu and his wife into the communal house with their children by a rope.

"Yes, sir." Their reply echoed throughout the five sections of the communal house. Then, the mayor held the rope that tied Mr. Dậu, his wife, and their two children, and dropped them there.

"Here they are, sir," the mayor said.

The mandarin stared at Mr. Dậu. "Are you attempting to evade the state tax?"

Shivering, Mr. Dậu replied, "I've paid my tax already."

"Why did you say that he has not paid his tax?" the mandarin admonished the mayor.

"He's a liar! He has not paid it . . ."

The mandarin did not let the mayor finish his sentence and immediately asked Mr. Dậu, "Show me your tax receipt."

"Your Honor, I don't have any receipt," Mr. Dậu said. "But the canton chief, the treasurer, and the other authorities saw . . ."

The mandarin looked at the treasurer and the canton chief, asking, "Did you see Mr. Dậu pay his tax to the mayor?"

The treasurer glanced at the mayor and said, "Last night, his wife gave our mayor two piasters and seventy cents in coins. The mayor told us to count it."

As the conversation progressed, Dần pulled his mother's blouse and urged, "Mom, take me home now. I don't want to be here."

The mandarin glared at the little boy and berated the mayor. "Why did you allow the children to come here, huh? Do you want me to slap your face?"

The mayor grew pale. He quickly wrestled little Tỉu from her mother's arms, grasped Dần by the hair, furiously led the two children to the communal house's veranda, took them to the gate, and left them there, tasking Dần with watching his young sister. Paying no attention to their cries, the mayor returned to the communal house.

The mandarin asked the treasurer, "After counting it, who did you hand the money to?"

"To the mayor," the treasurer said.

"That is Hợi's tax," the mayor chimed in.

The mandarin frowned. "Who is this Hợi? Why does Mr. Dậu have to pay Hợi's head tax?"

"Hợi was his brother, and he died at the beginning of the first lunar month," the mayor explained. "As they are brothers, Mr. Dậu is responsible for his payment."

"Why didn't you issue a receipt to Mr. Dậu? Did you plan to steal that tax money?" the mandarin retorted. He then turned to his stenographer and instructed, "Write an official report stating that I am here to supervise the tax collection and have caught the mayor having collected Mr. Dậu's tax without issuing him a receipt. Then tell the canton chief to sign the document. Understood?"

The stenographer affirmed. Obsequiously, the mayor moved toward the mandarin and, scratching his ears, implored, "I am your servant. I beg Your Honor to consider my case. . . . I am innocent."

The mandarin grew even angrier. "How much were you able to get from the transient tenants during tax collection? Why do you want to extract taxes from a penniless resident? Be careful. I'll dismiss you from your position!"

"I beg Your Honor to consider my case. I've been falsely accused," the mayor said, repeating himself.

Switching to a softer tone, the mandarin said, "Report to the district office tomorrow. You hear me?"

Thanking him, the mayor withdrew obediently.

The mandarin returned to Mrs. Dậu. "Did you beat the chief orderly and the mayor's servant so that your husband could evade paying his tax?"

"No, Your Honor. I didn't beat them," Mrs. Dậu replied with a trembling voice. "I only intervened when they were about to beat my husband. I was afraid that because he is sick, he would die."

"I saw with my very own eyes that she beat the chief orderly and my servant," the mayor interrupted.

"Shut up! I'm not asking you," the mandarin said and drew closer to Mrs. Dậu. "Intervening means you fought them. . . . You dared to beat an orderly on duty. Do you want to be in jail?"

Mrs. Dậu didn't know how to answer. The mandarin dismissed her.

When the official statement was drawn up, the stenographer presented it to the mandarin, who after a quick perusal, told the canton chief to place his seal on the paper with some nobles signing as witnesses. Then he began to review the tax collections.

In front of the canton chief and the other authorities, the mayor poured the cash out from the box for the mandarin's stenographer to count. The bills and coins all amounted to 610 piasters. Compared to the taxes listed in the record book, they were short five hundred piasters, but the sum exceeded the counterfoils by twenty piasters.

The mandarin banged his fist on the table and said to the mayor threateningly, "If you didn't commit extortion, why do the taxes exceed the amount on the receipts? When this campaign is done, I'll take back your seal and title."

The mayor grew pale. He wrung his hands and repeatedly implored the mandarin to pity him.

The mandarin softened his voice: "Tomorrow, come to my office and bring Mr. Dậu's wife with you. Understand?"

The mandarin then inquired about the men who hadn't paid their poll taxes. The mayor's servants then dragged them up in front of the mandarin. He slapped their faces and kicked their butts to demonstrate his authority.

Imposingly, he stood up and stepped down from the veranda. Then he walked to his car. Banners, drumbeats, and horn blasts accompanied him as far as the entrance to the village.

XXI

As soon as the trial was over, Mrs. Dậu hurried to the gate of the communal house to look for her children. But she saw neither of them. Frightened, she asked the people nearby and was told that after her children had been left there, a village woman who was passing by saw and felt sorry for them, so she picked up Tỉu and breastfed the little girl and took Dần back to Mrs. Dậu's house.

Not waiting for her husband, Mrs. Dậu raced home. Tỉu had been fed, so she had fallen asleep. Dần was cooling and gulping down porridge. When the woman stepped on the veranda, the boy lifted up his head and burst out crying.

"Mom, where's Daddy?" he asked.

Mrs. Dậu waved her hand, saying, "Don't speak so loudly. Let your sister sleep. Daddy will be home soon." She then quietly walked into the house.

The elderly female neighbor dropped by and inquired, "So, your husband wasn't sent to the district office, and they've released him. Right?"

She then stepped through the veranda and sat on the shabby wooden bed.

"I must say, you are very brave," the neighbor continued. "You, a woman and a mother of three, could beat two men. What would have happened to you had they been stronger and knocked you down?"

Tiu woke up and bawled loudly. Mrs. Dậu gathered her baby in her arms and replied, "I know that a woman making a scene is bad, but we had been persecuted constantly and I ran out of patience. As you saw, my husband was ill. How could he endure an attack from both of them? I had to risk everything for him . . ."

The old woman gave Mrs. Dậu a quid of betel and said, "True, nobody can stand the guards' cruel behavior. I am an outsider, but hearing about this enrages me. How's everything now?"

Mrs. Dậu took the betel and responded, "The mandarin released me but summoned me to the district office tomorrow."

"Where has your husband gone? Has he been taken to the district town?"

"No. In fact . . ."

Mrs. Dậu had hardly finished speaking when Mr. Dậu, groggy, came into the room and groaned. His face was red as if he had just come from a hot kitchen.

He bowed to the elderly woman and tremblingly stepped up onto the veranda, his hands then resting on his knees. Holding the baby, Mrs. Dậu got to her feet to help him up.

The elderly neighbor anxiously said, "You look so feeble. Do you have a fever?"

Mr. Dậu staggered to the bed and lay down beside Dần. He panted and said, "Yes. I've been feeling uncomfortable. I guess I am about to have a fever."

Dần finished his porridge and then went into the courtyard to dip his bowl and chopsticks into a water basin.

Mrs. Dậu handed little Tiu to the elderly woman, saying, "Please hold her for me for a while." Then she placed the tray of porridge on the Kitchen God's shrine and sat next to her husband.

"Do you have a headache?" she asked. "Let me massage your temples."

Mr. Dậu waved his hand. "I'm very tired. Leave me alone for a while. Take the child from our neighbor so she can . . ."

"No worries!" the elderly woman said quickly. "I don't have anything to do today so let me hold the baby so your wife can do what needs to be done."

Mrs. Dậu got up slowly and said, "Thank you. Please help me take care of the baby for a little while." Then she took the torn mat that Tiu had dirtied the day before and brought it to the pond to wash, leaving her husband alone with the elderly neighbor.

"I didn't expect the guards to be so cruel." Mr. Dậu said to the neighbor while groaning in pain. "This morning, if my wife had not intervened and resisted, they would have beaten me to death."

The old woman spat the chewed betel on the ground and said, "I couldn't agree more. The guards are heartless. It is lucky that you have nothing in the house. If you had chickens or dogs, they would have slaughtered them to eat. Where are those men now?"

"They probably have returned to the district town with the mandarin," Mr. Dậu said.

"Has your wife been able to find the tax money anywhere?"

"Not yet. Since yesterday, she has been busy taking care of me and has had no time to worry about that. Poor thing!"

Tears filled Mr. Dậu's eyes.

"I'm most sorry about your situation." The elderly woman comforted him. "Yet a river has many parts and a man's life has many ups and downs. If you live morally, Heaven will bless you."

The sun shone onto the veranda. Mrs. Dậu returned from the pond with the mat washed and a handful of medicinal leaves.

After she had dried the mat over a hedge, Mrs. Dậu plunged the leaves in a basin of cold water and placed it beneath the altar.

"Are they *dành* and *duối* leaves?" the elderly neighbor asked.

"Yes. I've been told that if someone has a fever, crush the leaves and keep them overnight in the open air. Then let the patient drink the potion. It will cure any fever. I want to give it a try to see if it works for my husband."

"True. I've heard the same thing but forgot to tell you," The elderly woman said cheerfully. She spat out the betel from her mouth onto the floor and asked, "Have you eaten anything since this morning?"

Mrs. Dậu took her baby and said, "We've had no time. This morning, just as my husband was holding a bowl of porridge in his hand and was about to eat it, they stormed in . . ."

"Leave the baby to me. Go and get your husband some porridge. He must be very hungry."

"My mouth is bitter. I have no appetite," Mr. Dậu said.

"Try to eat something," the elderly woman insisted. "Otherwise you will get weaker and sicker. Porridge is good for your health."

"She is right," Mrs. Dậu chimed in. "Try to eat to pacify your stomach. You don't want to get sicker and hungry at the same time."

She brought a bowl of porridge to her husband and insisted, "All right, try to sit up and eat this. Don't disappoint me."

In an attempt to please his wife, Mr. Dậu listlessly sat up, took the bowl, and begrudgingly swallowed half of it but could finish no more because his mouth was bitter.

"You should eat some, too, so that you have milk for your baby," the elderly neighbor advised Mrs. Dậu. "Think of your little daughter. If you don't have enough milk to feed her, she will likely contract a lasting and serious disease."

"Finish the remaining gruel before it goes bad. Then go out and try to borrow some money," Mr. Dậu also urged his wife.

Mrs. Dậu took the tray of porridge down from the altar and laid it on the bed. She kept a bowlful for Dần and gulped down some porridge with tears running down her face.

"Today, with the rice you lent us, we have something to eat. But tomorrow, who will be kind enough to help us?" Mrs. Dậu said.

The elderly neighbor was greatly moved. "Heaven has an eye on everything," she said. "I still have half a bushel of rice saved. Bring your basket, and I'll lend you some. When your husband is able to work again, he will give it back to me."

A horn sounded at the gate. The neighbors' dogs barked from all directions. Accompanied by two watchmen, the mayor furiously broke into the house. He pointed his stick at Mr. Dậu and shouted, "Pay your poll tax now! Right now!"

"He has just returned from the communal house and has no money on hand. Please let him pay tomorrow," the elderly woman hurriedly said on Mr. Dậu's behalf.

"It's none of your business! Don't poke your nose into this matter," the mayor reprimanded her. "If he has no money, I'll dismantle his house." He then pointed his stick at Mrs. Dậu and said sarcastically, "Thanks to the two of you, the mandarin has given me a hard time. If the tax is not paid by this evening, two piasters and seventy cents, you'll be so sorry!"

XXII

Dần and Tỉu were still sleeping soundly. Mrs. Dậu brought her husband the drink prepared with medicinal leaves. She placed the tray and bowls on the bed and went to the kitchen to fetch the pot of rice. She had prepared the meal with the rice lent by the elderly neighbor a little early that day because she had to go into the district town.

Mr. Dậu had recovered somewhat and ate with his wife. But he had no appetite and only ate a few bites. Mrs. Dậu had hardly finished her first bowl when the mayor broke in with a rope, followed by two watchmen.

The mayor rushed toward Mrs. Dậu and roared, "Stand up and go to the district office!"

Mrs. Dậu was furious. "Fine! I'll go. I won't run out on my obligations. But let me finish my meal."

The mayor looked at her threateningly. "I don't give a damn about your meal. I'm only doing my duty."

Then he grabbed Mrs. Dậu's arms and told his watchmen, "Tie her up and take her away."

Her bowl fell from her hands onto the tray, spilling rice across the floor.

Mrs. Dậu's arms were twisted behind her back and tied up with the rope. Mr. Dậu looked intently at his wife and cried.

His gaze like daggers, the mayor threatened, "You too. By noontime, if the tax is not paid, I'll chop you into pieces. Don't use your illness as an excuse for delaying payment."

The ruckus startled Tỉu, and she began to cry loudly as if someone had pinched her. Mrs. Dậu tried to pacify the mayor. "Please let me nurse my baby."

But the mayor pointed his fingers at her and said, "Do you want me to slap your face? What nonsense are you saying? It's time to go to the mandarin's office, and you ask me to wait for you so you can nurse your child! Do you think I will stand here and wait for you?"

Pulling on the rope, he dragged her down the steps. He didn't stop cursing her the entire way to the communal house, where he told a watchman to tie her to a column.

Mới brought in a tray of boiled pig offal and tofu and laid it on the mat in the communal house's central hall. Sitting cross-legged near the banister, the mayor drank, ate, and criticized other people. "Yokel Dậu, aren't you ashamed? I am doing this to take my revenge on you," he stated.

The poor woman was furious. Her face turned pale with rage, but she bowed her head without uttering a word. The mayor spoke, stressing each word. "It's because of you two that the mandarin chastised me yesterday. I don't know how to handle this situation. I might lose over one hundred piasters I embezzled from this season's tax collection. It's all your fault!" He thumped his fist on the floor and said, "Do you know how much trouble you have caused? If I were to kill you, it wouldn't be enough."

The mayor continued to bluster to himself until his bottle of alcohol was half empty.

Mrs. Dậu ignored his venomous talk, as she had no desire to argue with a drunk.

The sun had risen high above the bamboo clump.

The food was fully consumed. Only then did the mayor abandon the tray and stand up. However, his mouth was still full of rice that he was chewing with a splash of fish sauce.

Having no time to rinse his mouth and drink tea, he called a watchman and said, "It's already late in the morning. Take her to the district town, or she will miss the morning's trial."

Mrs. Dậu was removed from the column and followed him and the other watchman.

The sunny sky suddenly grew dark with black drifting clouds coming from the north and then floating to the south. Lightning bolts flashed across the horizon, followed by claps of thunder and torrential rain.

The road crossed an empty ricefield, and there was no shelter in sight. The mayor had an umbrella, but he was just as drenched as Mrs. Dậu and the watchmen because the umbrella was nothing but an ornamental accessory that couldn't be opened.

This unfortunate storm only made matters worse, and he went on insulting Mrs. Dậu.

Tears and rain mingled as they streamed down the woman's cheeks. Having no one to turn to, she could only release the occasional sigh.

After a while, the wind eased, the rain abated, the sky gradually cleared, and the hot sun again beat down.

By the time they arrived at the gate of the district office, their clothes had dried. But the morning office hours had ended. The mayor led Mrs. Dậu away to wait at a nearby restaurant until the afternoon.

During tax collection time, the district town's restaurants were always filled with people. Customers crowded their dining room seats and bamboo benches. They ate, drank, talked, and argued with one another. A tumult of people called for rice, wine, and fish sauce from every direction. The restaurant's waiter, a little boy, was kept perpetually busy. The indescribable scent of garlic, alcohol, and shrimp paste that mingled with the sweat of those who hadn't bathed in some time would have made anyone unaccustomed to it nauseous.

Mrs. Dậu was tied to a column. She heard the mayor curse whenever someone asked why he had come to the district town. This hurt her deeply.

She was thinking anxiously of her husband and children at home. She wondered whether his fever had broken, whether someone had fed Tỉu, whether Dần was behaving or annoying his father, and whether Tý was able to live peacefully in the deputy's house or was being poorly treated.

Such questions echoed in her head, and her eyes were red from weeping.

Suddenly, Mrs. Dậu heard a loud voice: "You wicked woman! Do you expect us to come back again?"

Startled, Mrs. Dậu lifted her head and saw a heap of torn, handle-less umbrellas and the restaurant owner preventing some village authorities from leaving the establishment. One of them pointed at the umbrellas and said, "You are not reasonable! We owe only twenty-five cents and are leaving eleven umbrellas as collateral and yet you aren't satisfied?"

The restaurant owner stood firm. "Do you think all these umbrellas are worth twenty-five cents? If you have no money, then leave a decent cloth tunic as security. These umbrellas are only good for making skewers to roast meat."

"We must see the mandarin right now. If we leave our tunics here, how could we go to his office?" one man argued.

"I don't care about that. If you don't give me a tunic, you must pay me cash," the owner demanded.

The men looked at one another, perplexed.

One of them nagged the others. "If you had listened to me and not had another bottle of liquor, we wouldn't be in this trouble. So embarrassing!"

Another of the men removed a square seal made of copper from his pocket and handed it to the restaurant owner. "Take this. It's worth five hundred piasters. Tomorrow I'll redeem it."

Three long drumbeats came from the district office. Red-faced authorities from various villages entered. The mayor of Đông Xá untied Mrs. Dậu and led her through the gate. He instructed her to sit under a *bàng* tree in front of the office and told her to wait for her name to be called.

This was the first time that the peasant woman had ever seen an administrative office. For her, everything was unfamiliar, especially hearing the words "Your Honor," "dismissal," and "jail" frequently coming out from the mandarin's office. She saw people enter with an empty saucer and exit with it still empty.[14]

---

14. A saucer was used as a sign of respect when presenting bribes to the mandarin.

Only when the sun had begun to sink did the mayor of Đông Xá have the chance to present himself before the mandarin with an empty saucer. After a loud reprimand from the mandarin, the so-called father and mother of the people, the mayor whispered something to the mandarin and ran to the tree to bring Mrs. Dậu into the office.

The mandarin glanced at her face and spoke with authoritative tone: "Orderly, throw this woman into jail."

XXIII

From behind the office building, a car horn blared, accompanied by the rumble of an engine. A car began to exit and stopped in front of the mandarin's office, its hood jutting out from the gateway. Through a barred window in the orderlies' house, Mrs. Dậu saw a sulky woman walk down the steps beside the mandarin. Even though it was getting dark, Mrs. Dậu could recognize her elegant gait and beauty.

The woman wore a tight-fitting thin blue tunic that showed off her enticing full and round breasts. She had a scarf thrown over her head and over her shoulders. The thick powder applied to her face couldn't hide the deep wrinkles on either side of her red lips.

Arriving at the car, the woman took a mirror out of her handbag and looked at herself.

The mandarin opened the car door and enthusiastically urged her in. "Make haste, dear. Today is Saturday. He might go out this evening," he said.

The woman acted as if she were displeased. "How shameful I am! I am worse than a dog. I am no better than a prostitute," she said.

"Why do you say that? I know that you don't like it, but that's life," the mandarin replied sweetly. "We must do the same as other people must. If I can bear it, surely you can, too. As the saying goes, *one's friends are stepping-stones to wealth, and one's wife is a stepping-stone to honor*. If I'm promoted this year, I'll give you all the credit."

After a pause to look at her, the mandarin went on, "After all, you have nothing to lose."

Only then did Mrs. Dậu understand that the woman was the mandarin's wife. Seeing her husband grin incensed the mandarin's wife. She raised her voice, saying, "This is not funny. I am not amused, so stop joking!" Then she stepped into the car. Once seated, she leaned her back against the leather seat, opened her handbag, removed the mirror, and again gazed at her reflection.

The mandarin shut the car door and whispered to the chauffeur, "Drive Madame to his residency and leave immediately. Return an hour and a half later and bring her back home. Only after an hour and a half, understand?"

The engine revved, drowning out the driver's reply as the car started. The chauffeur honked a few times—a way to show respect to the mandarin, who waved cheerfully at his wife, saying, "Good luck." He stood watching the car until it disappeared from view.

Mrs. Dậu was still trying to understand the meaning of the conversation between the mandarin and his wife when the chief orderly came in from the office building. He quickly opened a trunk, removed a woman's suit consisting of a black gauze tunic, handkerchief, satin headscarf, camisole with silk bands, gauze cummerbund, white blouse, and pair of silk, light-pink pants. He handed them to Mrs. Dậu and told her, "Take these and the clogs over there with you. Go to the washroom behind the house and take a bath."

"Are you talking to me?" she asked, astonished.

The orderly frowned. "Who else besides you would have to wear these things?"

Mrs. Dậu burst into tears. "Please reconsider my case, sir! I have only just been arrested. Why do I need to wear prisoners' clothing?"

The chief orderly burst out laughing. "You're so dumb! Do you think these are prisoners' clothes? They are a gift from Heaven. Take a bath and put them on. Don't ask any more questions."

Mrs. Dậu wiped her tears and said, "I won't bathe. I won't change my clothes. Let me wear my own."

The chief orderly was annoyed by her obstinacy, saying, "But you are filthy. Do you think the mandarin's bed is like yours? Take a bath and put on the clothes for just tonight. Tomorrow you'll be free to wear your own dress."

Mrs. Dậu did not understand. She started to mumble as if she had something to stay, but the chief orderly shouted, "I'll send you to jail immediately. Don't act up when I am being kind to you."

Frightened by the threat, Mrs. Dậu took the clothing and the clogs and went to the washroom behind the orderlies' house. Water, soap, a basin and towel—everything was there for her to use. She stayed inside for a few minutes, opened the door, and walked out to peer around the corner of the orderlies' house. The chief orderly snapped, "Are you afraid that your torn dress will get wet? Close the door! No one wants to sneak a peek."

With some hesitation, Mrs. Dậu stepped back into the washroom.

Half an hour later, the door opened again. The peasant had transformed into a beautiful woman.

The chief orderly threw her a comb and a square mirror, saying, "Comb your hair, and wrap it nicely in the shawl."

Mrs. Dậu was perplexed, uncertain what was to happen next. The chief orderly chafed. He hurried her on again. Shyly, she took the comb and mirror and tidied her hair.

Another orderly standing nearby smiled. "How lucky you are to be detained by the mandarin," he said to her.

"Really, she is quite pretty," another orderly added. "When well-dressed, she is as beautiful as anyone."

"If she were not beautiful, would we have to carry water for her?" a third orderly said. "But she seems gloomy, perhaps something is agitating her." He looked at Mrs. Dậu and asked, "Why don't you cheer up, dear? Be more cheerful so that we can admire your beauty as a way to make up for having to carry water in for you . . ."

The orderlies all burst out laughing. Mrs. Dậu ignored them. She kept silent, focused her mind on her husband and children at home.

XXIV

The clock on the wall struck seven. Drumbeats announced the arrival of the evening. The gas lamp had just been lit. The chief orderly arrived from the mandarin's private house and said to the house servant, "Our mandarin is eating dinner very early. He told the chef to set the table at only six-thirty. And he is already drinking ginseng wine."

The house servant nodded. "Sure. Today is the best time for him to drink ginseng wine. He already has a strong sex drive, and this tonic will make him even more . . ."

Three drumbeats came from the watchtower, and a blue car drove into the courtyard.

The house servant whispered to the chief orderly, "That's the Minh Hảo district mandarin's car." Then he ran to the front of the office building.

The Minh Hảo mandarin opened the door wide and asked the house servant, "Is your mandarin home, or has he gone out already?"

"Sir, he's dining," the house servant replied respectfully.

The guest mounted the steps majestically. "Why is he taking his dinner so early? It is only seven o'clock. Go and tell him to finish his meal, and I'll wait here," he said and walked into the office.

The house servant ran to his mandarin's private residence. After a short while, he returned to the orderlies' house and said half-seriously, half-flippantly, "Our master is furious today. Who will land in his crosshairs?"

The chief orderly smiled knowingly. "He is very angry because his plans have been upended by a visitor. Is he going to receive his guest, or will he go on eating?"

"Our guest will be lucky if our boss doesn't curse him, let alone welcome him," the house servant said. "When I came to inform our master that the Minh Hảo mandarin was here, he fumed and said, 'Let him wait! I've to eat first.' Then he went on eating as if nothing had happened."

"Today is Saturday, so maybe the other mandarin is coming by to invite our mandarin to go to town together."

"Normally our boss would do just that, but tonight nothing could make him leave his home."

"Yes, tonight you will be exhausted serving him. This month, you'll make plenty of extra money. Have you asked for your watching fee?"[15]

"I've had no time," the house servant replied. He then turned in the direction of Mrs. Dậu and said, "Pay me fifty cents due."

Mrs. Dậu, who was sitting on a bamboo bed in a corner of the room, remained silent. She'd heard the request but didn't know who it was aimed at.

"You, woman from Đông Xá, are you mute?"

"Are you talking to me?" Mrs. Dậu asked, nonplussed.

"Who else?"

"What is the fee for, sir?"

Balling his right hands into a fist, the house servant dashed toward her and roared, thrusting his head forward. "Do you want to argue with me?"

"Give her a few punches," the chief orderly chipped in maliciously.

"Sirs, I am only a woman, and I dare not argue with you," Mrs. Dậu said apologetically in a trembling voice. "This is the first time that I have been to a mandarin's office, and I don't know what fee I must pay. Please excuse me."

The house servant was placated. He explained, "You must pay for your bed and food. It's out of pity that I only charge you fifty cents because you're poor. Pay me now!"

---

15. Money paid to serve as a lookout during illegal gatherings (i.e., card games).

"I have no money on me. I can't even pay my husband's head tax."

The house servant grew angry. "No money? You'll be chained up."

He pointed at a long piece of wood lying in a corner of the opposite building. "Do you see the shackles there? If the fee is not paid, you'll soon have your feet bound."

A bell rang. The house servant and the chief orderly rushed off to the office building. After a long while, sounds of laughter and talking came from the office. Then the host saw his guest off at the steps. After the guest had gotten in his car, the host held the guest's hand and said, "Let's meet next Saturday then. Don't be late!"

The headlights of the car turned on and lit up the entire courtyard. The car exited through the gate and vanished into the darkness. The mandarin called to the house servant, whispering something in his ear before going back to the office building.

Three echoing sounds came from the gong of the orderlies' house and the big drum of the local soldiers' barrack at the same time.

Mrs. Dậu was apprehensive and bent her head in the dimly lit room when the house servant entered and asked, "Are you awake or asleep? The mandarin has summoned you."

Startled, Mrs. Dậu lifted her head. "Why does the mandarin call for me at this hour?"

The house servant was about to speak bluntly but instead said, "No point in asking. Go there and you'll know."

Startled and flustered, Mrs. Dậu lifted up her head and asked in a shivering voice, "Why does he call for me at this time of the day?"

The house servant pretended to look serious. "No need to ask me. Ask him when you see him."

"I thought he worked during the day, not in the evening."

The house servant feigned anger, saying, "Tax collection is in full swing, and there are so many urgent affairs to manage that the mandarin cannot get everything done during the day and thus must work in the evening as well."

Apprehensive and in pain, Mrs. Dậu sat with her head lowered beneath a lightbulb. "I'd be most grateful if you'd ask him to allow me to come tomorrow morning."

"Impossible," the house servant replied. "This is not a joke. If you're summoned and you refuse to come, you'll be shackled immediately."

Mrs. Dậu said nothing, but her heart beat violently.

The chief orderly came in and shouted, "If she is being stubborn, tie her up!"

The two cruel men rushed toward her and dragged her to the building opposite the orderlies' house. One of them lifted the shackles; the other crossed her legs and put them in place. When the wooden piece was lowered and bolted, Mrs. Dậu grimaced with pain. She was like a rat caught in a trap. At first, she tried to bear it, but the pain was soon so immense that she could endure the suffering no more. She cried out and begged the men to release her.

The house servant swelled with pride. "Damn you! Now you know this cross-shackling method," he said as he unbolted the wood to remove her feet. "So, are you ready to come with us now?"

"I dare not disobey you, but please wait until my swollen ankles are recovered," she said tearfully.

The house servant gave her a wet washcloth to wipe her face and sore legs. He told her to put on the wooden clogs and led her past the office building to the mandarin's residence. As soon as she entered, the door was immediately shut behind her.

XXV

A kerosene lamp stood on a wardrobe. It flooded the room with a bluish light. Beneath a gauze mosquito net that fell loosely to the floor stood a Hong Kong-style bed. The mattress was covered with a smooth sheet, white as snow. A brocade cover atop a pile of lacquered trunks, a creased turban and a gauze tunic hanging from a peg all reflected in a mirror hung high near the ceiling. The room was bright as day, but there wasn't a soul inside.

Mrs. Dậu understood at once that this was not a safe place to be. She tried to turn the doorknob in an attempt to flee, but the door opened, and a man suddenly appeared clad in white silk and Kinh Tự leather shoes. He entered and closed the door behind him.

By his peculiar mustache, Mrs. Dậu recognized him as the mandarin. Her heart throbbed fiercely, and her hands trembled as she joined them for a bow.

"Good evening, Your Honor!"

"Where do you want to go?" the mandarin asked, in a soft voice. "Stand next to the mirror. I want to ask you a few questions."

Obediently, Mrs. Dậu went where he gestured. The mandarin sat on the bed opposite her. After having contemplated her beauty, he stood up and moved toward her. He bent his head in an attempt to kiss her rosy cheeks, but Mrs. Dậu ducked past him and ran toward the door. The mandarin pursued her, grabbed her hand, and dragged her back.

"Come to the bed. You beat an orderly on duty—that is a serious crime. Come here, and I'll drop the case," he said in a sweet tone.

Mrs. Dậu trembled even more.

"I beg you, sir. I am a married woman. Please spare me . . ."

The mandarin snatched her arm and drew her to him.

"I don't care if you are married," he said lustfully. "Come to the bed now, and tomorrow you will be free to go back to your husband. Nobody will keep you then."

Mrs. Dậu resisted. She fought to free her hand.

"I beg you, Your Honor. I'm a married woman. Spare me," she repeated.

The mandarin became impatient. He picked her up and was about to take her to the bed, but she was stronger than he was. During their struggle, she let out her anger. "Gosh! What sort of man are you? Release me or I'll scream."

The mandarin said nothing. He tightened his lips and tried to nail her against his body, and she again attempted to wriggle free.

The struggle lasted more than ten minutes. Mrs. Dậu finally managed to knock her assailant down. She ran to the door and leaned against the wall in a defensive position.

Slowly, the mandarin rose to his feet. He opened his wallet, removed about ten piasters in paper currency, and held them close to her face.

"Is it money you want?" he asked, out of breath.

Mrs. Dậu took the bills and threw them on the floor, saying, "Fuck your money!"

Staring at her, the mandarin tried again to hold her tight. But she was able to push him away.

Suddenly, drumbeats and a car horn and engine were heard at the gate.

The mandarin found himself in an awkward position. He quickly opened the back door and shoved her out, saying curtly, "Go, go."

In the darkness, Mrs. Dậu could hear a voice whisper, "Grasp my shoulder. Hurry up if you want to survive."

Then a strong back was offered to her. Scared, she snatched the man's neck, and he carried her down the steps and made his way out via a winding route.

The car stopped in front of the office building. An angry female voice rose. "Are you awake, dear?"

The mandarin emerged from his residence.

"Yes, I'm waiting for you," he replied. "Why have you come home so early? Did you meet him?"

The woman's shrill voice, now inside their connubial chamber, could be heard as far away as the mandarin's office. "Why are you panting? Why is the back door open? Look at the banknotes on the floor. Whose clogs are these? Why is the sheet wrinkled?" Then she stamped the floor and shrieked, "Kill me. You've done something ignominious! Here's the knife. Stab me! How extraordinarily your behavior shames me!"

In the meantime, Mrs. Dậu was carried back to the washroom. The man put her down, told her to change, and vanished.

From the chamber, the woman's furious voice called the house servant to come immediately.

"Get your ass up here right now! Damn you! Who did you just bring in here? Tell me now, or I'll tear you into pieces!"

After a lull during which only grumblings and whippings could be heard, the bawling resumed. "You won't tell me? Damn you! Fuck your parents! You'll be sorry if I go to that other orderlies' house now."

The cursing that carried in from the mandarin's chamber to the orderlies' house was like a hammer knocking at Mrs. Dậu's ears that made her heart race.

A man crept into the washroom and told her to get out. Leading her by the blouse, he took her to the rear of the house, and then via a roundabout path, let her to the gate, and drove her out of the premises.

In the mandarin's residence, the accusations continued.

XXVI

Drumbeats from the watchtower announced the start of the fourth watch, 1:00 A.M. Drops of dew could be heard dripping from leaf to leaf. Outside the district office's gate, the fog was so thick that one could hardly see anything more than three meters away.

Via the glimmer of the moon reflected in the ponds and flooded ricefields, Mrs. Dậu made her way to the restaurant where she had been earlier to find shelter for the night.

The place was still open and bright inside. Groups of village authorities were playing cards.

Seeing someone peer in from outside, a woman wearing half-trendy, half-rustic clothes asked arrogantly, "Who's out there? Are you eavesdropping?"

Still frightened by the incident at the district office, Mrs. Dậu stepped in cautiously and said, trembling, "Good evening, ma'am. I've just been released from the district jail. It is very dark, and I cannot go home. Please allow me to stay here until dawn."

"Ask the owner of this place. I'm only a customer," the woman replied.

Coming out of her room, the restaurant owner asked, "Are you the woman who was tied to the column by the Đông Xá mayor earlier today?"

"Yes, I am," Mrs. Dậu replied.

"Pay two cents for the night if you don't plan to have any food."

"I have no money on me, and I dare not ask for a bed. I only ask for permission to sit here . . ."

"If you have no money, get out. Don't stay here to steal from my customers."

With affected generosity, the female customer intervened, "Be kind and let her sit here. She looks like a trustworthy woman, not a pickpocket."

Sitting on the plank bed, the woman inquired of Mrs. Dậu as to why she had been arrested and jailed. She then took pity on her situation and asked, "Do you want a job?"

"What job?" asked Mrs. Dậu.

"Wet nurse. I'm not a go-between, but if you want to work, I can help you."

"Where, ma'am?"

"I'm Dignitary Xung's wife. My husband works in a mandarin's office, and I am here on private business. Our mandarin is currently looking for a few wet nurses. If you wish, I can introduce you."

"I have a baby to nurse."

Madame Xung laughed at Mrs. Dậu.

"You're funny. How can you be a wet nurse if you don't have a baby? In the mandarin's family, you'll get to eat good food and wear nice clothes and receive high wages. It's better than wearing a patched dress and eating rice mixed with sweet potatoes all year round without earning a penny."

"But who will nurse my baby then?"

"Hire a wet nurse and pay her with your wages. You'll still have plenty of money left."

Finding Madame Xung's words agreeable, Mrs. Dậu asked, "When would I have to go?"

"Tomorrow would be best."

"If so, I cannot, because I have to consult with my husband first. I can't go without his permission."

"How far away is your house?"

"Not far. Only eight kilometers from here."

"Is the road accessible to vehicles?"

"Rickshaws can go straight to the center of the village."

"All right, I'll go with you to discuss the matter with your husband. If he agrees, I'll lend you ten piasters to buy clothes, and you can pay me back as soon as you get your first wages."

The gambling had just ended because some of the players had lost all their money. The winners noisily called out to the restaurant owner to serve alcohol. Madame Xung also ordered her food and invited Mrs. Dậu to partake with her. But the peasant woman refused her offer.

The day grew brighter. Madame Xung told her to call a rickshaw, and together they went to Đông Xá Village. On the way, Madame Xung told the poor woman about the privileges she enjoyed under her mandarin's protection and his servants' comfortable lives. Her optimistic stories made Mrs. Dậu forget her terrible experiences in the district office. She considered Madame Xung a kind woman in every respect.

The rickshaw arrived at Đông Xá Village in mid-morning—the time when the villagers were carrying meals out to the plowmen. The villagers were all astonished to see Mrs. Dậu sitting in a rickshaw behind a woman who appeared quite distinguished. They stared inquisitively at the two women from the moment they got off the rickshaw to when they reached Mrs. Dậu's home.

Mr. Dậu and his son were at first overjoyed to see Mrs. Dậu arrive at the gate, but their joy disappeared as soon as they saw her followed in by a stranger.

After Mrs. Dậu invited Madame Xung to sit on the ramshackle bamboo bench, she gently asked her husband what had been going on since she had left the previous morning.

She learned that Mr. Dậu's fever was gone and that in her absence, the neighbor woman had taken good care of Tiu.

When the latter heard of Mrs. Dậu's return, she came to return Tiu and asked Mrs. Dậu what had happened in the district office.

With tears in her eyes, Mrs. Dậu told Madame Xung that the neighbor was the greatest source of support she had ever known. Taking the baby, she thanked the woman for her kindness with visible emotion.

Dần ran up and hid behind his mother. Mrs. Dậu stroked his head. She gave a shy glance to her husband, and her cheeks grew red.

She started with this remark: "Mandarin Tư Ân is a wicked man." Then, she told her husband all the details of the incident at the district office.

Mr. Dậu listened anxiously as his wife described her struggle to defend her chastity against the lascivious devil. He was proud and happy when the story ended in triumph for his wife.

Madame Xung chimed in to conclude Mrs. Dậu's story, saying that she had met her at a restaurant and was willing to introduce her to her mandarin as a wet nurse. She said that she had come to get Mr. Dậu's opinion on the matter.

"If you agree," she said, "I'll remain here to wait for your wife, and we'll go to town together. If not, I'll leave right away."

Mr. Dậu was perplexed. He wanted to think it over. Outside at the gate, the mayor's servant came to ask for the tax.

Madame Xung took the opportunity to return to the subject that brought her there. "If your family is in such a predicament, you two can't just stay here and see your entire family starve to death. You ought to let her go. If your wife takes my advice, I can lend you some money to settle your debts."

"I'm quite willing to let my wife go," Mr. Dậu said with some hesitation and then, pointing to Tỉu, asked, "But I am concerned about our little girl. If my wife is not around, how can I handle Tỉu?"

"Excuse me for what I'm going to say . . . , " the elderly neighbor chimed in.

"Please go on," Mr. Dậu said.

"My eldest son lost his little girl a few days ago. His wife is heart-broken now and weeps all day long. She still has milk and since yesterday morning she has nursed Tỉu. It seems that she adores your daughter very much. May I suggest that you allow my daughter-in-law to raise Tỉu until she turns twelve years old? Then you can take her back."

"That's wonderful!" Madame Xung said to Mr. and Mrs. Dậu. "You should accept her kind offer."

Mr. Dậu was moved. "It's very kind of you," he said to the elderly neighbor. "We agree."

Madame Xung opened her purse, removed five piasters, and handed them to Mr. Dậu.

"When your wife arrives in town, I'll lend her another five piasters to buy new clothes," she said.

Mrs. Dậu put her baby in the care of the elderly neighbor and ran out to buy eggs and fish sauce to have a feast for Madame Xung. She invited the neighbor to stay and entertain her guest while she was gone.

The sun was sinking. The neighbor's son and his wife came and took Tíu home. Mrs. Dậu could not help crying as she handed her baby to the neighbors. Her tears fell faster when she said goodbye to her husband, her son, and the thatched hut hidden snugly behind a bamboo grove. She followed Madame Xung to the railway station, where they would take a train to Trung Sơn to start a new life.

XXVII

The rice in the pot overflowed and doused the fire.

With his hands on his hips, the cook laughed appreciatively.

"She eats nothing but sweet potatoes and yet she is truly beautiful," he said. "Mother of three children but she still looks like an eighteen-year-old maiden. It's a pity that her breasts sag a bit."

Slowly, a chauffeur came in from the courtyard. "What a pity for me," he said amorously to Mrs. Dậu. "I'm still a bachelor, but when I see you, I like to imagine you as my wife. Listen, dear, how about getting remarried? Why spend the rest of your life with that mud-stained peasant? *To marry a driver is a blessing; to marry a plowman is a curse.* Have you ever heard this song?"

Mrs. Dậu pretended not to hear him. She puffed up her pink cheeks to blow on the fire. Her blouse was damp with sweat.

For the last three days, she had had to help the cook with washing the dishes and vegetables before she officially became a wet nurse. Today, the weather was extremely hot, and none of the mandarin's servants wanted to work near the fire, so she was assigned a new task: cooking rice.

When the rice was cooked, Madame Xung arrived in a sunny mood.

"Where is the Đông Xá woman?" she called. "Is the rice ready? Go and take a bath and change your dress. You have been offered the job. The doctor said that your milk is very good. Our mistress will give you five piasters a month. If you are docile and work hard, she will increase your wages later."

Mrs. Dậu gladly took her clothes to the pond to bathe. Then, on the instructions of the mandarin's wife, she followed Đình, another wet nurse, to the chamber of the mandarin's mother.

The old woman was not far from eighty. She had no teeth left and thus could not eat any solid food. She had been drinking beef broth every day, but the doctor had said that nothing was more nutritious than human milk and she had to drink some to maintain her health. That is why the mandarin hired Mrs. Dậu.

Like Đình, Mrs. Dậu had to milk herself several times a day with a rubber pump applied to her breasts. It was a little painful, but the tank was light, and it was easier than toiling under the sun all day.

From then on, apart from her work feeding the mandarin's mother and serving his sisters, Mrs. Dậu devoted all her free time to thinking of her husband and children and waiting impatiently for the end of the month to receive her wages and send them home.

The food in the mandarin's house was a healing holy water—her sun-tanned skin became fair and smooth. The contrast between her sharp eyes and red lips enhanced her beauty.

The mandarin showed his feelings for her privately. During his wife's absence, he would call her to his room to perform various tasks. Sometimes he was in a good mood and inquired whether her husband would like to be a mayor, explaining that he could help. But knowing that her family was destitute, she never dreamed of such an honor and politely turned down the offer.

One autumn night, it was Đình's turn to go to the chamber of the mandarin's mother. Mrs. Dậu was alone in the nurses' room, which was dimly lit with an oil lamp placed atop the trunk that contained Đình's belongings.

July's[16] dull, unceasing rain increased her homesickness. Her family's poverty and misery suddenly entered her mind.

She felt uneasy. Downcast, she unpacked a bundle of worn-out clothes cast off by the mandarin's family to patch and mend so that when she was allowed to go home, she could bring them to her children.

It was late at night. Her back ached, and she stretched out on the bed to take a short rest before resuming her needlework. But overtired, she fell asleep.

All of a sudden, she felt a hand touching her breasts and woke up. The door was closed tightly, and the American oil lamp had been turned off. The room was completely dark. Frightened, she grasped the hand and shouted, "Who are you?"

---

16. July of the lunar calendar.

A short beard brushed her face, and she heard a voice whisper, "I . . . I . . . I'm . . . the . . . mandarin. Be quiet!"

"I'm only your servant, sir," she said.

"Lower your voice. When the light is out, a tiled house and a thatched house are the same. I don't care one way or the other . . ."

She let go of his hand, leaped up, opened the door, and ran out into the courtyard.

Outside it was pitch black—as dark as Mrs. Dậu's future.

Light Out

Contexts and an Overview of Criticism

Ngô Văn Giá

The opening chapters of Ngô Tất Tố's *Light Out* were first published in 1936 in the newspapers *Future* (Tương lai) and *Vietnamese Women* (Việt nữ). The entire novella was published in 1939 by Mai Lĩnh-Hà Nội Publishing House. Since its first publication, the novella has been reprinted nearly sixty times in Vietnam, and not all editions are the same, because the author constantly revised a few chapters. For nearly a century, *Light Out* has been positively received by the Vietnamese reading public, both during the pre-1945 semifeudal, semicolonial period and during the post-1945 communist regime. The Vietnamese government has never imposed censorship on the novella, scholarly critiques of the work, or the translation of the novella into other languages. The novella has been widely taught in the national curriculum and was made into a movie in 1980. However, the readership of each period interprets the work differently, depending on the sociohistorical and cultural context in which the readers live.

The feudal society in the rural areas of northern Vietnam operated under structures imposed by the colonial French government. Historians call this a semifeudal, semicolonial society. The colonial French government ruled hierarchically, from the political headquarters to the hamlet. The French exploited Vietnam, which it claimed as a colony, aggressively. More specially, the colonial government did not appoint its own people to hold administrative positions in the rural areas, but it did mandate that each male individual between the age of eighteen and forty-nine pay his capitation tax. This is the central issue that Ngô addresses in great detail in *Light Out* because it imposes pressure on the penurious civilians. Other conflicts in the rural areas were related to landownership. Primarily, land was in the hands of wealthy landowners, and peasants were compelled to work for them as plowmen and field hands. The desperate peasants had to pay a high interest rate if they borrowed money from the wealthy, and thus they became pauperized.[1]

The rural region in northern Vietnam was organized in a rather complicated fashion. First, a village was established based on the villagers' consent. Oftentimes, a village was established by a distinguished person or a group of people who directed the clearing of the land for cultivation. Thus, the village culture always was characterized by collective love and solidarity. Nguyen Khac Tung notes, "The village is the unit of settlement of peasants linked by relations of neighbourhood."[2] Under the feudal government, the village became an administrative unit that reported directly to a commune. Above the commune was the district, and above the district was the province. Therefore, each village had a mayor and officials who reported up the hierarchy to the ruling government. In his novella, Ngô depicts members of the various social classes in depth. They are, from the top down, the mandarin, the mayor, the deputy, the canton chief, the treasurer, the chief orderly, and the watchman. Each official in turn reserved the right to oppress the peasants or the powerless. Ngô's novella demonstrates his profound knowledge of how the village operated and was governed, primarily because he was himself a farmer but also an intellectual who had a strong affiliation with village culture. He was not an advocate of the Retrospective Movement (1936–1939), which many of his intellectual contemporaries supported. Rather, he was more ideologically progressive, condemning the

---

1. Nguyễn Hồng Phong, in his *Vietnamese Villages and Hamlets* (Xã thôn Việt Nam) [NXB Văn Sử Địa, 1958]), states in his discussion of landownership under the French occupation that, in rural Vietnam under the primitive communal system, land was the property of a clan, and peasant households benefited from it; under the feudal system, land was in the hand of wealthy landowners, prosperous peasants, and village tyrants. Landowners and village tyrants maliciously took over public land, causing peasants' poverty. This book was reprinted as a chapter in *Nguyễn Hồng Phong: Some Research Projects on the Humanities and Social Sciences* (Nguyễn Hồng Phong: Một số công trình nghiên cứu khoa học xã hội và nhân văn [Hà Nội: NXB Khoa Học Xã Hội, 2005]), 1:21–291.

2. Nguyen Khac Tung, "The Village: Settlement of Peasants in Northern Vietnam," in *The Traditional Village in Vietnam* (Hà Nội: The Gioi, 1993), 7.

cruelty exercised by the village's corrupt authorities and supervisors, and criticizing regressive customs and cultural practices, while showing empathy for the poor, the oppressed, and the exploited.

The village was considered by the French occupational government to be a functional economic unit, although the rural reality was that of a backward and barely self-sufficient agricultural enterprise. According to Cao Van Bien, "a 1921 decree regarding village administration reform stipulated that those villages and communes with at least 500 tax-payers had to establish village and commune budget book-keeping."[3] Its residents worked as hired plowmen or farmhands, and oftentimes landowners rented their land to peasants for cultivation, and at the end of the year the landowners collected a large portion of the agricultural products, mostly rice, in return. The peasants, deprived of the fruits of their means of production, became impoverished beyond the possibility of economic recovery.

An image that appears often in *Light Out* is of the bamboo grove, which is a symbol of a traditional Vietnamese village in the North. Nguyen Khac Tung observes that the village and its hamlets are "girdled by bamboo hedges which constitute their inviolable boundaries. The bamboo belt is in some cases reinforced by an earth wall and a moat against raids by pirates."[4] The residents of a village generally shared a common culture of spiritual beliefs and practices. Generally, the villagers relied on the same traditional indigenous medical treatments for specific illnesses and collectively adhered to the same superstitions. All of the aforementioned characteristics of the village are sociologically and anthropologically observed by Ngô, because he thoroughly depicts them in these modes in his novella, and especially in his two famous journalistic projects, *A Report on the Village's Communal House* (Tập án cái đình, 1939) and *The Village Affairs* (Việc làng, 1940).

The policies of the 1936 French Popular Front government, headed by Léon Blum, had a direct impact on Vietnamese society and an indirect impact on *Light Out*. This antifascist government fought for the working class's political and economic rights, endorsed peaceful and diplomatic actions, and attempted to improve the living conditions for the populations of France's colonies, referred to as *la France d'outre-mer*.

---

3. Cao Van Bien, "The Economic Basis of Tonkin Community in Villages and Communes Prior to the August 1945 Revolution," in *The Traditional Village in Vietnam* (Hà Nội: The Gioi, 1993), 263.

4. Nguyen Khac Tung, "Village," 13.

Therefore, a wind of democracy blew into colonial Vietnam, and the Vietnamese became more aware of the concept of democracy as introduced from the West. The Vietnamese Communist Party was founded in 1930, and it operated freely. Publication censorship was abolished; public strikes and meetings were no longer oppressed. Writers, artists, and the progressive intelligentsia gradually became more active in their demands for social reorganization, rural reform, the abolition of social injustice, and the improvement of living conditions for the poor and the working class. Realist authors wrote about these issues in their short fiction and novels. Some authors of the Self-Reliant Literary Group published works that focused on rural reform based on the motto of the Light Association and other statements of social ideals.[5] For instance, Nhất Linh published *Two Beauties* (Hai vẻ đẹp) in 1936, Khái Hưng *Family* (Gia đình) in 1937 and *Happy Days* (Những ngày vui) in 1938, and Hoàng Đạo *A Bright Road* (Con đường sáng) in 1938. Thus, Ngô's *Light Out* also was published in this democratic climate of the time.

As stated earlier, Ngô was familiar with village life in rural northern Vietnam, and it would be amiss not to contextualize his work within the literary thought of the 1930s. From 1936 to 1939, there were three major literary movements in Vietnam: romanticism (the New Poetry and the fiction written by members of the Self-Reliant Literary Group), realism (which critics often refer to as the literature of critical realism), and revolutionary literature (which reflects the Marxist-Leninist ideology promoted by the Vietnamese Communist Party). There were several famous novels authored by writers employing romanticism and realism in the 1930s. For instance, some prominent romantic novels include *The Autumn Sun* (Nắng thu), *Severance of Ties* (Đoạn tuyệt), and *Estrangement* (Lạnh lùng) by Nhất Linh; *A Butterfly's Soul Dreaming of a Fairy* (Hồn bướm mơ tiên) and *Halfway through Youthfulness* (Nửa chừng xuân); and *A Flower Street Vendor* (Gánh hàng hoa) and *A Stormy Life* (Đời mưa gió), coauthored by Nhất Linh and Khái Hưng. Some highly acclaimed realist novels are *Jade Leaves on Gold Branches* (Lá ngọc cành vàng), *A Female Wage Earner* (Cô làm công), and *The Impasse* (Bước đường

---

5. The Self-Reliant Literary Group founded the Light Association and publicly called for advocacy in the newspaper *Today* (Ngày Nay), no. 38, 13 December 1936. Nhất Linh was its chairman. The architects Nguyễn Cao Luyện and Nguyễn Như Tiếp designed the model Light House to get rid of dark houses that looked like rat holes, hoping to help poor people improve their living conditions. The association's motto was "Society, Humanism, and Reform."

cùng) by Nguyễn Công Hoan; *The Storm* (Giông tố), *A Damaged Dike* (Vỡ đê), *Dumb Luck* (Số đỏ), and *Prostitution* (Làm đĩ) by Vũ Trọng Phụng; *Alone in the Night* (Một mình trong đêm tối) by Vũ Bằng; and *The Thief* (Bỉ vỏ) by Nguyên Hồng. All these authors and their works undoubtedly had a significant influence on Ngô's writing. The modern novel, which differs greatly from the classical Chinese episodic novel, was adopted from the West. The Vietnamese intellectuals who were fluent in French, or had been educated in France, not only helped introduce the modern novel into Vietnam but also wrote their own fiction using the *Quốc ngữ* script.

Proficient in reading Vietnamese, French, and the Han script, Ngô read both contemporary Vietnamese novels and works by the Russian author Maxim Gorky and by other noteworthy international authors in French and Chinese translation. Thus, a wide range of modern novels influenced his fiction. Ngô also published one of his short stories titled "A Mother Dog, Its Puppies, and a Daughter" in the newspaper *Future* in 1936, which later became a chapter in *Light Out*. His other stories, such as "A Bundle of Vegetables in the Trunk" and "A *Bánh Chưng*," depict the misery and poverty of indigent peasants. However, the author seemed to be dissatisfied with the short-fiction genre because its brevity did not allow him to portray the realities of life in rural northern Vietnam fully and thoroughly and to utilize his vast knowledge of village culture.

Ngô became interested in journalism very early in his career. In 1926, he wrote for *Annam Magazine*, and later he wrote for several other newspapers, such as *The Eastern France Times*, *The Bee*, *Vietnamese Women*, *Tuesday's Novel*, *Future*, and *Hà Nội's New Literature*.[6] His articles usually focused on topics related to the countryside and peasants' plights deriving from exploitation, unemployment, and natural disasters. Investigative journalists must search beneath the surface of events and report their discoveries to the public. Engaged journalists must also delve into the multifaceted current issues in society in a timely manner. Ngô's critical approach to journalism made full use of his acute good sense and alert mind as he examined and investigated the underlying causes of the inequities and injustices of his time. His novella *Light Out* and his novel-reportage *The Tent and the Bamboo Bed* (Lều chõng) demonstrate his journalistic expertise in exposing the too-often ignored social realities of colonial Vietnam. Ngô is known for his democratic positions,

---

6. Annam was a French protectorate encompassing the central region of Vietnam.

his enthusiasm in learning new things, his well-informed knowledge of current events and political issues, his intellectual tenacity, and his eagerness to adopt Western progressive values. He publicly resisted outdated customs and traditional conservative Confucian dogmas. These assets and values raise the significance of his novels exponentially.

Little notice or appreciation was given to Ngô's *Light Out* in the 1930s. Contemporary critics and authors tended to interpret the novella through a sociological lens, which focuses its attention on the description of social actualities, rather than through a Marxist lens, which focuses on issues of class consciousness and class struggle. For instance, in the late 1930s and early 1940s, Vũ Ngọc Phan, Vũ Trọng Phụng, and Phú Hương discussed primarily the peasants' tribulations, the rural authorities' exploitation, and the author's humanistic concerns as presented in *Light Out*.[7] The critics had not yet assimilated the interpretive values and importance of Marxist theory.

Since 1945, critics have become more aware of the nuances offered by Marxist thought. Their critiques have become more willing to consider whether a text addresses class struggle and class conflict. This Marxist influence can be discerned in the assessments of *Light Out* by such authors as Nguyễn Tuân and Nguyễn Công Hoan, and in the comments or reviews made by such literary critics and scholars as Như Phong, Phong Lê, Nguyễn Đăng Mạnh, Phan Cự Đệ, and Hà Minh Đức. Their assessments have been influenced by the communist journalist Trần Minh Tước since 1939.[8] Below are some key points found in their reading of *Light Out*.

First, they affirm that Ngô is a prominent and talented author of the literature of critical realism and that his novella *Light Out* proves this fact.

Second, *Light Out* truthfully depicts the tension between the local feudal government and the exploited, impecunious peasants. The Dậus are shown to be maliciously victimized, mistreated, and oppressed by members of the classes that own or control the means of production. The novella is an indictment of the crimes committed through

---

7. The best-researched articles on Ngô Tất Tố and *Light Out* appear in Mai Hương and Tôn Phương Lan, eds., *Ngô Tất Tố: Về tác gia và tác phẩm* (Hà Nội: NXB Giáo dục, 2000).

8. Trần Minh Tước published "*Light Out* by Ngô Tất Tố, an Author of the Peasantry" ("Một nhà văn của dân quê Ngô Tất Tố trong *Tắt đèn*"), an article in the newspaper *Mới*, no. 4, 15 June 1939. His article is reprinted in *Ngô Tất Tố: Về tác gia và tác phẩm*. Trần viewed the novel through a Marxist lens. Trần was born in 1911 and wrote under the pseudonym Xích Điểu. He became a member of the Vietnamese Communist Party in 1930.

an inhumane tax policy and the actual physical abuse experienced by dehumanized peasants. Although the novella does not address the colonial government and its minions directly, the reader can see clearly how the French colonialists colluded with the feudal puppet government to exploit the indigenous and impoverished colonized people.[9]

Third, the revolutionary spirit of the Vietnamese peasants cannot be extinguished, and in the novella Mrs. Dậu embodies this spirit because she dares fight the mayor's servant and the chief orderly to defend her ailing husband.

Fourth, the novella's ending is pessimistic because, at the time of writing, the author had not yet come to a thorough understanding of socialism and communism. He was, therefore, unable to see that the Vietnamese Communist Party could help liberate the peasants from their class oppression and ignite a revolution against the social injustice of the colonialization of Vietnam.

The four major points listed above are relevant because they clarify the novella's humanistic themes, and when Ngô wrote the novella, he was not fully aware of how the social superstructure was determined by the economic base, as observed through the Marxist lens. The author's humanistic concerns for the well-being of the subalterns are exhibited and amplified in his fully transparent detestation of the wealthy and heartless exploiters. *Light Out* highlights the themes of love, empathy, and humanity that are treasured by the enlightened humankind. Ngô's perspective helps explain why the novella is considered a classic in Vietnam.

However, if the novella is viewed from the lens of cultural studies, a few significant cultural elements enrich our reading of *Light Out*. It is crucial to note here that an author sometimes is not conscious of cultural factors that become embedded into his or her writing.

First, *Light Out* depicts a typical village in the pastoral North. It is a tight-knit village, with only one entrance (that is, the village gate), and the villagers must go through that entrance when they exit to work in the rice paddy or to go to another village. A watchtower is erected next to the entrance, and for security reasons a watchman or guard is tasked with checking the identity of everyone who enters or exits the village.

---

9. The author mentions the French only once in the novel: The village mayor says, "Go ask the French. I don't know," when Mrs. Dậu asks him to explain why she has to pay her dead brother-in-law's poll tax. The author Nguyễn Tuân argues that, with this detail, Ngô indirectly condemns the colonial French government.

In the opening chapter of the novella, the author describes a scene in which many villagers and their buffaloes are not allowed to go through the entrance to work because the mayor wants to know who among them have not paid their poll tax. The villagers talking, begging, and complaining amid the sounds of drumbeats, the noise of the buffaloes, and the scolding chief watchman create a cacophony, foreshadowing turmoil that will soon break out.

The capitation tax, which the author Nguyễn Tuân refers to as a "bizarre poll tax," was implemented as a form of exploitation by the semifeudal, semicolonial government at the time. All men from the age of eighteen to forty-nine had to pay the poll tax—a regulation that originated from the Trịnh lords in the second half of the eighteenth century. This mandatory assessment was continued under the French occupation of Vietnam, and it became a nightmare for the peasantry and the indigent classes in society. They became desperate and even more destitute. The fact that the novella's Mr. Dậu has to pay his deceased brother's tax intensifies the financial distress that the family is experiencing, and it emphasizes the irrationality and inhumanity of the system enforced by the village officials. Nguyễn Tuân commented, "That cruel tax is a shame that was inflicted on Annamese society."[10]

To pay Mr. Dậu's and his brother's poll taxes, Mrs. Dậu has to sell their oldest daughter Tý, as well as the family's dog and her puppies, to Deputy Quế. Many Western readers might find this detail hyperbolic or not a factual reality, but in the 1930s, it was not an uncommon occurrence in rural Vietnam: destitute and desperate families often did sell their children to wealthy families who either had no children of their own or who needed servants. Normally a rich family would buy a child simply so that they could easily exploit the child's labor. Deputy Quế and his wife buy Tý, a seven-year-old girl, to be their house servant. There were no child protection laws in Vietnam at that time, so children often became objects for trading, physical abuse, and labor exploitation. It should be noted that recently, some readers argue that Mrs. Dậu selling her daughter to save her husband violates traditional concepts of Vietnamese motherhood. However, the reader should take into consideration her dilemma. Mrs. Dậu has to choose between saving her husband and selling her daughter. If she did not sell Tý, she would not have the money to bail her ailing husband out, and he would

---

10. Nguyễn Tuân, "Lời giới thiệu truyện *Tắt đèn*" ("An Introduction to *Light Out*" [Hà Nội: NXB Văn Hóa-Viện Văn Học, 1962]), reprinted in *Ngô Tất Tố: Về tác gia và tác phẩm*, 213.

very likely die. Although Tý is sold and lives a hard life in Deputy Quế's residence, she will not die, and there is hope that one day Mrs. Dậu can buy her back. However, Mrs. Dậu is genuinely heartbroken when she makes this decision. Her tears fill the pages that describe the separation. Selling one's child to a wealthy family was common, and neither illegal nor morally condemned by society. It was simply a painful reality that many families had to face in order to survive, however sorrowful the parting was.

Second, the author depicts a scene of revelry in which the elder village nobles and landowners quarrel boisterously while eating and drinking in the communal house. Their mannerisms, as described, are despicable. In villages in northern Vietnam, this kind of activity in the communal house was seen as a social ill. Similar scenes appear in Ngô's *A Report on the Village's Communal House* and *The Village Affairs*. In Vietnamese culture, the way one eats reveals a lot about one's social class and status. As a Vietnamese proverb says, "A bite in the communal house equals a tray of food in a kitchen corner."

The relationship between a village leader and his officials was complicated. The formalities establishing the hierarchy were not absolute. The members competed maliciously against and were envious of one another. The author Nam Cao compares them to "a school of fish fighting over bait" in his famous short story "Chí Phèo."[11] Such Vietnamese people were, and are, obsessed with power. They study hard, trying at all costs to join the ruling class, and thereafter they battle with each other to remain and to rise within the hierarchy. For instance, Ngô sarcastically refers to the mandarin as "the father and mother of the people." The irony in Nam Cao's reference is transparent to any Vietnamese reader: even a person with no power or high social status sometimes acts pretentiously to demonstrate their self-assumed authority or to intimidate others. The Taiwanese author Bo Yang, in his book *The Ugly Chinaman and the Crisis of Chinese Culture*, refers to this habit as "the mandarin trait," which exists within each individual.[12]

In *Light Out*, the former mayor is invited to partake in all events in the communal house. He is portrayed as an alcoholic who knows that he

---

11. Nam Cao, *Đôi lứa xứng đôi* (Hà Nội: NXB Văn Học, 2017), 20. The author later changed the title of the story to "Chí Phèo."

12. This book was translated into Vietnamese by Nguyễn Hồi Thủ as *Người Trung Quốc xấu xí* (California: NXB Văn Nghệ, 1999), 97. The author's name, Bo Yang, becomes Bá Dương in Vietnamese.

no longer possesses a voice or authority. He feels forgotten and ignored, so, to appear to be a figure of significance, he acts arrogantly toward those currently in power and to everyone beneath him. For instance, in chapter 18, the former mayor engages in a quarrel with the current mayor, and he eventually throws a bowl onto the current mayor's tray of food. The author notes that when the chief orderly escorted him out to the communal house's courtyard, "The former mayor grabbed a sharp piece of the broken pot from near the column and was about to slash his own forehead, but the chief orderly rushed in, grabbed it, and threw the shard away." In this scene, he raises a ruckus to show his disobedience and to cast blame on the current mayor. A few years after the publication of *Light Out*, in 1941, Nam Cao depicts such ridiculous behavior more vividly when he portrays the male protagonist Chí Phèo in the story of the same name.

Third, Ngô is familiar with Vietnamese folk spirituality, and he incorporates it in his fiction. In chapter 18, when the orderlies carry Mr. Dậu to his house and he lies unconscious like a corpse, many villagers come over and offer help. The author describes this scene in detail to illustrate the villagers' spontaneous compassion and concern for his health. In the northern countryside, residents practice this custom: whenever anyone faints or loses consciousness, someone must go to the gate or an alley nearby to summon the unconscious person's soul(s). Ancient Vietnamese people believed that each male individual had three souls and seven *vía*, while each female individual had nine *vía*. The three souls refer to a person's consciousness, energy, and mood. *Vía* refers to each orifice in the human body. For a man, the seven *vía* are his eyes, ears, nostrils, and mouth. For a woman, besides the same seven *vía*, she has two additional *vía*—her nipples. Tradition holds that when one gets sick or faints, one's souls and *vía* have left their body, and someone must call them back in order to save the person's life. This chapter also details the villagers' collective kindness toward Mr. Dậu and his wife. A neighbor lends them some rice to cook porridge. Someone shows Mrs. Dậu a folk treatment for her husband's ailment. The Vietnamese people, collectively speaking, maintain this noble concern for members of their community. Their caring gestures and empathy for the Dậus are in stark contrast with the insensitivity and vicious behavior of the village mayor and other officials at the communal house, especially with the inhumanity of Deputy Quế and his wife.

In terms of plot development, *Light Out* follows a conventional arc: exposition, rising action, climax, falling action, and resolution, and the events are narrated chronologically. Nevertheless, further discussion helps clarify the novella's ending. As stated earlier, critics have pointed out that the novella ends on a note of pessimism, perhaps because its author had not yet assimilated the nuances of communist ideology.[13] The concluding sentence of the novel reads: "Outside it was pitch black—as dark as Mrs. Dậu's future." I argue, however, that the author provides the novella with an open ending. Although Mrs. Dậu is able to resist her ruthless oppressors, how can she, a member of the lowest class, continue to survive in a society that is fraught with traps, malice, and injustices? The unhappy ending suggests the complicated relationship between the character and her society. The author does not offer a clear and definite ending to encourage the reader to imagine what will happen next, to Mrs. Dậu and to her family.

In terms of characterization, two categories of people are portrayed: the oppressed victims and the victimizing oppressors. Such construction is typical in conventional novels from the first half of the twentieth century in Vietnam. Some critics note that Ngô depicts the characters' physical appearance, speech, and mannerisms in detail but not their internal conflicts, psyches, and streams of consciousness. Although Ngô was well-read, and particularly familiar with French literature, he was not formally trained to examine the complexity of human psychology as many Western contempories were. For instance, Ngô was not aware of Freudian and Jungian psychoanalysis, which became important in late nineteenth- and early twentieth-century Western literature. Therefore, his debut novella does not examine the effects of the subconscious and the nuances of human behavior.

Ngô constructs the character Mrs. Dậu as the embodiment of a traditional Vietnamese woman whose life is directed by Confucian values. She is beautiful, strong, honest, and naïve. Despite her destitution, she refuses to be seduced by money or tempted by lust while demonstrating bravery and chastity. Thus, she represents a moral and virtuous rural woman, despite being caught up in a net of misfortune and malice. Most of the characters in *Light Out* are presented as flat characters. Nevertheless, the author succeeds in creating a few recognizable characters whose names have entered into verbal lore. In modern Vietnamese

---

13. See Hồng Chương, "*Tắt đèn*: Cuốn tiểu thuyết hiện thực xuất sắc" (1956); Phong Lê, "Những đóng góp của Ngô Tất Tố trong *Tắt đèn*" (1963); and Nguyễn Đăng Mạnh, "*Tắt đèn* của Ngô Tất Tố" (1963). These essays/articles were published in the 1960s and thus reflect the literary ideology of the period. They are reprinted in *Ngô Tất Tố: Về tác gia và tác phẩm*.

parlance, a penurious and miserable person is often called a Mrs. Dậu, and an affluent but heartless person is sometimes called a Deputy Quế, even by people who have not read *Light Out*.

All the events in Ngô's novella take place within five days. His contemporary Nguyễn Tuân notes that the novella delineates a setting that "suffocates life" and represents "a suffocating Annamese village."[14] The author Thạch Lam, in his 1941 collection of essays titled *Going with the Flow* (Theo dòng), states, "Authors need to revive the atmosphere that surrounds a text."[15] The atmosphere here refers not to the physical but to the artistic atmosphere that originates from the author's perception of the world around him. *Light Out* takes place in Đông Xá Village, and, as noted earlier, Ngô is skillful in referring to the constant sounds of drumbeats and gongs, barking of dogs, and the scolding of village officials—sounds that are background counterpoint to Mr. Dậu groaning and panting, his wife pleading and crying, and their children squalling and screaming. Moreover, the author effectively depicts the hot, stifling atmosphere of the communal house, the roasting sun over the village road, and the cacophony of dogs disturbing a dark night. The depressing setting and its auditory accompaniment make Mrs. Dậu and her loved ones all the more anxious, nervous, and frightened.

Also noted earlier, Ngô employs sarcasm and irony to depict Deputy Quế, the mandarin, and some village nobles. For instance, he describes Deputy Quế's ostentatious residence, ludicrously designed in a semi-Western, semi-Vietnamese architectural style. His body language and mannerisms are the traits of a caricature. He achieves upward mobility through bribery and flattery. In meetings, he discusses nothing and listens to no one. He yawns but does not fall asleep, because he is afraid that someone might steal his leather shoes. Although Ngô's sarcasm and irony are not as scathing as those of his contemporaries Nguyễn Công Hoan and Vũ Trọng Phụng, his sardonic tone is effective in ridiculing the novella's most contemptible, avaricious characters.

Another linguistic element is Ngô's use of the passive voice in the narrative. At that time, the passive voice was often employed by French and British writers but not generally by Vietnamese authors. The scholar Vũ Ngọc Phan noticed this when the novella was first released in the late 1930s, while the majority of Vietnamese writers were promoting

---

14. Nguyễn Tuân, "Lời giới thiệu truyện *Tắt đèn*," 213.
15. Phong Lê, ed., *Tuyển tập Thạch Lam* (Thạch Lam's Selected Works, [Hà Nội: NXB Văn học, 1988]), 289.

Vietnamese literature written in the *Quốc ngữ* script. Vũ says that the sentences in the passive voice read as if they had been translated from French.[16] In the first half of the twentieth century, several Vietnamese authors who were fluent in French, or who had been educated in France, translated French literature into Vietnamese, so Ngô's writing style must have been influenced by his reading of their works.

In addition, Ngô occasionally overuses parallel sentence structure, which was popular in Han dynasty literature. For instance, the opening passage of chapter 5, in which he describes Deputy Quế's residence, includes five sentences that have the same number of words and rhythms. Of course, in this English edition, it is impossible to capture this stylistic quality due to linguistic differences. The parallel structure might seem awkward. The critic Nguyễn Đăng Mạnh remarks that Ngô's desciption of Mrs. Dậu's face at the end of chapter 10 sounds a bit forced:[17] "Wisps of hair fell over Mrs. Dậu's arched eyebrows and fluttered like tenuous strands of smoke in the wind. A few drops of tears ran down her rosy cheeks like drops of glittering dew on rose petals."

Obviously, in his debut novella, Ngô's writing style sometimes reflects that of his French and traditional Chinese influences too strongly, but it is a reflex of the literary movements in Vietnam in the 1930–1945 period, in which writers were attempting to bring modernism to Vietnamese literature while choosing what to adopt and what to reject from outside influences. Despite these shortcomings and some incongruencies, Ngô deserves admiration for his skillful portrayals of the atrocities of the powerful and the miseries of the powerless, as well as for his candid exposure of the harsh realities of life in Vietnam under the French occupation.

Bibliography

Bá, Dương. *Người Trung Quốc xấu xí.* Translated by Nguyễn Hồi Thủ. California: NXB Văn Nghệ, 1999.

Cao, Bien Van. "The Economic Basis of Tonkin Community in Villages and Communes Prior to the August 1945 Revolution." In *The Traditional Village in Vietnam*, 262–78. Hanoi: The Gioi, 1993.

---

16. Vũ Ngọc Phan, *Nhà văn hiện đại* (Modern Authors [Hà Nội: NXB Khoa học xã hội, 1989]), 1:569.

17. Nguyễn Đăng Mạnh, *"Tắt đèn của Ngô Tất Tố"* [Ngô Tất Tố's *Light Out*], in *Ngô Tất Tố: Về tác giả và tác phẩm*, 259.

Hà, Đức Văn. "Ngô Tất Tố: Nhà văn tin cậy của nông dân." In *Ngô Tất Tố: Về tác gia và tác phẩm*, edited by Mai Hương and Tôn Phương Lan, 186–90. Hà Nội: NXB Giáo dục, 2000.

Hồng, Chương. "*Tắt đèn*: Cuốn tiểu thuyết hiện thực xuất sắc." In *Ngô Tất Tố: Về tác gia và tác phẩm*, edited by Mai Hương and Tôn Phương Lan, 233–42. Hà Nội: NXB Giáo dục, 2000.

Nam, Cao. *Đôi lứa xứng đôi*. Hà Nội: NXB Văn Học, 2017.

Ngày Nay 38, no. 13 (December 1936).

Nguyễn, Mạnh Đăng. "*Tắt đèn* của Ngô Tất Tố" (1963). In *Ngô Tất Tố: Về tác gia và tác phẩm*, edited by Mai Hương and Tôn Phương Lan, 259–74. Hà Nội: NXB Giáo dục, 2000.

Nguyễn, Phong Hồng. "Chế độ sở hữu ruộng đất ở nông thôn Việt Nam dưới thời Pháp thuộc." *Nguyễn Hồng Phong: Một số công trình nghiên cứu khoa học xã hội và nhân văn*. Vol. 1, 21–291. Hà Nội: NXB Khoa Học Xã Hội, 2005.

Nguyễn, Tuân. "Lời giới thiệu truyện *Tắt đèn*." In *Ngô Tất Tố: Về tác gia và tác phẩm*, edited by Mai Hương and Tôn Phương Lan, 213–32. Hà Nội: NXB Giáo dục, 2000.

Nguyen, Tung Khac. "The Village: Settlement of Peasants in Northern Vietnam." In *The Traditional Village in Vietnam*, 7–43. Hanoi: The Gioi, 1993.

Phong, Lê. "Những đóng góp của Ngô Tất Tố trong *Tắt đèn*." In *Ngô Tất Tố: Về tác gia và tác phẩm*, edited by Mai Hương and Tôn Phương Lan, 243–58. Hà Nội: NXB Giáo dục, 2000.

——, ed. *Tuyển tập Thạch Lam*. Hà Nội: NXB Văn học, 1988.

Trần, Tước Minh. "Một nhà văn của dân quê Ngô Tất Tố trong *Tắt đèn*." In *Ngô Tất Tố: Về tác gia và tác phẩm*, edited by Mai Hương and Tôn Phương Lan, 195–97. Hà Nội: NXB Giáo dục, 2000.

Vũ, Phan Ngọc. *Nhà văn hiện đại*. Vol. 1. Hà Nội: NXB Khoa học xã hội, 1989.

PART II

Modern Vietnamese Stories, 1930–1954

1

Carrion Eaters

Nguyễn Công Hoan

Because Xích had never experienced death before, he had no specific plan for his own death. Generally, if a person were to die in a city, he would do well to choose his death for a Friday night so that his wife and children might have enough time to publish the obituary in the news. Then on Sunday, the funeral would take place. Elderly neighbors, notables, friends, and relatives would attend the burial ceremony. In the countryside, however, if one dies in an accident, it is wise to avoid Sundays or holidays so the burial won't be delayed by legal investigations.

As a twist of misfortune and irony, no one ever dies twice and learns the valuable lesson of how and when to die properly. Thus, many people die foolishly. Xích was one such person. An illiterate peasant, he was such a fool that he inadvertently drowned last Saturday night. His father, Mr. Cứu, had rented a lotus pond located near a bamboo grove from the village. When the lotus season arrived, he put up a small cottage in the middle of the pond. He and Xích took turns sleeping there to watch out for thieves. That Saturday afternoon, Xích became inebriated at a gathering at the village's communal house. When Xích got home that evening, Mr. Cứu told him to take his tobacco water pipe and pillow with him and leave for the cottage immediately. Xích staggered away, and no one saw him the following morning. At about eight o'clock, his body was found floating in the water near the edge of the pond.

Several assumptions about his death arose. The two that made the most sense were either that he fell into the deep water while clumsily managing his little boat because he was so drunk or that he unconsciously rolled into the water while turning over in his sleep. There was no way he could have committed suicide or been beaten to death by thugs.

Out of curiosity, Mr. Hương Lý, the village leader, asked Mr. Cứu's neighbors if they had heard any kind of quarrel between Mr. Cứu and his son the day before. Other village officials paid special attention to the corpse but were unable to find any clue that might indicate a logical cause of Xích's death. Upon hearing the news of his drowning, the villagers rushed to the pond and felt pity for him—he was a nice and kind man—and no one was unmoved by the sight of his corpse floating in the water.

Mrs. Cứu wailed miserably over her lost son and attempted to jump into the water to embrace his body, but the villagers stopped her. In her grief and emotional turmoil, she tore into the village leader for not allowing her to bring her son's body onto the shore.

"I can't stand this any longer. It's breaking my heart," she said, bemoaning her son's death.

"We have to wait for the district coroner to investigate your son's death first. Once we have his official report on the accident, you may do whatever you want to prepare for his funeral. As for now, you'd best not touch the body because we don't want it disturbed. They would never let you bury him anyway if you took him ashore and claimed that he drowned. His body must remain in the water," a villager said, trying to console her.

"Why wouldn't the coroner let me bury my son?" Mrs. Cứu asked loudly.

"Because he wants to have a doctor perform an autopsy. That takes time, you know," another villager explained.

Mrs. Cứu understood, then blew her nose and wiped away her tears. She sat by the empty coffin under a tree and waited, wanting to bury her son as soon as possible. Her relatives had gone to the district office to file a report on Xích's death early that morning, but no one had returned yet, even though it was not far. One hour, two hours, three hours passed. Mrs. Cứu grew exhausted and started to lose her patience. She kept walking around, trying not to look at her son's body. Then she sat on the ground with her head resting on her knees. She waited for the honking sounds that signaled the arrival of the coroner's car. Occasionally, she heard the squeaky noise of a nearby rice mill and thought the coroner had finally arrived, but then sighed. Her hope was crushed.

It was quite hot outside, as if the ground were burning under the roasting sun. Xích's corpse started to decompose. His limbs were curling up, and his hair was becoming disheveled like the roots of Japanese hyacinth. A breeze ruffled the water, and the waves rubbing against his body created sounds like flatulence. Xích's body bobbed around in the water. Then suddenly, his body flipped over and he looked like a barbecued animal. His belly was filled with water. His cheeks and face were bloated. His eyes were closed tightly. His limbs were twisted. His deformed, ghostly appearance was frightening.

The villagers gradually started to avoid the morbid scene. Nobody dared come close to the pond. Those passing by who did not know about the corpse covered their faces, closed their mouths, and spat after they had passed the pond.

Mr. Cứu stayed home and waited for the officials to carry out the investigation. His anxiety tormented him, but he must be courteous to the guests and visitors coming to offer their condolences. He wanted to be left alone so that he could lament the death of his son. He worried about his wife, who was still at the pond, because she might do something crazy, like jump into the water. His regrets would never end if there were another death in the family.

Relatives came over and helped prepare for the funeral. Some set up a small altar and placed two white candles on it. Others prepared a shroud for the deceased and mourning headbands for the children.

Because it was a Sunday, the coroner was not in his office all morning. He had gone dancing and did not return home until three or four o'clock in the morning. His office remained closed that afternoon. Once Mr. Cứu found out about this, he screamed, and Mrs. Cứu collapsed by the bamboo grove and remained unconscious for five minutes. The entire village had no choice but to keep waiting.

Relatives left after their tasks at Mr. Cứu's home were finished, and they came back the next morning. Friends and neighbors stayed around awaiting the burial, accompanied by the sounds of drums and gongs. Mr. Cứu had someone bring his wife home, and the old couple lay on their bed waiting for the coroner. The corpse became even more deformed and bobbed around not too far from the open coffin into which it would be placed. Everything was quiet, and the leaves drooped in the extreme heat.

Yet amid silent sorrow, lively activities took place. While the deformed corpse disgusted the villagers, who were terrified of standing close to it, the fish and insects found it appealing. In the water, the fish merrily swam back and forth. They swam into his armpits and ears, snapped their jaws, and disappeared swiftly. In the air, flies and bugs landed on the corpse, searching for food. Every now and then, a yellow bamboo leaf suddenly fell into the pond and disturbed their feast. They flew away with a buzzing sound. After a short while, they returned and formed black patches on the gray corpse.

In the afternoon, a nauseating stench began to spread. At the top of the bamboo grove, a crow steadied itself with its claws on a branch and moved its tail feathers, trying to keep its balance. Then it looked with keen interest at the floating corpse below. Another crow perched on a different branch, and both uttered low, coarse sounds as if calling to each other. Then two or three more crows joined them. One crow flapped its wings and landed on the belly of the corpse. Noticing that there was no danger, all the crows started attacking the dead body. Meanwhile, Xích's body remained a feast for the fish and flies. His limbs were all curled up, his face distorted, but his ghostly appearance did not frighten them away. They seemed to enjoy the flesh of the dead.

At nine o'clock the next morning, the coroner's car's horn filled the air. The crows were startled and flew away noisily, as did the bugs and flies. The fish hid themselves under rocks. The district official of legal affairs finally appeared, escorted by a clerk and a police officer. They talked and spat simultaneously. The police officer turned the corpse over with a stick while the other two examined it carefully and jotted down some notes. Mr. Hương Lý, Mr. and Mrs. Cứu, their relatives, and the villagers stood quietly by and swallowed their saliva as they stared at the body. Some signed. Some wiped away tears.

After the investigation was complete, the coroner ordered the police officer to send the spectators away. Then he asked Mr. Cứu, "How much money do you earn from this pond, including the fish and the lotus? A few hundred piasters?"

The coroner's question had nothing to do with his son's death, but Mr. Cứu still replied, "Yes, sir."

"How many *mẫu* of land do you have for cultivation?" the coroner asked.[1]

---

1. 1 *mẫu* = 39,000 square feet.

"Twenty-two *mẫu*, sir," Mr. Cứu responded.

"This is just to let you know that I know about your financial situation. Based on my investigation, you may not bury your son yet because I must send a doctor here to verify a few things," the coroner said as he nodded his head.

"Sir, please have mercy on us," Mr. Cứu trembled and begged.

"Your son was murdered." The coroner shook his head. "We need a doctor to perform a thorough autopsy."

"Oh! My poor son!" Mrs. Cứu screamed as she covered her face with her hands.

Everyone, except the coroner, was moved by the grief she showed over her drowned son. The coroner represented the law and justice, and even though he was a human being, he acted like an unfeeling, heartless stone statue, impervious to Mrs. Cứu's grief and Mr. Cứu's plea. There was, however, one thing that could change the coroner's coldhearted attitude—money.

Noticing that the coroner was contemplatively looking at the rotting, drowned corpse, Mr. Cứu sadly proposed, "Sir, it's hot out here. Please come over to my house to rest for a while."

"Sure. It's disgusting here. Look at the dead body's bloated shape and discoloration, and the flies, bugs, fish, and crows keep attacking it. It gets worse under this hot sun. I don't know when you may bury your son because we must wait for the doctor's report," the coroner said as he raised his hands to chase off the flies and then spat.

As he was walking, he told the clerk, "It's a murder, unlike what you read in the initial report."

"I swear in front of my son's spirit that I am not concealing anything from you. Punish me if I lied to you. Please allow me to bury my son. I'll show you my eternal gratitude," Mr. Cứu said softly as he walked closer to the coroner.

The coroner turned his face toward Mr. Cứu and looked at him sympathetically. "How much would you offer to demonstrate your gratitude?" he asked.

"Ten piasters, sir."

"You should know that the gas alone for my trip here already cost that much." The coroner laughed.

"Sir, this is a serious murder," the clerk walked up and said to the coroner, who then grimaced and told Mr. Cứu, "Look at your land and estate. You want to bury your son immediately, but you're not offering enough. It should be a hundred piasters, at least."

"Sir, country folks are naïve. They want to get things done, but they don't want to pay," the clerk said to the coroner.

"Please tell the coroner that I don't have a hundred piasters. Would he accept fifty?" Mr. Cứu frowned and whispered to the clerk.

The clerk glared and waved his hand, a clear demonstration of his disapproval. "Not a chance. How could that be possible?" he told Mr. Cứu. Then, he whispered, "I guarantee you I can persuade the coroner to accept your offer. How about eighty piasters for him and ten for me?"

"At the moment, I don't have that much money," Mr. Cứu replied softly.

"Don't worry. You can make a promise first and pay later. I'll help you. You can't leave your son in the water like that forever."

Mr. Cứu became quiet and sighed. He turned back and saw his wife's grief. He could no longer control his tears. Then he and the clerk agreed to settle for a total of seventy piasters. An hour later, the flies, bugs, crows, and fish lost their feast. It was the coroner who had taken it away.

2

The Teeth of an Upper-Class Family's Dog

Nguyễn Công Hoan

At about six o'clock, an automobile approached. Its headlights illuminated the horizon. The car crossed a bridge, and as it came closer to the front of a French-style house enclosed by an iron fence, its honking sounded like a frog's croaking. Then the car stopped. But just before the car came slowly to a full standstill, a dog jumped out from the car onto the ground, wagging its tail and barking. The dog reared up on its hind legs to greet the two people who then were getting out of the car—one was the owner of the house, and the other was his guest.

The car lights were turned off, and the doors closed. The host and his guest entered the house. They both wore French clothes designed for hunting, and their shoes were covered in mud. Hunting guns rested on their shoulders, and they each held a heavy string of game birds. As the dog ran ahead, it looked back, wagging its tail and yelping. The host invited his guest to have a seat on the living room couch. The room was built and decorated in the modern style, with a shiny wooden floor and light, sky-blue paint on the walls. The mantled gas lantern was also light blue. One could tell from looking at the living room that its owner was a wealthy, sophisticated, and extravagant gentleman. His wife had just finished her makeup and came to the living room to greet the guest. The dog sat on the fourth chair, panting with its tongue out while observing each person in the room. It is a universal truism that rich people love to show off, and the host was no exception. To him, the mansion, the automobile, the living room, and the dining room were somewhat out of date, and he was no longer enthusiastic about showing them off. Thus, he acquired something new—the dog that he named Lu.

"My dog's breed is Braque d'Auvergne. I got it for seventy piasters from a Frenchman who offered me a good deal because he had a high opinion of me. The dog should've cost at least four hundred piasters! Few breeds are better than this one, and generally, they cost more than five hundred piasters, but rarely do you see an Annamese spend even four hundred piasters on a dog—quite an extravagant expense.[1] Moreover, there aren't many Annamese people who know the value of these dogs, so they would consider it a waste to spend their money on one. Take a closer look at it. Its ears are large, its nose is always wet, its legs are long, and it's a spotted dog. If you don't notice these characteristics, then you might mistake this particular breed for others. I love this dog most of all for its square-shaped head, like the Chinese ideograph for *field*. Look, here is a horizontal stroke. Here is a vertical stroke. Isn't that great? If a dog of this breed has a sleek belly, a short muzzle, and ribs that swell like those of a goat, it's definitely a healthy and fast dog. You surely appreciated my dog's stately posture earlier. It is always ten meters ahead of me, isn't it? It's true—you could use a yardstick to measure the distance. My dog looks great, especially when it shifts its gaze and sniffs with its nose. If it catches the scent of a bird hiding in a bush, it ducks its head and quietly puts its tail up as a signal to me. After I have loaded bullets in the gun and made a clicking sound with my tongue, the dog leaps toward the bird. The bird then flies out, and *bang*—how can the bird escape my shot? It's always just like that, ten times out of ten!"

The dog sat on a chair across from its master, swiveling its muzzle slightly as if listening attentively to the conversation.

"My dog not only hunts well, but it also finds lost items. Why don't you let it get the smell of your eyeglasses, hide them in the garden, and I then will order it to find them for you?"

---

1. The French divided Vietnam into three regions: Tonkin (the northern region), Annam (the central region), and Cochinchine (the southern region). Because the Nguyễn dynasty was retained in Huế, a province in central Vietnam, the French called all the Vietnamese people *l'Annamite*.

The guest was also a dog lover and wanted to test Lu's talent. Not surprisingly, in less than five minutes, Lu held the eyeglasses tightly between its teeth, wagged its tail, and returned them to the guest. The host was quite satisfied and laughed loudly, caressing the dog, embracing it affectionately, and then kissing it, just as if he were overjoyed at a son who had earned excellent grades in school.

"I take care of my dog very carefully. I never let it eat from the ground. That's why it is hygienic and quite smart. No wonder French dogs are always better than our Annamese dogs. Annamese dogs not only have ugly fur but also indiscriminately eat food and snap at people. Sometimes they sneak up behind you and bite your pants. Very dangerous, indeed! But my dog is different—if it barks, there must be a burglar attempting to break in. It will leap at the burglar and maul his face. If a burglar breaks into my house, he is out of luck. He may lose his head and have nothing to put his hat on! But my dog barks only after ten o'clock at night."

Dinner was ready and placed on the table. As the host invited the guest to sit, the dog sprang onto the table and sat in front of the host.

"My Lu is very respectful. It took me a long time to train it. Here is its own plate of food—rice mixed with meat, so delicious—but if I don't permit it to eat, it doesn't dare take a bite, even when I am not here."

The host then took the dog's plate out to the front yard. The guest and the dog followed. Lu wagged its tail, signaling its happiness. The host placed the plate in the middle of the front yard. The dog bent its head to sniff it. When it was about to eat, the host cried out in French, *"Attention!"* Realizing its master was not addressing it as usual, Lu stepped back slowly.

"I don't need to stand here and keep an eye on it. I bet you, after we have finished our dinner, this plate of food will remain untouched. Please go in and dine with me."

At that moment, if the host had been paying attention, he would have noticed something large and dark at the gate. It was a beggar, sitting with his arms around his knees. His peasant hat was so frayed that it revealed its lining. He wore a loincloth, and his tattered shirt had only one sleeve and exposed his long, scrawny, darkened arms and legs. His beggar's sack was wide open and lay next to his thin, worn-out shoes.

The beggar had been waiting there a long time. He heard the sounds of plates and chopsticks in the kitchen and smelled the aroma of stir-fried food that the breeze had carried out from the house. He cried out loudly, begging for some food, but no one heard his pleas. When he saw two people walking into the yard, he knelt down and begged until froth covered his mouth, but the two men were too busy playing with the dog to pay him any mind. The beggar tried to cry out even louder, but when the host heard the beggar's cries, he glowered and yelled angrily, "What are you crying for? You interrupted our conversation. Get out of here now. If not, I'll kick you to death!"

The miserable man said nothing. The host and his guest went inside to have dinner. The beggar stared at the dog's plate. He was starving and started to drool. He didn't have even enough control to swallow his saliva. He wished to steal a bite from the dog's plate of food, but he was fearful that the dog might bite him. He couldn't understand why the dog kept standing close to the plate without eating. He thought that the dog didn't like the food, and he wished he could be the dog in a rich family, rather than a mere man.

If the dog knew human language, the beggar would have approached it to tell it about his starvation. Hopefully, the dog would have some empathy and exercise some "humanity" by giving the beggar its unwanted food. Or was the dog guarding the food because the beggar was sitting at the gate? The beggar quietly walked behind the gate to take a better look. After a while, the dog went slowly toward the wall and lay down. Seizing this opportunity, the beggar risked his life and stepped forward. But suddenly, the dog stood up, moved forward, and snorted. The beggar stared at the dog, and the dog, in return, stared at him. The plate of food rested between them. If the beggar took a step forward, so did the dog. They were two adversaries refusing to yield to each other.

After about ten minutes, the beggar came up with a plan. He grabbed a rock and hid it behind his back. Then he ran toward the dog's food, quickly picked up a piece, and voraciously ate it.

But the dog acted faster. It ran toward the beggar, jumped up, opened its mouth, and snarled at him. The beggar lifted his arm and hit the dog in its mouth with the rock. The creature yelped and in the blink of an eye, pinned the man to the ground, scratching his face and biting his mouth. The man punched the dog in the head and knocked it over. The animal lay on its back with all four legs in the air, yelping loudly.

Hearing the dog cry, the host quickly put down his bowl and chopsticks. He didn't even have time to excuse himself to his wife and guest. Carrying a lamp, he ran toward the scene.

"Oh no! What's happened to my Lu? Gosh! Two of its teeth are broken!" he cried. He then yelled at the house servants, took the dog in his arms, and walked inside.

The host then ran back outside to see who had beaten his dog. He saw a black shadow running away. He got into his car, turned on the headlights, and recognized that it was the beggar who was running.

"You bastard, you broke my dog's teeth. My car will run over and kill you. Then I'll pay a fine for homicide. Thirty piasters at most."

He turned off his headlights and accelerated to catch up with the shadow.

3

Hunger

Thạch Lam

A breeze stole into the room and awakened Sinh. He could feel the wintry cold under his thin blanket. Curling up all night on a hard wooden bed had left him extremely tired. Sinh wrapped the blanket around his body and sat up. As on other mornings, he was sickened by the same sadness and morbidity in his soul. He studied the unobtrusive furniture in the dimly lit room: a wobbly table in the corner, a broken bamboo bed, an earless teapot, some stained, chipped saucers, and finally a leather trunk—the last vestige of his former luxurious life. Looking at these simple possessions, he thought about his current misery. He had been living among this discarded furniture, in this same dark and dank room for a long time now. He had become so familiar with the sound of gusts at night and the exhaustion caused by hunger that he couldn't remember how many days he had been suffering from hunger and winter cold.

Sinh sighed. He recalled the day that he had been laid off, his boss's nonchalant but firm voice, and the despondent faces of the co-workers sharing his fate. Since then, life had become destitute and miserable.

Suddenly he heard the sound of wooden clogs in the front yard and looked up. It was his wife coming home. She lifted the red curtain at the main entrance and entered. The sight of the thin shadow that her shirt cast onto the ground moved him deeply. She walked toward his bed and looked at Sinh without saying anything. Sinh held her hand and asked affectionately, "Dear, you left quite early this morning. Where did you go?"

"I went to see Mrs. Ba to borrow some money," she replied.

"Did she lend you any?"

His wife looked at him, sighed, and shook her head. "Nobody will lend us money recently. Mrs. Ba has already forgotten about the time when she needed our help."

"That's life. No need to blame her. So what should we do now?" Sinh asked sadly.

He thought about the empty rice jar. They didn't have even a single penny. It had been two days since they had eaten a meal together, and the hunger made him miserable.

"What should we do?" His wife repeated Sinh's question and then began to cry. Sinh loved her dearly and held her tightly and affectionately. He wanted to die—that would be better than suffering this poverty-stricken life.

Afternoon came and carried with it cold winds. Sinh sat on a chair on his small balcony and looked down. The room he rented was part of a long, narrow house divided into many small rooms. An entire family was crowded into each room, and all the tenants, who came from various places, were poor vendors.

It was dinnertime. Sinh saw other tenants busy preparing meals and thought about his empty kitchen. He wondered where his wife had gone all day, and whether she would bring home any food or disappoint him again. The more he thought about his destitute situation, the more he loved his wife, who used to enjoy a comfortable life but now had to suffer because of his unemployment. They had first met at a party in another village. Back then, he had a job and plenty of money. They fell in love, and he married her despite his family's disapproval. They had lived a wonderful, happy life together, but now that was only a distant memory. He missed those golden days, which had been replaced by poverty, hardships, hunger, and misery. Despite his current predicament, his wife's love for him did not fade, and they felt sorry for each other. Her weak, small shadow on the floor, which he had seen that morning, reappeared in his mind. He recalled her disappointment, her sad eyes, the way she looked at him affectionately, and her sacrifice.

A cold wind blew past, and he could feel a chill run through his body. He was starving and exhausted. His blurry vision made everything he saw, near and far, hazy. In his former comfortable life, he had never thought about hunger. Only in his misery did he understand how hunger tormented a person. He trembled as he thought about the power of hunger. One could use one's physical strength to control one's mental weakness, but hunger had already deprived him of that strength. The smell of food from downstairs tormented him. Sinh looked down and saw his neighbors cooking dinner. Although their food was not special—just some fried tofu and fish—he longed for it.

In the past, when he heard stories about people fighting one another for food, he smirked. To him, eating was a trivial matter, and possessing a noble, dignified soul was the most important thing in life. However, in that very moment, he realized the necessity of food. When he was rich, he looked down on poor, filthy people. He asked himself why they needed to live lives of suffering and he questioned the purpose of their existence. Now, he wished he could have something to eat just to survive.

A hand softly tapped on his shoulder. His wife smiled and showed him some boxes neatly wrapped in shiny plastic. He knew that there was delicious food in the boxes from an expensive French restaurant. He could smell the flavorful meat, and his hands trembled as he untied the strings around the boxes.

"How can you afford these, Mai?" he asked ecstatically.

"Go ahead and enjoy the food, then I'll tell you. Fortunately, a kindhearted woman . . ."

"Who is she? Tell me, please," he insisted.

"Honey, eat first, and I'll tell you," she replied affectionately.

She then quickly placed the boxes on the table and unwrapped them. Sinh saw slices of delicious meat and pork pâté and some red and yellow cakes.

"I took a chance when I left the house. You know how friends are nowadays. If we are poor and needy, nobody wants to help us because they know we would never be able to return their kindness. So, I wandered around town and wanted to commit suicide. Fortunately, I ran into Mrs. Hiểu, and she was delighted to see me again," Mai said cheerfully. "Mrs. Hiểu is so kind," she continued. "She lent me money and promised to help me open a small business. Such a kindhearted woman! Honey, soon I will sell betel nut."

"Without her help, we would be starving again today. But why did you spend so much money on food?" he asked.

Mai bowed her head and smiled. Her rosy cheeks and a few disheveled hairs made her look even more beautiful. She pulled a stack of paper bills from her pocket and placed it on the table, then walked away happily, saying, "I'll be right back. I'm getting a knife to cut the cakes." As she left, Sinh noticed a piece of folded paper on the floor. He picked it up and recognized the handwriting of an unknown male: *Mai, here is the amount of money I promised. If you need more, I'll give you the rest, but you must not miss our appointment. I'll be waiting for you . . .*

The piece of paper fell from his hand without his noticing. He felt like he was suffocating. Within an instant, his joy vanished. The discovery hurt him tremendously; he was not dreaming. Undoubtedly, the money and the note were related. But who had lent Mai the money? Sinh recalled the times when his wife returned home with great disappointment and sighs. All the people she knew had greeted her pleas for help with coldhearted indifference. Mai must have fabricated the story about Mrs. Hiếu to deceive him. Furious, Sinh curled his lips in disdain. His body trembled, and he cursed, "Bitch!"

He felt as if someone had stabbed his heart. He grasped the arms of the chair he was sitting in, looked at the roll of money on the table and the half-unwrapped boxes of food, and bent down to pick up the note again.

It was quiet. Then, he heard the sounds of the curtain curling up in the wind, and the sounds of his wife walking toward him. He bit his lips to control his anger and held the chair tightly. Mai stood next to him and caressed his hair. She opened the boxes and cut the cakes.

"Look at these delicious cakes. I bought them at Hàng Trống. I paid five pennies for this top-quality meat. Let me cut it for you. You must be very hungry. Let's eat first, and we'll . . .," Mai said happily. She then cut the meat, placed it on a plate, and continued, "Dear, please eat. What are you waiting for? We are very fortunate. If I hadn't run into Mrs. Hiếu, I wouldn't know what to do." Tapping him on the shoulder, she added, "I guess we would be starving still, wouldn't we? You should be grateful to Mrs. Hiếu, a kindhearted woman. She handed me the fifteen piasters as soon as I asked her. Did you count the money? I am not lying."

Sinh grew furious and couldn't control his emotions. He was enraged by his wife's lies, which she covered so tactfully. Was Mai that wicked? How could she deceive him with her gentle eyes and beautiful face?

Sinh pushed Mai away as if she were a filthy creature. She trembled and fell. Her shawl fell off, her hair was disheveled. She opened her eyes wide and looked at Sinh in astonishment.

"What's wrong with you?" she asked.

"What's wrong? Don't pretend!" Sinh laughed like a maniac. He showed her the folded note held in his hand. "So, what's this?"

Mai's face went pale. She held her head in her hands and trembled. Sinh's voice was bitter and sarcastic as he said, "A kindhearted Mrs. Hiếu! Yeah! Why didn't you tell me you had an appointment with her tonight?"

Mai bowed her head and sobbed. Her crying didn't alleviate his fury. Instead it outraged him. Mai was frightened and called her husband's name hesitantly, "Sinh, my dear . . . "

"Stop crying and get out of here," Sinh ignored her words and said. "I don't ever want to see you again. Here, take this with you." He grasped the roll of money and threw at Mai. The paper bills fell off her and scattered over the floor. Then he threw the food and cakes onto the floor. "I don't want to eat this dirty food!"

Ignoring his wife's plea for forgiveness, he collapsed into the chair. His greasy hands held his forehead. Mai sobbed, used her shirt to cover her face, and walked out.

Sinh bent his head and agonized over the situation. His rage had vanished, leaving him nothing but endless sadness. He felt emotionless and empty. He hated his cursed life and his poverty. When would the suffering end? Why had Mai deceived him, despite everything they had gone through together?

Sinh couldn't make sense of the situation and could bear no more suffering. He dropped his head onto the table. A breeze suddenly startled him, and he smelled the delicious aroma of the meat. His hunger started to torment him again. He forgot his anguish. He wanted to control his hunger but failed. He inhaled the smell of the meat and the cake voraciously, then bent down and looked at the food scattered on the floor. He looked around and didn't see Mai. Hesitantly, he reached for the meat and began to eat ravenously, without thinking.

No food was left, except for a few cake crumbs on the wrappers. Sinh felt relieved and stretched out his body. Then he recalled the note, the money, Mai's sobbing, his insults, and his anguish.

An infinite dreariness ran through Sinh's mind. He held his face in his hands and sobbed.

4

An Early Morning

Thạch Lam

Bính had tossed and turned all night, unable to get a wink of sleep, although he had gone out and not returned home until very late. The pillow was damp with sweat as he lay on his side with his eyes shut. Strange and incoherent dreams had haunted his sleep. Bính opened his eyes and gawked at the mosquito net. Then he looked at its quietly undulating surface amid a faint light emitted from the oil lamp. The wall clock made mournful sounds to signal each passing hour, and a consistently ticking noise marked each second. Bính was drained. He could feel exhaustion entering his toes and fingers and spreading throughout his body—a consequence of his decadent lifestyle. A feeling of fatigue permeated his entire body.

A rooster crowed softly in the distance. The night was advancing toward dawn. Faint sunlight began to enter his room through the windows and through the palm-leaf roof that had been slightly damaged by the daytime heat. The early morning sunlight was dim but clear. Bính pushed open the flaps of his mosquito net and sat up. The air in his thatched house was becoming humid and unpleasant, and he could feel the heavy, fetid atmosphere on his eyelids.

Out of habit, Bính thought about lying down again, but this time he slid out of bed and stood up. The cool floor gave his feet a comforting sensation. He opened the door and walked outside. Bính sat by an areca tree on the front yard's bricks. The tranquil, peaceful early morning engendered a peculiar feeling within him. He was uncertain whether it was cool stillness or still coolness. The cool water in the small cement tank was covered with morning dew. The ground surrounding it was clean and orderly. The coolness of the night remained on the surface of the tank's water and on the rose bushes nearby. Bính's exhaustion began to gradually subside, and blood circulated more rapidly through his body, as if it were rushing up to catch the fresh air.

It had been quite a while since he had last gotten up early, and he had almost forgotten the experience of an early morning. For years, he had been indulging himself in late-night revelries and social gatherings, and he often arrived home as people were preparing for the early market. Normally, as he reclined with fatigue on the bus with sleep-deprived eyes on his way home after his parties, he saw women carrying baskets of vegetables heading toward the market. Their newly cut, crisp, fresh vegetables were in great contrast to his limp, spent body at three or four o'clock in the morning. People in Hà Nội were still sleeping at those hours; their doors remained shut. Outside, streetlights illuminated the long, quiet, empty streets. Dry leaves fell on the ground. Only at such hours did he walk out from dark alleys, wearing a hat partially covering his face, trudging along the brick sidewalks with his hands in his pockets. He saw a carmine light coming from an outdoor lamp at the end of the street. He could not remember how long he had been leading such a wasteful life. It must have been years—since he was laid off, became penniless, and had to return to his mother's dilapidated house, his family's only property.

Bính looked around the small garden. The ground still bore some marks left by his mother's sweeping the afternoon before. This familiar scene looked new to him because he always got up too late to appreciate the simple beauty of an early morning. The miniature mountain landscape his father built and often had looked at for hours when he was alive, the fish pond encircled by moss, the gray and moldy trunks of the areca trees, his mother's well-tended beds of vegetables, and the bushes with red roses blooming in early mornings—they all became recognizable to him again.

The atmosphere and scenery evoked memories from his youth. He used to get up early like everyone else, and he had been energetic and healthy. He would pour water from the tank into a basin and wash his face, his skin absorbing the coolness of the water. He had enjoyed those early mornings tremendously. He used to stare up at the vast blue sky and around at the lush vegetation in the garden. Everything in him had awakened. Through the thin hedges, he had caught a glimpse of people going to the market, listened to their laughter and chatter, and heard the creaking sound of shouldered bamboo poles laden with heavy bags of rice. While he was reviewing his lessons at his desk in the living room, he would hear the prolonged cooing of the pigeons next door.

Rarely did he recall those days. He wanted to forget everything after a long night of revelry. He had always been too lethargic to remember those sweet moments. He was troubled by his disturbed sleep but had no time for reminiscence. And when he sobered up, he only wanted to continue his meaningless existence.

Bính did not excuse his degeneration. Since his father's death, Bính had become ever more decadent and wasteful. His nocturnal lifestyle appealed to him, as a fire appeals to moths. The colorful lights of night-clubs made the red lips and rosy cheeks of flirtatious women irresistible. He immersed himself in alcohol and drugs. Several times, he had pushed his mother away as she begged him to stay home and left the house quickly to avoid hearing her crying in a dark corner. He had squandered all of his family's money and ruined his health. A bitter feeling and a sense of ennui penetrated his heart. Perhaps he had fallen into the desperate abyss because he saw nothing left in life to strive for. Deep inside, he vaguely noticed a light glimmering in darkness, but he had refused to follow it.

However, the early morning's cool air refreshed him and cleansed him, awakening memories of his happy youth. The cooing from the neighbor's pigeons had given way to the chattering of people on their way to the market on the other side of the thin hedges. The rainwater in the tank was cool and fresh, the azure sky was cloudless, and very soon everything would brighten in the warm sunlight.

Bính stood up and walked toward the red rose bushes by the water tank. He bent down and plucked a rose, as he used to do in the past. He put the flower on a plate and observed its petals, which gently held a clear, pearl-like drop of dew. The rose emitted a lovely, familiar scent, a plain scent typical of homegrown roses, and he thought about his mother, who loved him dearly. The flower embodied her, and Bính felt a burst of love for his mother. That morning, he wanted his miserable mother to see a rose gracefully positioned on a plate as she got up, something that she had enjoyed seeing a long time ago. The rose was the early morning's precious gift that contained a sublime freshness within its petals after a rain. A pleasant and serene feeling entered his heart. He felt younger, and he found himself bending down, appreciating the beauty of dewdrops on fresh roses. The common sounds of early mornings and the cooing of pigeons seemed to return to him, freshly.

Bính stood up. The cool breeze from a rice field brought the gentle smell of wet grass. The sky's color had changed from blue to pink. The sun started to rise on the horizon. Inside, his mother had just woken up. She pushed open her mosquito net and chanted the Buddha's name with a beaded rosary in her hands. Her voice was as clear and gentle as it had always been.

Bính quietly walked inside, afraid to disturb his mother's chanting. He went toward the ancestral altar, placed the plate with the rose on it, and emptied the water from an antique offering bowl. When his mother finished her chanting, she asked him gently and affectionately, as she did when he was a child, "Why did you get up so early, dear?"

5

Moonlit Nights

Thạch Lam

It was still sunset when the moon rose. A big, red, full moon slowly appeared on the horizon from behind a high clump of bamboo near a distant village. A few threads of cloud crossed in front of the moon, became tenuous, and gradually vanished. A gentle breeze brought the pleasant scent of a field. About an hour after the great bell of a local Buddhist temple emitted its early evening toll, the sky became high and vast, while the moon became smaller but brighter. It resembled a flute-kite flying high in the sky. Moonlight poured down from the sky, illuminating tree branches and leaves and bathing the streets with its silver beams. In the small garden by a pond, Tuân lay on a narrow bamboo bed in a dark corner, looking up at the night sky. He observed the moon through sharp, dark bamboo leaves, and the scene resembled a pastoral Chinese painting. Cool air emerged from the moss around the pond. A flower wall glowed in the middle of the garden, and thick, tiny pomegranate leaves sparkled like crystals.

Shadows from trees made the place comfortable and private. Tuân's heart beat faster. He reached out his hands and listened carefully to the subtle sounds of quivering leaves and someone's gentle steps. A tree branch bent down, then suddenly returned to its original position, its shadow reflected on the pond. A flower was blossoming slowly. Tuân saw a woman's shadow walking toward him. He extended his arms to embrace her and whispered affectionately, "Honey . . ."

Without responding, she quietly fell into his arms. Tuân bent his head down and smelled the familiar scent of her hair. He embraced her and kissed her passionately. After a while, he released her slightly. Mai straightened her disheveled hair. A melancholic feeling overwhelmed Tuân. The couple were so intimate that they never got bored of looking at each other. Mai's eyes glistened endearingly in the shadow cast by her scarf. Tuân held her gently and bent down to appreciate her eyes more closely. He was attracted to her symmetrical face, tiny chin, and ivory-colored neck. He was mesmerized by her beauty. She laid her head on his arm, and he bent down closely, as if she were a precious flower.

Ever since that moonlit night, they continued to see each other in his garden. At first, their meetings lasted from the time the moon rose until it set. Then they stayed together as long as the moon's glow remained, and their love grew stronger and more passionate. He was eighteen, she sixteen, and both were as youthful as fast-growing buds.

●

Mai and Tuân were next-door neighbors. As children, they had often played together. In the evenings, Mai would cross the hedge between the houses to visit Tuân. Then they would whisper in the dark as if they were doing something wrong. Not until Mai's mother called her did she leave Tuân and quickly run home. When he was thirteen, and she eleven, his uncle took Tuân to the city for school, and gradually he forgot Mai, his childhood neighbor. Tuân, however, did not know whether Mai had forgotten him as well. Sometimes, during his homecomings, from his garden, he saw her shadow fluttering through her garden. He heard her voice clearly, and at night, he could hear her laughter or conversations with the seasonal field workers.

One day, Tuân returned from the rice paddy and ran into Mai at the gate of his house. Shy and blushing, she covered her face with a conical hat. Tuân stood there and did not know what to say. After a moment of silence, Mai left. Tuân's eyes followed her as she walked in the sunlight, and he was overwhelmed with sweet memories of their childhood. That afternoon, Tuân sat on a rock by the pond in his garden and realized that the path on which Mai once had trodden when she came to see him was now covered with brush.

After his vacation ended, Tuân returned to the city and to school. He did not have another chance to visit his family. One year, two years, three years passed, and Tuân did not know how Mai was faring. The image of her covering her face with a conical hat, revealing only her smile, became a blurred memory, just as the fading image of his village receded into the hazy twilight of his memory.

Before summer ended, while Tuân was getting ready for a trip to Sầm Sơn Beach with some friends—some of whom were his pretty female classmates—his mother, who was visiting him in the city, asked, "Do you still remember our neighbor Mai? She's getting married very soon. This year!"

All of a sudden, Tuân stopped packing and remained quiet, as if he were thinking about something serious. Before his mother left, she asked, "So have you changed your mind? Are you not going to Sầm Sơn as planned?"

"No, Mom. I am going back with you."

Upon arriving home, Tuân went to the garden. It was the first day of the month, and a crescent moon hung in the quiet sky. He then saw Mai in a white blouse in her front yard. He was overwhelmed with strong emotions. He felt nervous, as if anticipating a joyful event. He did not call Mai but stayed in the garden until it got very cold.

After that night, the moon gradually became fuller and brighter. A breeze carried with it a pleasant scent, a dark red rose remained invisible in the dark while a white rose became more conspicuous. Tuân sat on the flower wall in the garden and felt elated. He assured himself that on that night Mai would return his love, and that she desired his love, just as he did hers.

Tuân bent down to smell a crimson rose. Its petals, dotted with yellow pollen, were as dark as the night and emitted a pleasant scent. The moon was high above the treetops. Tuân walked toward the gate. In the dark, Mai was already there, waiting for him. He extended his arms to embrace her, heard the fast beating of her heart, and felt her warm breathing. In the quiet, they kissed each other passionately without exchanging a word.

When Mai gently pushed his arms away, Tuân saw tears in her eyes. "Are you crying?" he asked affectionately.

Mai did not reply but laid her head on his shoulder. Her small, slender body trembled with her sobbing. Tuân felt strong emotions for her, and their reunion was fraught with sorrow and tears. In the dark, she told him how much she had missed him. Mai had been in love with Tuân since childhood, thinking about him constantly since he left for the city, although Tuân had been oblivious to it. He was overjoyed to learn of her love for him. Unfortunately, it was too late; she would be married very soon.

They continued to meet in his garden on moonlit nights. They sat on the rock, spoke affectionately, and expressed their love for each other.

●

Tonight was their final evening.

Tuân and Mai sat on the rock and waited for the moon to rise. After midnight, it was cold and misty. In the tranquil night, they heard dry leaves falling from branches. In the pond, a fish stirred in the water, creating concentric circles. Mai leaned her body against Tuân's and asked, "You're leaving tomorrow, aren't you?"

She then cried without any further utterance. Tuân held her hands tightly, not knowing what to say. He wanted to comfort her but decided not to. He was still very young and did not understand her desperation. He could not imagine that they would soon be parted forever.

Love could not be extinguished by sorrow. Mai and Tuân were like two dreamers. She put her arm around his neck, and her lips found his in an ardent kiss. Her lips bled, and it was painful. Mai, however, was happy in that moment of pain, and she offered him her most precious gift—her virgin body and purity of soul.

●

Three days had passed since Tuân departed.

During those days, Mai could focus on nothing, as if her mind had followed him. She sat quietly for hours, having no more tears to shed. This morning, the groom's family arrived to present wedding offerings to her parents. Her mother greeted and welcomed them warmly and joyfully. Her fiancé donned his best clothes. He was somewhat shy but cheerful. Mai sat in her chamber and heard the conversation between her mother and the groom's family in the living room.

At night, after everyone had gone to bed, Mai quietly crossed the hedge and went to Tuân's garden. She sat on the rock by the pond—the same spot where she and Tuân used to sit. Tonight, the moon rose late. She sat there as the cold mist penetrated her skin. The garden became darker. A few roses blossomed, and she could smell their gentle fragrance, which reminded her of the first time she was held in Tuân's embrace.

It was quite late, and the moon did not rise until near dawn. The moon looked melancholic and blurry behind the trees at the end of the garden. When the moon showed its light on her body, she put her head into her hands and sobbed. Broken-hearted, she cried for her ill-fated love and life.

The next morning, Tuân's parents saw her body in the pond. Her hair was loose, floating freely among the hyacinths.

6

Two Sisters

Nhất Linh

Mrs. Xã Vực had two daughters, Bìm and Lạch. Bìm, only two years older than Lạch, looked much older than her sister. Her body was buxom and sturdy, her legs and arms large, her eyes small and slightly rheumy. Her fat upper eyelids, chubby cheeks, and thick lips made her look like a clumsy dolt. Although Bìm toiled from sunrise to midnight and ate sparingly, she remained rotund. She was quiet—never talked back or argued—and always remained reserved. Seldom did she reveal her true feelings, whether she was melancholic or exuberant. Mrs. Xã's affection for her older daughter only increased with the thought that Bìm would be single forever because men found her undesirable, and this disheartened Mrs. Xã greatly. She comforted herself with the thought that, although Bìm was unattractive, she was kind, industrious, and imbued with quiet dignity.

In the village, there was an affluent family, the Lýs, who owned more than twenty hectares of farming land. The Lýs had only one son, who was thirteen. Mrs. Xã knew that the Lýs needed a house servant, and she hoped that Bìm might thus have a chance to become their daughter-in-law. Mrs. Lý, for her part, had already noticed Bìm and considered her thoroughly. Because Mrs. Lý had only one son, it was crucial that she take great care in determining his marriage prospects. Mrs. Lý defended Bìm against people's negative comments about her slowness and clumsiness. "She's slow, but she does things properly," Mrs. Lý would say. "Her physique proves that." Then, suddenly, she'd think of the water buffalos in the corrals.

The day Mrs. Lý came to Mrs. Xã's home to propose marriage on her son's behalf, Mrs. Xã said she would need to consult her daughter first. But in fact, she didn't need to consult Bìm because she knew that Bìm would definitely accept. Bìm learned about her marriage by overhearing other people talking about it. She did not think about her thirteen-year-old betrothed. He was just a child, and there was no need to give him much serious thought. Her primary interest was that she was to become the Lýs' daughter-in-law, and it would be a great honor to become a member of that wealthy family.

On the day of the wedding, a misunderstanding occurred that almost ruined everything. After some negotiations between the two families, Mrs. Xã understood that the groom's family would pay her eighty piasters before her daughter joined their family. However, the groom's family thought that Mrs. Xã had agreed on sixty piasters. When the two families met, Mr. Xã at first complained about the monetary issue and insisted that his daughter be granted some extra days before she joined the Lý family. After some further negotiations, Mr. Xã finally agreed to let his daughter go because the Lýs had promised to pay him the rest eventually.

"Please be kind to our young children. Letting them be husband and wife is the most important thing at this point. We have waited so long for today, an auspicious date, to take your daughter home with us. We will settle the monetary matter later," the Lýs said.

The Xãs knew that once their daughter left, they had no hope of receiving the rest of the money, so they knew they were being deceived. Mrs. Xã cared very much for her daughter and didn't want to ruin the wedding, so she accepted the fact that she would lose the anticipated twenty piasters.

"Just let it go. A string will break if stretched too much," she whispered to her husband.

Things did not get complicated. But there were still obstacles after Bìm joined her new home. She had, after all, married a thirteen-year-old boy for sixty piasters.

In caring only about Bìm, Mrs. Xã had given up hope for her younger daughter, Lạch, who was disobedient and rebellious. The more dignity Bìm maintained, the more debauchery Lạch pursued. Lạch would not listen to anyone's advice. She was like a beautiful, lovable bird, chirping and singing ceaselessly. When she looked at someone, her eyes turned flirtatious. Her lips puckered, suggestive and kissable, when she talked, as if she were expressing romantic words. Lạch also sang beautifully. On moonlit autumn nights, her voice was clear and resonated throughout the village. Sometimes, she hid in a bush and sang to tease and flirt with men along the quiet village paths. Because she was such a libertine, she looked condescendingly upon men. She laughed loudly when she heard about her sister's marriage to Ngẩu, the Lýs' son. One day, she saw her brother-in-law and hid behind a bush. When Ngẩu sauntered by, she called, "Hey, Ngẩu. Come over here. I wanna tell you something." She pulled the boy toward her, rubbed his head, and then let him go.

Lạch thought that her sister's marriage was untenable and unacceptable. Her stubborn, obdurate personality could not accept such a peculiar marriage. Her mother kept telling her, "You sooner or later will become a whore. Your sister at least was able to bring home some lucre. I won't get a penny out of you, but I will have to bear your bad reputation."

Later, Lạch joined a traditional operetta group that traveled to various villages, giving performances, but she soon quit because she couldn't earn enough money. With her physical attributes and lovely voice, she became a well-known singer in a licensed district in Hải Phòng. Meanwhile, Bìm still lived a normal domestic life in the Lý household, fulfilling her duties as a daughter-in-law. She lived a life of work, serving her husband's family. She got up at four in the morning to chop hyacinth, cook bran for the pigs, and prepare breakfast for the live-in field hands. She spent the rest of her day taking care of the house, preparing meals for her father-in-law, and serving her husband and his younger sisters. On important familial events such as anniversaries honoring the dead and New Year celebrations, she, as the only daughter-in-law, had to do everything. Her hair became full of ash and dust; her face was smeared with soot. She wore a mended blouse and a dress that was never washed. She busied herself with tending the fire in the kitchen while cooking rice and running back and forth to serve food and alcohol to the elderly male guests. Her jobs were the same every day. She could never rest, but she didn't need to rest anyway.

A few months after the wedding, Bìm and Ngẩu finally slept together in the same bed because he had grown used to her and was no longer afraid of his wife, as he had been at first, and because his parents insisted that they share the bed together. Bìm worked hard all day, so she fell asleep immediately after she lay down and was soon snoring like a freight train. To get warm, Ngầu crawled into her arms like a child being embraced by his mother.

One day, on a quiet, less-traveled village road, Bìm encountered a man. She did not regret what happened between her and the stranger, though she was a bit frightened. But when she arrived home, there was no sign of suspicion, and she accepted that nobody knew of the affair. Also, if she became pregnant and gave birth to a child, it would be assumed to be Ngầu's. Thus, she didn't worry a bit, and she did not regret her actions morally. Like a castrated rooster, like a pig with no perception of living in a sty but still fat and healthy, Bìm became sturdier, and her eyes became rheumier.

The Lýs had a live-in tutor who taught Chinese to some kids in the village. Ngầu was also his student, learning some words so that he could read documents and his family tree. One might wonder whether Bìm's life or a pig's life was preferable. Sometimes, while Bìm was feeding the pigs, her smeared face and filthy body appearing no better than the pigs', she heard Ngầu in the study spell the letters *e* and *a* as if some ancient sounds were echoing around while he was reciting Confucian philosophy on the purposes of Great Learning. Then, he translated the Chinese words into some intelligible Vietnamese.

Bìm no longer thought about her depraved sister, who had already abandoned her home. If someone asked about Lạch, she only cursed her silently, "What a whore!" She considered Lạch a stranger. Lạch was a teahouse girl, and she frequented dancing parties with male clients. After a boyfriend taught her some dancing techniques, she became a dancer and worked at a bar in Hải Phòng. At night, while Bìm snored loudly next to an unkempt boy and slept on a torn sedge mat, Lạch, like a beautiful flower, held a female coworker and danced happily to melodious music under the colorful lights of the bar, awaiting the arrival of clients. She put her hands on her friend's back, dancing and joking. Every now and then, she grew excited, moving her head around along with the music, tapping her feet on the brick floor, and then twirled her friend around a few times. She sang to the music and suddenly thought about moonlit nights in her village, the bamboo, the guava trees—those long-gone images associated with her childhood. She became emotional, and sang in a low voice: *When I left the village, they were only shoots. Upon my return, they have grown into tall bamboo trees.*

One day, by chance, a boyfriend drove her in his car through her village. She asked him to let her visit her family and told him to meet her at the beverage stand at the village entrance. When Mrs. Xã saw Lạch coming home, she held her face with her hands and cried, "Why didn't you die in a street corner already? Why do you want to humiliate me with your bad reputation?" Seeing Lạch, Mrs. Xã thought about Bìm and comforted herself that at least she could take pride in her older daughter.

"Please let me visit my sister and my brother-in-law. I want to see how much he has grown up," Lạch said. "What was his name again, Mom?" She then laughed loudly and continued, "Ah, I remember it now—Ngầu."

"Do not go over there. You're going to embarrass both your sister and me," Mrs. Xã advised.

But Lạch refused to listen to her mother's plea. When she arrived at the Lý household, Bìm was picking lice out of her mother-in-law's hair, and they were sitting next to a haystack. Lạch pulled up the back of her shirt slightly and sat on the low brick wall surrounding the Lýs' flower garden. The sunlight made her yellow silk shirt and flowered velvet pants glisten. One could smell the scent of her perfume.

"Are you here for a visit?" Bìm asked indifferently. Then she felt embarrassed, bowed her head, and continued to search for lice. She picked out some of the nits and bit them, and then said, "How gross! Mother, your hair is too infested with lice."

Ngầu was sitting on the front porch, reciting, "Great Learning makes one virtuous . . ." when he noticed a stranger wearing beautiful clothes. He ran toward her but stopped because he was afraid. He stood there sucking his fingers, amid some wandering pigs, and stared at her. Lạch saw Ngầu. She smiled, closed one eye, and blinked her other eye to tease him, as she had done once before. She then burst out laughing but decided to control her laughter. Lạch then stood up and left because neither Mrs. Lý nor her sister had invited her inside.

As Bìm watched Lạch leave, she pouted. Bìm was embarrassed in front of her mother-in-law because she had a slutty sister. Fortunately, she had just caught a big louse and placed it inside her mother-in-law's palm and said, "Here, Mother. This is a really fat louse," to hide her embarrassment.

●

As my friend told me this story, he concluded:

"Of course, Bìm is respected while Lạch is derided. Nevertheless, it is also dreadful and degrading to sell oneself into a marriage for sixty piasters and become the servant to a child who can't even keep his nose clean just so that one can be honored as a dutiful daughter and dedicated wife. How awful it is to live such an 'honorable' life. I myself wonder if we should consider Lạch a whore. Even though Lạch lives a degraded life, she lives the life of a human being, and although she is a woman of ill repute, she is not passive and submissive like a water buffalo that is purchased and exploited for its labor. Bìm may disrespect Lạch, but Bìm should not compare herself to Lạch, who lives as a human being."

"Is this a true story?" I asked.

"Not really, but there are more Bìms than Lạchs in our society nowadays. I told you this story because I just saw a ten-year-old, rheumy-eyed little boy with a shaved head who has been married already for three years. Recently, I went to a dance club in Hải Phòng where I saw a country girl arm-in-arm with a female friend dancing wildly under the colorful lights. The farm girl—who resembles the Lạch of my story—had very beautiful but very morose eyes, as if she missed her village and wished she could lead a better life. I imagined her saying to me, desperate and sad, "I have to live like this so that I won't suffer like my sister."

7

An Insipid Life

Nhất Linh

Khương put his hands on the mat, crawled slowly toward the corner of his bed, and opened a table drawer. He took a careful look inside, but it was too dark in the room to see clearly, so he had to feel through the drawer blindly. After searching for a while, he closed the drawer, disappointed. Khương remembered throwing a half-smoked cigarette in there a few days ago but could find it nowhere now.

"It must have been that bastard servant boy, Nhỏ, who stole it," he frowned and mumbled.

Suddenly, Khương saw a used cigarette lying on the floor right next to a trestle's foot. He picked it up, blew off the dust, and smelled it.

"An English cigarette. It must have been left here by Hạp, who visited me a few days ago," he said. He sat up and used his fingers to dig out the tobacco. Then he placed the tobacco into his palm and, amused, said, "It's enough to make a small cigarette."

After searching through his pocket, he pulled out a pack of cigarette papers and started to roll a smoke. He rolled leisurely, as if he wanted to extend the process so that he would enjoy its production to the fullest. It had been seven years since his legs were paralyzed—the circumstance that had confined his life to that bed. He couldn't work, and his addiction to smoking was the only pleasure that could alleviate his dejection. His family gradually became more destitute, and his survival was dependent on his wife, who had some money saved and had opened a small rice business at home.

Khương struck a match to light the cigarette, but because the tobacco was damp, he couldn't inhale any smoke. The cigarette wrap became wet with his saliva and tore apart. Khương spit hard so that the tobacco wouldn't stick to his lips, and he then threw the cigarette away. Khương lay down for a while, and when he was about to call Nhỏ, he heard his wife's shouting in the living room. He was going to tell Nhỏ to ask his wife for some tobacco money, but hearing her scream, he decided to wait. Half an hour passed, and noticing that no client was in the shop, Khương called softly, "Nhỏ."

He waited, but Nhỏ didn't appear because the boy was always busy. Every now and then, he called again in a soft voice, hoping that the servant boy would hear him. Eventually, Nhỏ showed up, and Khương hesitantly said, "Go ask Auntie to give me some tobacco money and then go get me a pack of smokes."

When Nhỏ went to talk to Khương's wife, Khương was not surprised to hear her complaining, "Uncle smokes too much! If he smokes, so do you. You never learn a lesson from being punished for stealing." After her rebuke, she gave the boy a hard knock on his head, but Khương only paid attention to the sounds of her opening the money box and the clinking of coins. After she gave the boy some money, she mumbled, "Smoking more, coughing more. There's no good reason to smoke."

After a while, the boy went into Khương's bedroom, placed a pack of tobacco on a teapot warmer in a somewhat disrespectful manner, and hastily left the room. Khương didn't mind his disrespectful behavior, but he felt uneasy about having to crawl to the teapot warmer to get the pack. He slowly opened the container, rolled a large cigarette, lay down on his back, and smoked with great enjoyment. When the smoke wafted across the sunbeams pouring in through the window, they looked like patches of clouds that eventually passed into the darkness of the room. Khương painfully recalled the golden days between his twenty-fifth and thirty-fifth birthdays—a period during which he had lived with boundless hope about life, a time when he nurtured great enthusiasm and ambition. After attending law school for two years, he faced academic expulsion, and his life was never the same again. His wife, Liên, who used to be a gentle, delicate lady with beautiful, dreamy eyes, was now an unattractive, sharp-tongued rice seller. Liên married him because she admired his ambitious goals, but his ambition and her beauty were like the smoke that crossed the sunbeams and vanished into the darkness.

Since his paralysis, Khương sometimes considered his former aspirations but decided to clear them from his mind because they now seemed so pointless. He became indifferent toward everything, even toward his wife—a person to whom he had believed he would devote all his affection until he died. Liên no longer loved him, and after seven years of suffering, she considered him a burden, but one for whom she still had some small vestiges of sympathy. Khương wished that Liên would abandon him so that he could determine his own life. As long as she took care of him, he would continue to live like this—a life in which he had already lost his energy and was incapable of making a new start.

Khương rolled another cigarette and smoked. The room was smoky as if fog had descended. He felt both headachy and excited. He closed his ears to avoid hearing his wife, who was scolding Nhỏ in the other room. He could still hear her clearly, but this time, unlike before, he paid close attention to her words: "I just saw you right here, but you already disappeared into the bedroom. How can a person sleep that much? I don't feed you so that you can sleep all day and become a burden, do I?" She cleared her throat and continued, "Why am I so unfortunate? I have too many debts and heavy burdens on my shoulders."

Khương turned his body and lay on his side with his ear close to a pillow. He didn't want to think about anything, but he couldn't free his mind from his wife's rebukes. *I close my ears so that I can't hear her, but her words still hang in the air*, he thought. He suddenly sat up, and anger reddened his face. Then he called, "Nhỏ."

Liên ran into the bedroom on hearing his unusually loud call, because she thought there was an emergency.

"What's going on?" she asked.

"Please take a seat. I want to talk to you," Khương said.

Liên looked around and didn't know what was happening. "What's going on with you?" she raised her voice.

"Just take a seat first," he said.

"I'm quite busy now," Liên said. "So be quick."

"I told you to sit down!" Khương yelled.

"You really want to raise your voice with me, do you? How unusual!" Liên yelled back.

"I have always hoped that when you discipline our house servant, you might at least think about me and watch your tongue. You should be more tactful with your words." Khương lowered his voice.

"Now you forbid me to discipline the servant. When I'm angry, I don't care what I say, and I don't have time to think about anyone. Why is my life so cursed? I want peace, but you won't leave me alone. I'd be better off dead than having to live like this!"

Khương waited until she was quiet and then said slowly, "You suffer, but so do I. However, you ought to think of the past and show me some compassion. Why don't we . . . ?"

Khương wanted to remind her of their romantic past, but seeing her nonchalant grimace and emotionless eyes, he knew that there would never be a day when they could again live blissfully as they once had. Liên didn't quite understand what her husband wanted to say, but before she left, she grinned and said, "You're just wasting my time. Good for nothing—only good for making a fuss."

Her words "making a fuss" evoked a sense of self-loathing in Khương, because they reminded him of his former energy and enthusiasm. Another person wouldn't be able to detect the utter deterioration of his soul. He clenched his teeth and raised a fist in front of Liên's face and said, "If I weren't disabled . . ." Ironically, his anger only made her smirk.

"You don't need to threaten me," she said. "You've done it several times. You think I am afraid of you, don't you?" She walked out, mumbling, "What a phony hero!"

Khương grasped a teapot lid and was about to throw it after her, but he decided not to. *Things can't get better. She is sick and tired of me anyway. That she has become a shrew is not her fault*, he mused to himself. He became despondent and lay back on the bed. He tried to raise his legs but failed. *I am a dead man!* he thought.

Suddenly, he saw a pointy jackknife that had a thin blade because it had been sharpened several times. He had bought it when he was an able-bodied man, and he'd often used it for self-defense, because he, at one point, had had many enemies. The pointy blade reminded him of his earlier meetings with friends at the homes of teahouse girls, where he would use the knife to open newly purchased opium boxes. He remembered a teahouse girl's beautiful hand trying to find a good spot on the box for him to insert the knife, after which red opium would erupt from the opening, like fresh blood. Khương held the knife and tested its sharpness against his index finger. Holding it tightly, he lifted the blade close to his throat—just a slight thrust into his neck would drain out enough blood to put an end to his suffering. Echoing in his ears were the words *Phony hero! Phony hero!* He would remain quiet. He wouldn't scream to prove his courage to his wife—his last act of courage: to die in silence.

But all of a sudden, he became frightened. He opened his eyes wide to take a closer look at the knife. His hand automatically fell down on the mat, and his palm opened up. The knife slowly left his fingers and fell quietly to the floor. "*Non! Je ne peux pas,*"[1] Khương mumbled in French.

A strong wind slammed the window shut. The room grew dark. Khương felt a chill crawl over his body. His wife's scolding and his suicidal cowardice made him realize the morbidity of his soul. He perceived that emotional death was more devastating than physical death, because he must exist and suffer on. Khương stretched out his arms and looked at the ceiling. A sunbeam traveling through leaves reminded him of a happy life beyond his walls. In his imagination, he saw green trees dancing happily in the wind, in the sunlight, and white clouds floating gently above. He saw some girls chatting and walking by. They were beautiful and lively. Their cheeks were rosy under the sun, and their eyes reflected the clear, azure autumn sky. Then he imagined that he heard a joke, followed by laughter, and that the laughter came from beyond, and his dark room was a large coffin in which he had been buried alive.

---

1. No, I can't.

8

Two Eyes

Khái Hưng

Mr. Cửu Niệm had been very sick for nearly two months. He suffered from a disease that the herbalists diagnosed as a delirium typical of the elderly, even though he was not yet sixty years old. His illness didn't get worse or improve. Every night, at around one or two o'clock, he would mumble and scream for help, waking up his children and grandchildren. They would run to his bedside. While panting, he recounted his nightmares: two eyes haunted him and stared at him closely. The two eyes were huge, white, and round; the pupils were black and square.

"Gosh! Two eyes! Two square eyes!" he moaned. Then he remained awake until the morning.

One day he called all his children and grandchildren together and said, "I'm sure this is a matter of revenge or a request for money to be returned."

Mr. Cửu seemed hesitant, scared, and embarrassed as he lay quietly, thinking. He looked up at the mosquito net while his children and grandchildren stood quietly, worried, and waiting respectfully. After a while, he could no longer hide his secret, so he sighed and told them a story:

You probably don't know why I own this property today. My parents left me nothing, and I was illiterate. I used to be poor and hungry, really hungry, and one day I suddenly became rich. I built this house and purchased land. All the villagers made assumptions and gossiped about how I made my fortune. But I've never told anyone the truth about how I became rich. I was fortunate. In the old days, I was very poor. I worked as a hired laborer carrying water-pipe tobacco for other people and did any kind of work available to feed myself twice a day and earn some extra money. In difficult times, all I wanted was two meals a day.

One day, in the late afternoon, when everybody had stopped working to get ready for dinner, I was still digging the foundation for the house of the district mandarin, Mr. Thà. I don't know why I continued working that day—nobody forced me to, and it wasn't even my house.

Suddenly, amid urging cries, "Niệm, come and eat with us," I heard a deafening clack. My shovel's blade hit a hard object. It seemed to be an urn of some kind. I bent down and looked. It was a small jar covered with a lid and carefully sealed with clay and mud. I thought that there had to be something valuable inside it, so I calmly covered it with soil and went to have dinner with everyone.

That night, I asked for permission to sleep at the construction site, which was a normal thing, because I worked for Mr. Thà. Sometimes I didn't go home for a few days or even two weeks. I waited until night came and everybody was gone, and then returned to the foundation. I dug around and pulled up the small clay jar, about the size of a jar for pickled eggplants, but it was very heavy. The new house's foundation was in a garden. Mr. Thà was very rich and had several acres of land. I took the jar to a dense clump of banana trees, opened the lid, took out everything, and wrapped it in a rag and hid it. I didn't know what had been inside. Only the next day when I brought it home did I realize it was gold, all gold bars . . .

Mr. Cửu stopped talking. His children and grandchildren remained standing silently, waiting for the connection between his story about the jar and the two square eyes. After a long while, he continued, "I'm sure the ghost of Mr. Thà's father . . . wants the gold back. He has followed me around and wants it back. Look! His two eyes appear again—they want to tell me that I'll die soon."

Mr. Cửu choked as if he were being strangled by two invisible hands.

His eldest son comforted him, "Dad, what you got is a gift from Heaven. If it belonged to Mr. Thà's father, then Mr. Thà would know about it. He has never mentioned it, and his dead ancestors have never told him about the gold in his dreams. And it is strange that in the dream, the pot of gold is never in Mr. Thà's hands. One more thing that makes us believe that it is a gift from Heaven for you: why did you find it during a break? If you had found it in the morning or around noon, then everybody would have known, and Mr. Thà would have claimed that it was his gold, and you would have nothing. So, I'm sure that it is a gift from Heaven and not something that belonged to Mr. Thà's ancestors. You must have cultivated good karma in your past lives."

Mr. Cửu smiled and repeated, "I have cultivated good karma?"

He thought about what he had done. He had worked as a loan shark and hoarded rice without selling it, and thus made the price go up while so many people were starving to death. Then he muttered, "I guess those eyes are of the starving people who are dead. They want me dead."

Strangely, although he was sick, his brain was exceptionally sharp. He then said, "If those were their eyes, why would the eyes look so weird? Why are the pupils square and so big? No, it must be the eyes of a god."

Suddenly in his imagination, a goddess appeared naked and sitting on a brick pedestal, a goddess with a mouth filled with plastic teeth and big eyes—the scleras were white and the pupils square and black. The statue gradually disappeared, leaving only her two eyes staring at him.

"Oh gosh! Two eyes! Two square eyes!" he shouted. He shook his head and waved his hand to chase his children and grandchildren out of the room.

Mr. Cửu's children discussed their father's illness. They guessed that it had something to do with his bad karma. They immediately invited respectable Buddhist monks to pray for him for three days, hoping to set him free from it. On the third night, a monk with a great voice summoned the souls of all the dead beings and invited them to listen to the word of Lord Buddha. Many of them were miserable and poverty-stricken spirits.

When the monk prayed, "To those homeless and starving spirits . . .," Mr. Cửu screamed and fainted.

Mr. Cửu dreamed that he was walking on a sunny road, his feet were tired, his stomach empty. On both sides of the road, green rice stalks grew and many people were busy working. They sang folk songs that he knew and used to sing during harvest seasons.

When he arrived at a small shrine hidden in the shade of a luxuriant banyan tree, he stopped to rest. A ray of hope suddenly shone into his eyes. He saw a big bamboo tray full of solid coins and coins with square holes in their centers. He looked around and saw no one. A few incense sticks placed on a gold paper offering to the supernatural emitted a cold fragrance and further enhanced the site's serenity. He thought to himself, *I just need to take a handful of coins and put them in my pocket, and I'll never starve to death*. He extended his arm but immediately withdrew it as if someone were watching him. He thought of Mường stories and Thổ stories, ethnic minority stories of ghosts guarding a house: if you enter the house and steal something while the owner is away, the ghost will say the name of the object you have stolen, follow you, and strangle you to death. He shuddered, became scared, and walked away.

After walking for a while, he returned to the tray of coins. He intended to just take a few and eat something, and if he died, he would be content. He would rather die than be hungry. Suddenly, a man walked toward him. Mr. Cửu became scared and hid behind the banyan tree. The man walked past the shrine, and Mr. Cửu saw him throw a coin with a square hole onto the center of the tray. He waited for the man to disappear and then moved to the tray and looked at it. He dared not take any coins from it—they belonged to the goddess. He mumbled to himself, "It's sacrosanct . . . I would be punished." Then he decided to walk away.

He walked a long distance until he made a turn into a busy market where he saw a female beggar sitting beside a basket and a cane. Her white eyes were looking into the sky, and she was whining about her fate in a sing-song voice, "I have my body but no eyes." Her basket held two coins. Mr. Cửu stared at them. He stood quietly for a long while as if listening to the beggar's pleas. But in fact, he was thinking, *She's blind. She can't see me, and nobody is here.* He bent down and quietly took the two coins from her basket and put them in his bag.

Afraid that the blind beggar would chase him, he ran away very fast. He went into the market and bought a full bowl of rice and ate it voraciously. After that, he returned to the path and saw the beggar still sitting there. The two coins were still in her basket. He was delighted, and said to himself, *Ah, I dreamed that I had taken her two coins, but in fact I never had.*

When he reached the shrine, he looked at the tray of coins again. Strangely, all the coins with the square holes in the middle had been paired up, and suddenly transformed into eyes. The eyes became bigger and bigger and glared at him—white eyes with square black pupils. Then he heard the voice of the beggar coming from all directions, "Sirs and Madams, please help me. I have a body but no eyes." Then several square eyes flew toward him and surrounded him.

He screamed, "Gosh! Two square eyes!" He then woke up from his nightmare.

Outside, in the yard, the melodious voice of the monk summoning the souls of the dead was just like the pleas of the beggar. Mr. Cửu panted and fainted again.

The next morning, Mr. Cửu called his children and grandchildren and said his last words, "I've done sinful things. I've treated people wickedly, and those two square eyes are not some god's holy eyes or saint's divine eyes as I thought. They are human eyes. That day . . . a long time ago . . . But never mind. You're all here, and you will atone for my sins. Today, you'll beat the wooden fish and make a public announcement that for the next five days, I'll offer food to all the hungry in this entire region. You give each of them a bowl of rice and two coins *with square holes in the centers*. Remember that? The coins pay for my debts, and the bowl of rice is interest for my debts."

That afternoon, Mr. Cửu heard the sound of the wooden fish. He knew that his children would do as he had told them. He was elated and smiled in his death, knowing that he would never be haunted again by the two square eyes.

9

You Must Live

Khái Hưng

At Yên Phụ Dike, one summer afternoon.

The water of the Nhị Hà River had just started to rise, rushing and flowing as if it wanted to drag away the small island in the middle of the river.

The red water took with it tree trunks and dry branches from the forest; they floated like a row of small boats racing toward an unknown destination.

Standing on the embankment, Thức, a mason, looked at the logs and hankered for them. Then he turned around and looked at his wife attentively, as if asking for her opinion. She looked at the river and the sky, shook her head, and sighed.

"The wind is very strong, but those dark clouds on the horizon are gathering very quickly. The rain is coming soon, my dear!"

Thức sighed and puttered around. Then he suddenly stopped and asked his wife, "Have you cooked dinner?"

"I have. But there's only enough rice for our two children to eat this afternoon," she said sadly.

They looked at each other in silence . . . Then it seemed that something hypnotized and suppressed them, so they returned to the river. The tree trunks were still floating in the red water.

The husband smiled—a goofy smile—and said, "I'll take a risk."

She shook her head, saying nothing.

"Have you talked to Mrs. Ký yet?"

"Yes."

"So?"

"It won't work. She said she would hand me the money only after I brought her the wood collected from the river. She won't advance us any money."

"Is that so?"

The words *Is that so?* sounded as hard as the last two strokes of a trowel hitting the brick of a wall under construction. Thức was determined to do something extraordinary, so he turned his head and said, "You go home first and take care of Bò."

"No need to. Nhớn and Bé are playing with him."

"But it's better if you are home with them. Nhớn is only five; she can't take care of her two younger siblings."

"All right, then. I'll go. But why don't you go home, too? You don't need to stand here, do you?"

"You go home first. I'll see you later."

She complied with his request and went to Yên Phụ Village.

●

Arriving at their home, which was a low-ceilinged, damp, and dark dwelling, Mrs. Thức stood in the doorway and was heartbroken by the sight of their family's poverty.

Crowded on the wooden bed without a straw mat, their three kids were crying and calling for her. Her son Bò was screaming; he wanted to be nursed. He hadn't eaten anything since that morning.

The oldest child, Nhớn, attempted to comfort him but failed, so she said to her younger sister, Bé, "Go find where Mom is so she can breast-feed him."

But Bé refused to go. She lay down and screamed and yelled.

Mrs. Thức ran toward her son, picked him up, and held him in her arms, saying, "Poor thing! I've been away, and you're hungry and crying."

Then she sat down to breastfeed her son. But the boy sucked her nipple for a long time and couldn't get any milk, so he let go of his mother's breast and cried even louder.

Mrs. Thức sighed; two tears glistened in her tired eyes. She stood up and walked around while singing a lullaby to her son. Then she said, "Gosh! I have nothing to eat, and no milk to feed my child."

After a while, the boy grew tired and fell asleep out of exhaustion. She told her daughters to go outside and play so that their brother could get some rest.

Mrs. Thức sat quietly as she reflected on her life. As a woman from the countryside, her simple mind never knew how to use her imagination nor how to arrange her memories in a logical order. The things she remembered were a mess—they resembled human figures and objects in a photograph. But she did remember one thing clearly: in her entire life she had never once enjoyed any leisure time as wealthy people did.

When she was twelve or thirteen, Mrs. Thức, whose maiden name was Lạc, became a bricklayer. There had been nothing extraordinary about her life. Day after day, month after month, year after year . . .

When she was seventeen, she and Thức worked at the same construction site. She was a bricklayer, and he was a roofer. They joked with each other, and somehow fell in love and got married.

For five long years, in their damp and dark house at the foot of Yên Phụ Dike, there was nothing peaceful worth remembering about the miserable couple's two empty lives, and they became even more miserable when she gave birth to three children in three years.

It was a tough time financially, for everyone. There was not much work available, and the wages were low. The couple struggled day after day and never earned enough money to feed themselves and their children.

Suddenly, during the previous year's wet season, Thức came up with a new way to make a living. He borrowed money to buy a bamboo boat, and he and his wife rowed to the middle of the river to collect wood. Two months later, he had not only paid off his debt but also had more than enough money to enjoy life.

This year, without money and without food, he and his wife desperately waited for the day the water would rise again.

The day before, it had rained, which meant his family would have food to eat.

Thinking about it made Mrs. Thức smile as she laid her baby down on a diaper, tiptoed outside, and walked along the dike. She appeared determined to do something.

●

When she got to the dike, Mrs. Thức couldn't see her husband.

The wind was blowing violently, whirring, roaring fiercely, and the water was flowing like a waterfall. She looked in the dark sky.

She stood there, thinking. Her blouse fluttered and made a sound like the crashing of waves against the shore. Suddenly a thought came to her mind, causing her to panic and run down to the foot of the dike by the river.

When she got to where the boat was tied, she saw her husband using all of his strength to tighten up the knots of the bamboo strings. She stood quietly, watching him and waiting until he finished his work. She then stepped into the boat and asked, "Where are we going?"

Thức glared at his wife and spoke harshly, "Why don't you stay home with the kids?

She stammered in fear, "They . . . are . . . sleeping."

"What are you doing here?"

"But where are we going to take the boat?

"Stop asking. Go home, now!"

She held her face and cried. Moved by her emotions, he asked her, "Why are you crying, dear?"

"Because you're going to collect firewood alone, and you won't let me join you."

He was deep in thought for a while, looked at the sky and water, and said, "You can't go. It's dangerous!"

She laughed and said, "We'll face danger together. Don't be afraid. I can swim."

"Okay!"

The word *Okay!* sounded so cold. She shivered. The wind remained strong, the water fierce, and the sky was getting darker.

"Are you scared?" he asked.

"No," she said.

●

They started to take the boat to the middle of the river; the husband rowed while the wife swam alongside it. To resist the force of the water, he turned the prow of the boat upstream, but it still drifted downward, sometimes emerging, sometimes sinking, sometimes hidden and some-times visible in the alluvial water, like a dry bamboo leaf floating in a puddle of blood, like a mosquito drowned in a pot of red ink.

Half an hour later, the boat reached the middle of the stream. The husband held the oars firmly while his wife collected floating wood.

Not long after, the boat was almost full of wood, and when they were about to return to shore, it started to rain. . . . Then lightning seemed to tear through the dark clouds, and thunder shook the earth.

The small boat was full of water and heavy. They tried to swim but were pulled away by the violent water. . . .

Suddenly, they both shouted, "Oh, no!"

The boat had sunk. The collected wood rejoined the floating wood and drifted away, dragging with it their overturned boat.

"You think you can swim to shore?" he asked.

"Of course!" she affirmed.

"Swim and follow the current. Rest your head on the waves."

"No need to worry about me."

The rain was still heavy; the lightning was still terrifying. It felt like they had fallen into a ravine. After a while, Thức saw that his wife was exhausted, so he swam closer and asked, "How are you doing?"

"I'm okay. No worries."

As soon as she said those words, her head sank. She struggled to raise her head above the water. He rushed toward her to help. He used one arm to hold her body and the other arm to swim. She smiled and looked at him affectionately. He smiled back. After a while, he said, "I'm very tired. Why don't you hold on to me so that I can swim? I can't use my arm to keep your body from sinking any longer."

A few minutes later, he grew exhausted, and his arms were tired.

"Do you have enough energy to swim?" she asked softly.

"I don't know. If it were just me, I'm sure I could."

"Allow me to let you loose so you can swim to shore."

"No. If we die, we'll die together." He smiled.

A few minutes had gone by, but she felt as if it had been an entire day.

"Do you think you can make it?" he asked her.

"I'm . . . okay."

"Oh, no! We'll die together."

"Bò, Nhớn, and Bé . . . !" she then said in a trembling voice. "You must live, my dear."

Thức felt his body become lighter as her heavy body was no longer attached to it. His wife had thought of her children and quietly released her hands to allow herself to drown. This gave him enough strength to make it to shore.

●

Electric lights lit the riverbank. The wind had stopped; the waves had calmed down. A man held a crying son; his two little girls stood next to him. It was Thức's family on the riverbank saying farewell to the soul of the woman who had sacrificed herself out of love.

In the vastness of the scenery, the river flowed calmly downstream.

10

From Theory to Practice

Vũ Trọng Phụng

He was Westernized. People told him that he was not yet *completely* Westernized, but he firmly believed he indeed was. After returning from France, he socialized only with French people and adored only them, especially his chief administrative officer. He spoke only French, even to his own people, who all had flat noses. Playing the role was easy for him because it cost him nothing.

Things that cost him money concerned him. Although he did not always eat French food, he didn't want the Annamese folks to know that he sometimes ate Vietnamese food as well—even water spinach and pickled eggplant. Deep in his heart, he thanked God for bestowing on the Annamese their water spinach and eggplant—so cheap but so delicious that they made people forget their desire for meat and fish. But he never told that to anyone.

All that people could see in him was his assumed Western lifestyle, behavior, and language. He placed his ancestral shrine amid his French furniture, and he explained with a shrug, "I do that to stop my mom from screaming—which requires paying due respect to tradition." He made that statement in French, and to prove he did what he said, he sometimes invited his French friends over to dance. Of course, they danced in front of his ancestral shrine, because in his house only that area was spacious enough. The elderly folks would have "admired" his extreme Westernization until they were pale in the face, had they not already lost too much face through his behavior.

But that is not what this story is primarily about.

The most crucial element has to do with his 100 percent Westernized, Europeanized opinions, particularly regarding a scandalous problem that was imported into the antiquated culture of our yellow-skinned and flat-nosed Vietnamese folks from the West. He stated his position on this issue to draw people's attention to his completely Westernized lifestyle. The scandalous matter was about the "wearing of horns," or cuckoldry.

●

Let's take a look at him. He stands up and walks back and forth. He tucks his hands into his pants pockets, and if he is in the right mood, he argues about an issue and sometimes elaborates on his argument with a few nods of approval. No one can act the part better than he! His audience listens attentively and quietly. Even if they want to refute him, they remain silent. From the speaker's mouth comes odd, or even shocking, statements. Regardless of whether his statements reflect his predilections for controversy or his eccentricities, they always affirm his presumed enthusiasm and understanding. Thus, those who would like to interrupt him remain sitting calmly and listen attentively. Of course, we should never scorn anyone's devotion and profound insight, if one were truly an authority on a subject, but about him we have some doubts: was the speaker actually one who "had deep experiences in life"?

But . . . let's take a listen to him.

"The wearing of horns, if considered a scandal at all, is merely a minor scandal, which shouldn't draw too much attention. I don't understand why people deride a cuckold. Even in France, they ridicule cuckolds. This is cruel because a cuckold should be pitied. However, he might not be pitied, if you consider the matter more carefully. First, his wife must commit adultery, as I have mentioned earlier, and cuckoldry is not that serious! Second, the wearing of horns, if it is to be considered a source of anguish, is merely a source of mental anguish in the husband's weak imagination! To reinforce this argument, we need to add this: a society that has either adulterous husbands or cuckolded husbands is a civilized society. Why is this so? Because marriage, by nature, is a mistake, when it is instituted to resolve the urges of romantic love. Marriage is a contract that forces two people to commit themselves to each other for all their lives, while in each of them, as God has created, there lies an abstract something—a something that always desires change and the disposal of the old for the new. Let's examine men's perspectives in order to understand this more clearly. Men sometimes get sick and tired of their wives and feel that they no longer can live compatibly with them under one roof; thus, divorce is the only solution. But fortunately, husbands find an alternative solution that helps them not only to endure a dysfunctional marriage but also to avoid permanent separation and the abiding hatred of their wives and innocent children. They comfort themselves, every now and then, by cheating on their wives for an evening, finding temporary happiness and illusory bliss in the arms of a one-night stand. Is that not simple? Occasional promiscuity gives the husbands smug satisfaction and encourages them to continue to put up with their annoying wives. Smart wives, who realize the instability of nuptial realities, simply ignore their husbands' adultery. That's what they *should* do. They must put up with minor infidelities now to avoid more serious disruptions later. God created men, and His primary goal was to make them betrayers. If their pride is constantly nurtured, they will treat their wives properly and kindly. If a husband cannot cheat on his wife, he will surely take revenge on her."

Some people in the audience burst out laughing. Others do not say a word. He continues his oration: "Now, let's put ourselves in the position of the wife. Why are we so selfish? Why are we so unfair? Why are we so cruel? We men are promiscuous with impunity, but if our wives behave as we do, then nothing remains the same. If a wife commits adultery, how can you call it a scandal when the husband has been cheating for years? Women should be able to act just as men do. It's as simple as that. Like men, women cheat as an alternative to getting a divorce—women also find satisfaction and rejuvenation through acts of infidelity. So, why are men so selfish? That's not right. Cheating is nothing extraordinary—merely a diamond cutting a diamond—isn't it? Moreover, wives who commit adultery should be considered brave and enlightened. They are like workers who dare to organize demonstrations against the government or like those women who carry revolutionary flags, demanding freedom and equality! So, as I have said, the wearing of horns signals an advanced civilization. A woman who cheats on her husband shows her abandonment of our negative, traditional customs in which women were unpaid maids."

"So, is the blame on the cuckold, no matter whether he is a good or bad husband?" a member of the audience inquires.

The speaker responds confidently, "That's correct, sir. It doesn't matter how talented, healthy, and wealthy we are, if we wear the horns, we must bear the blame, as we have erred, and only our wives are aware of our faults. So, as I have said earlier, a cuckold never should be pitied, if we consider the situation carefully. If we are clever, dignified, and healthy, both mentally and intellectually, our wives will never cheat on us. So, definitely, a cuckold always must bear the blame and kindly tolerate his wife's indiscretions. In addition, we, as civilized people, should consider adultery insignificant. Adultery is necessary. For example, we must eat when hungry, drink when thirsty, or urinate when our bladder is full. Let me add this: if a husband is absent from home for a long time, for instance, and his wife sleeps around, the husband should look upon this as necessary, just as one must urinate when one has to. What is sexual intercourse? Traditionally, it has been cast as a taboo. But why do we think of it as a taboo and ascribe to it characteristics that it doesn't possess? So, is the wearing of horns distressing enough to force one to commit suicide?"

"So what should be a cuckold's philosophical position on the matter?" another member of the audience asks.

"Just ignore everything," the orator replies. "We must admit that *we* have erred, even though we don't know what we have done wrong! If we were perfect, our wives would be loyal to us, wouldn't they? The best thing to do is not to make the situation worse. As I have stated earlier, adultery is a sign of civilization. This is undeniable. If marriage is the tomb of love, adultery is a natural reaction to commitment. If we want to be truly civilized, we should consider even incest as an attempt to gain freedom, as we all naturally desire change. What is progress, if not an attempt to live a freer life? In the West, they enjoy the freedom of assembly, freedom of thought, freedom of speech, and freedom of protest, after millions of people sacrificed their lives to gain these rights. But they still need to gain public approval for their freedom of copulation! With this freedom, our society truly becomes divine. Thus, if a husband or a wife cheats, each should disregard the indiscretion, because each errs. Also, that kind of adulterous behavior, if we appreciate it as a cultural value by considering the freedom of copulation to be like other forms of freedom, human beings will no longer face the problems associated with adultery, which have ruined many families and individuals' lives."

"Such provocative thoughts!" another member of the audience smiles and comments. "You've made all the men here lose their dignity."

"Sir, about cuckoldry, who can guarantee that any man will never be cuckolded during his life?" the Westernized orator asks. "Let me remind you of this: the most attractive hero in human history is Emperor Napoleon, but he too was also a cuckold! His cuckoldry should be a lesson for all men all over the world. If we don't appreciate cuckoldry as a cultural fact, then men are quite short-sighted."

"Have you finished your speech on cuckoldry?" another person asks.

"I have drawn my conclusions," the speaker nods.

"He is too Westernized! Very dangerous!" many people in the audience complain. "He is not only Westernized in his dress, in his manner, and in his language, but he has Westernized his soul!"

The speaker smiles in satisfaction, knowing he has been successful. The primary goal of his eccentric words and argument has been to make people perceive him as a "100 percent Westernized" person. He considers their critical mutterings to be compliments. And while everyone was listening attentively to him, nobody noticed a handsome young man staring flirtatiously at the speaker's young and beautiful wife, who was making some tea in a separate room while concentrating on her husband's speech. Personally, I thought that because he must already be a cuckold himself, he was defending cuckoldry through his shocking argument.

•

But I was in error.

The scandal in his marriage occurred only later—not previously, as I had thought. About a year later, I happened to see the Westernized speaker lying on a bed in an opium den. People told me he had divorced his wife. How sad! No one knew the cause of their separation. They could say only that he lived in deep sorrow. The opium den became his only refuge, as he had grown so weary of life.

In his conversation with some close friends, he alluded vaguely to the source of his sorrow: "I fell in love with a woman!"

But one day, when another close friend who was unaware of his situation criticized him for being a cruel, thoughtless, and treacherous husband and called him by various epithets, the Westernized man exclaimed, "You're so stupid! If your wife cheated on you, would you want to continue to live with her?"

That was that.

I myself, only an observer, suddenly became dismayed and skeptical of life. I thought of Annam as an impoverished land, and even if a theory were great elsewhere, when it was imported to this country, it could well become corrosive. I still believe that our Annamese folks have no consistent theory of life. For this reason, the extremely Westernized man could attempt to talk the Western talk, but he could not walk the Western walk. Good Lord! From the case of one man, conclusions might be drawn about the whole society.

11

Overweening Pride

Vũ Trọng Phụng

When her husband got home, Mrs. Quang hurriedly inquired, "So, is she any better? Is she going to make it?"

Phạm Quang stood there, breathing heavily as if he had just walked ten kilometers, although he had walked only from the end of the street back to his home. He gently hung his hat on a deer-horn coat rack, took off his coat, and lay down on the floor. It took him a while to reply, "The situation is grave. Not sure if she's going to make it this time."

"So, how is she doing?" asked his wife, who stopped her sewing and frowned.

"Last night in her sleep she was delirious, but once awake, she sobbed continuously. Mr. Dần told me that in her delirium, she kept calling my name. We've got to be very careful, or we'll destroy everything. It turns out that I have committed a crime—killing a woman!" Mr. Quang said wearily, as if he were half awake.

●

"I'm unable to understand the conversation between you two! Who's this person you are talking about?" I asked Mrs. Quang.

"A cousin of mine," she responded.

Her very brief clarification caused me even more surprise and confusion. How could that be? I wondered how Mr. Quang could have the guts to talk about something that sounded like a tragic love triangle, and to mention his wife's cousin right in front of her.

"I'm sorry, but I still don't get it."

Mrs. Quang started to look at me mischievously and at her husband slyly. She then cleared her throat and smiled, "The patient, Oanh, is actually my cousin. Before we got married, my husband had been infatuated with her, but sadly, when he proposed to her, she declined. Then, he proposed to me, and she married someone else. Very unfortunately for her, however, she married a wicked man, a good-for-nothing—he lives a decadent life and beats his wife. He has abandoned her and their son, and we don't know which whore he is living with right now. This depressed Oanh greatly, and she became ill, probably because she still thinks about and loves the man who truly had loved her but whose marriage proposal she turned down. My husband, I mean—as I have told you."

Mr. Quang, probably embarrassed because his wife talked about the past at an inopportune time, covered his forehead with his hands discreetly to indicate dismay, because it seemed abnormal to act indifferently in this situation. However, Mrs. Quang was smart and could read her husband's mind immediately.

"So during your visit, did you observe anything that you should be concerned about?" she asked her husband in a serious tone.

Mr. Quang quickly sat up and stared at me to avoid embarrassment in his response to her inquiry.

"As I pulled up a chair and sat at the head of her bed," he said, "Oanh pulled down her blanket and looked at me. Her eyes contained the countless unspoken things endured by her suffering soul. But in the eyes of this ailing woman sparkled an unusual beam of light. I sensed a mixture of regret, hope, and anxiety in those eyes. Then she stammered, 'Do you still love me as you used to? Don't you hate me?' I didn't know whether I should nod or shake my head, or how otherwise to answer those questions. Later, outside, while Mr. Dần was holding her son Chắt on the hospital's playground, I took the boy's hands and placed them on my chest affectionately. He stared at me skeptically, withdrew his hands, and turned his face to a wall. Then he kept sobbing and crying. I lost my patience, stood up unsteadily, and left. Gosh, what should I do now?"

Mrs. Quang showed no facial expression for a few minutes. She then looked genuinely sad, sighed, and slowly said, "I feel sorry for her. Oanh is to be pitied."

Her attitude toward Oanh astonished me. If others were in her shoes, how much jealousy, anger, and resentment would ensue; how miserable their faces would look. But Mrs. Quang showed none, expressing only sympathy for her cousin.

I felt it necessary to offer her a compliment. "Mrs. Quang, you're a model wife."

●

My friend, Mr. Quang, is a fortunate man to have married a woman like her. Although he was a destitute author, he still could claim to be the happiest man in the world. It seemed that he had obtained all the happiness one could obtain in life, as he had found his other half—a trustworthy and faithful soulmate.

I thought I might be able to alleviate his anxiety a little bit, so I tapped him on the shoulder and said, "You probably don't know how lucky you are."

"Nothing unusual here. Why are you being so generous with your compliments?" Mrs. Quang asked me excitedly.

"I think it is unusual. Jealousy is a woman thing. It is proverbial that in order to be happy, one must love madly, and to love madly, one must show jealousy. You're not jealous at all, but happy."

"I really am generous and kind. That's all," she smiled calmly and explained. "So I can't forbid my husband to be forgiving. Also, Oanh should be pitied because she made a bad decision. She declined his marriage proposal, and then he proposed to me. You should be aware of the fact that I come from a wealthy family, but she does not. Although I'm not obliged to act kindly, I do believe that she has contributed to our current nuptial bliss. Isn't that so? If she had accepted his proposal, we wouldn't be married today. That's why I feel sorry for her. Other women surely would act jealously and then suffer through suspicion. They would hate her and want to see her suffer so that they could gain satisfaction. But I am not like them. Right now, Oanh has regrets, which is understandable. It is humbling when one has lost one's pride and self-esteem. When one suffers due to resentment and hatred of someone else, it leads to self-loathing. In this situation with Oanh, how could I be jealous and vent my anger on my husband? What's in it for me to hate her? Those are the reasons for my sympathy, and not because she is my cousin."

"You're definitely right. Even siblings can stab one another due to jealousy, and in this case you two are just cousins."

"I don't know much about her actual health condition yet," Mr. Quang interrupted our conversation and said angrily. "The charlatans at the hospital have been discussing her illness loudly and nonsensically, but no one knows what is really going on with her health. One said she has lung problems. Another said she has some kind of brain damage. Another said she has heart problems. Even Heaven doesn't seem to know!"

Mrs. Quang looked at her husband and forced a smile. "You're being irrational. She definitely has mental problems, which affect her entire body, and her heart too. I think she is suffering from two kinds of pain: physical pain and mental pain. If you want to cure her, first, you must attend to her emotional distress. Those quacks at the hospital don't know anything!"

"You're so right. Why don't you suggest a method of treatment? It's easy to talk about it but *not* so easy to do it," Mr. Quang said.

"Now, listen to you. That's your business, not mine."

I was on my friend's side, defending him. "Please be kind and think of a way to help your husband."

She then continued with her sewing but looked contemplative. I didn't know for sure whether she was considering a cure for the miserable woman's anguish—a woman whom she should regard as a rival—or whether she was regretting her previous extraordinary declaration of kindness and forgivingness, which had been elicited by my earlier compliments. There are duplicitous people who talk the talk of generosity but who do not walk the walk. To find the truth, one must give them rope to see if they hang themselves.

That night, my friend rushed me to a private room to recount in specific detail the story about Oanh, while his wife continued to sew until very late.

●

The following morning, when my friend called me for breakfast, his wife asked him cheerfully, "So, have you come up with a solution?"

"I can think of nothing," Mr. Quang replied jokingly and grimaced.

She looked at me, smiled, and then said to her husband sardonically, "Poor thing! Your hair has turned gray because you've been seeking a solution all night, like Wu Zisu."[1]

My friend pressed his forehead with his hands, and I interpreted the significance in his gesture. I thought that his wife had just ridiculed him and found gratification in doing so. By speaking ironically, she no longer seemed so extraordinary a woman.

"It's such a simple matter. Can't you think of anything at all?" Mrs. Quang continued.

Suddenly, I was embarrassed. Her comment targeted not just my friend but also me. Honestly, I had spent the entire night thinking of a way to help my friend, but I had failed. Men, through vanity, often underestimate women, but now a woman's mockery of another man for his naïveté humiliated me. And this gave me a sense of extreme uneasiness.

But Mrs. Quang was clever. Noticing how I blushed with embarrassment more than her husband, she continued, "Well, in your situation, how can you think of anything while you are deeply saddened and distracted by your emotions? Although I'm not very smart, as an outsider, my mind at least is clearer than yours."

"Then what do you think I should do?" Mr. Quang looked up, gently asking his wife.

Before speaking, his wife lowered her head. It seemed as though she were attempting to articulate her thoughts tactfully.

Probably to cover his embarrassment while waiting for her answer, he sighed and said, "This is a sad situation. I predicted that this would happen sooner or later. Currently, Oanh's husband has left her to pursue a slut, and she is considering submitting to the court her request for divorce. Even now, I don't know why she declined my marriage proposal when the entire village thought she should have felt fortunate to marry me. Very strange! Even my wife was surprised at Oanh's decision. Could it be that she was in love with another man back then? Did she and her present husband marry each other out of true love? Was she acting through arrogance toward me or loyalty to another? It doesn't matter anymore. I used to love her sincerely, and now she must accept her decision with regret."

---

1. A famous Chinese scholar and military general who fought for the state of Wu during the Spring and Autumn Period (1476–771 BCE) in China.

"You should find a way to make Oanh stop regretting the past. I'm sure she then will recover," Mrs. Quang responded delicately to her husband's original question.

"Ah, I've got it," Mr. Quang said.

"So, what are you waiting for?" she asked.

"But . . . what if . . . will she resent me?"

"Of course, it's inevitable."

Mr. Quang thought for a long while and shook his head.

"No, I can't. Right now, Oanh is suffering from regret, which means she still loves me. She is madly and genuinely in love with me! Would it be wise to ruin the beautiful romantic love that she holds for me—a person who once loved her, too? She must have loved me greatly to have such strong feelings for me now. I can't deceive her. In the past, she didn't reciprocate my love, but I enjoyed being in love. If I now must make her hate me, I inadvertently would compromise my true feelings and love and justify her hatred all the more."

"You must make the sacrifice. Be brave. *Loving a person to have her love you is narcissistic!* I know, of course, that if you lie to her, she'll hate you. But I beg you, at least to give it a try. Then you will learn how it feels to love someone who hates you," his wife advised, raising her hand.

Buried deeply in his thoughts, Mr. Quang frowned and shook his head. "No. I cannot make Oanh hate me. I'm sorry. You are a forgiving and understanding woman. You should know . . . I still love Oanh very much."

"But if you refuse to lie to her, you are torturing an already wounded heart. You simply don't want to be hated. You're so selfish! Just wait until she dies and then grieve," Mrs. Quang rebutted, showing signs of anger.

Mr. Quang dropped into his chair like a falling tree. He nearly wept.

"I'd rather see her die now. If that happens, I can tend her grave and grieve properly. If she dies now, her soul can rest in peace. But if she lives, as you suggest, not only will her body become decrepit, but her soul will never rest due to the resentment and hatred that would occupy her heart."

"You're so wrong. Resentment is nourishing, not detrimental. Resentment gives birth to an inflated ego and overweening pride. And it is that pride that becomes one's defense. It is one's regret and self-hatred that kill," Mrs. Quang said, forcing a smile.

He remained unsatisfied.

"But I don't want to kill Oanh's love for me. Hatred is an ugly thing that shouldn't exist in a woman who simply made a bad decision.

Rather she should be pitied. Isn't it better for Oanh to keep her regret, to remain desperate, and to die of love, so that her love can follow her into eternity, and her love can become eternal?"

"Okay, let Oanh die, then. But what about her six-year-old son, Chắt? He is my nephew—our nephew. Killing his mother means killing him, too. You cannot kill that innocent boy," Mrs. Quang said. Her voice trembled.

Mr. Quang looked at his wife for a while, and then departed. He went to Oanh's home. He returned half an hour later with a grimace and said, "It's over now. I have acted cruelly."

"What happened?"

"I told Oanh this: 'I have only pity for you. You asked me if I hated you. I did not love you, so how I could I hate you? Why did you reject me? You've ended up in a miserable situation and you want to love me now. . . . That kind of love has no value.' Oanh was so overwhelmed that she became speechless. She choked, and I left immediately."

"Only by doing that could you prolong her life," Mrs. Quang shrugged her shoulder satisfactorily.

"You should be patient and stay with us longer, to see the end of all of this," she then said to me.

●

A week passed.

One day, Mr. Quang called out to me from their open window. Oanh was holding her son, leisurely enjoying the atmosphere on the street. Only then did I see her face, for the first time, which looked so unusually calm, indicating that her regret over her lost love had dissipated. Although she still looked pale, her gait was firm. I had the feeling that the woman would not die. Oanh held her son affectionately, as if she had laid everything to rest to focus on raising him well.

"I am very grateful to you. You have taught me a lesson about sacrifice, which has saved two lives," Mr. Quang said, holding his wife's hands.

I lit a cigarette to reward myself because I knew so well how overweening pride and vanity both wounded and heightened a woman's dignity.

I wanted to take a look at Oanh again, but she had disappeared behind a fence.

1 2

The Gold Teeth

Vũ Trọng Phụng

An eighty-year-old man had promised his two beloved sons that he would die three months ago, but for the last three months, he just lay in his bed, moaning, eating his meals as well as urinating and defecating right there.

He was an utter scrooge. Even on his deathbed, he measured how much fish sauce had been consumed, counted how many onions he possessed, and was tightfisted to the point of miserliness. He kept his keys with him at all times and refused to unlock the wardrobe to take his property title documents out and share them with his sons.

Now he was dead. Such a relief!

As soon as he took his last breath, his sons and their wives grabbed the keys from him, thinking about their shares.

They could care less about his corpse lying there. For two days they busied themselves with thousands of things. The younger brother let his older brother have the wooden altar and the entire altar set, on the condition that he be in charge of the funeral, the feast for the commune officials, and the slaughtering of his sow for the province officials.

The next day, their relatives remained in the dark about the old man's death because his sons were still debating matters.

Around midnight, they reached an agreement. In bed, the older son dreamed about his libertine life to come, while the younger son was overjoyed by the thought of bribing higher authorities to obtain an official position in the village.

The sons and their wives whispered and giggled, while the corpse remained covered by a thin blanket next to a tiny, dim oil lamp. Because the old man left no will, his death was considered an unexpected death. His sons didn't inform their relatives and the authorities of the day and time their father had died, so grieving would be pointless.

When the older son and his wife were asleep, the younger son and his wife tiptoed outside for a private talk.

He was smarter than his older brother. He remembered that when the old man was alive, he had wanted to replace some of his broken teeth, so he had gone to a dentist in the city and had them crowned in gold.

The couple quarreled. The husband suggested that they remove the gold teeth from the corpse and sell them. His wife objected vehemently, saying that when there was a death in the family, the living often put some gold in the dead's mouth, hoping that his sacred spirit would bless the living who remained.

"You women are stupid!" the husband said angrily. "When one is dead, commemorating his death anniversary is just like putting on a performance. Those gold teeth are worth money. I don't care if you agree with me or not, but don't let my brother and his wife know about this."

Then he walked inside, leaving her standing there alone.

The corpse was inside the house. Outside, fireflies hovered in the yard. The leaves of an areca tree fluttered against those of a banana tree. A dog suddenly bit at a shadow and made a sad, frightening sound.

The wife was startled. She ran inside to try and stop her husband from removing the gold teeth, but when she saw the corpse, she became scared and dared not go close.

The husband knew she had to stay away from the scene so that he would be free to do whatever he wanted. He looked around and listened carefully. Assured that his older brother and sister-in-law were snoring, he tiptoed to the deathbed and lifted the blanket.

He pressed the dead man's eyes closed with one hand and used his other hand to squeeze the corpse's jaws. The jaws were sealed tight, so he had to use all his strength to open the dead mouth to remove the gold teeth. Like a malaria patient with a bucket of cold water poured over him, he trembled violently. The gold teeth fell onto the floor, but the son couldn't catch them, because when he looked at the dead eyes, the eyelids were open, because he had used his hand to press them force-fully. The dead mouth without the teeth resembled a dark and deep hole, and it refused to close. The dead man seemed to bulge his eyes and open his mouth wide to curse his unfilial son—it was horrifying.

The son just stood there, petrified, without blinking for quite some time. Then he screamed, held his face in his hands, and ran away.

Hearing the younger brother scream, the older brother and his wife sat up, unsure what was going on. Surprised, they looked at each other and quietly climbed out of bed. They walked to the door of the room where the corpse was kept and just stood there, staring at it. The corpse stared at them, open-mouthed, as if cursing someone.

The couple was terrified, so they just stood close to each other and quivered. Their hearts beat fast. The older brother was baffled and con-sumed by thoughts of a spirit entering a living person's body, and he didn't know whether he should remain there motionlessly or run away. Suddenly, thanks to the oil lamp's light, he saw the gold teeth under the bed.

He immediately understood why his younger brother had been in the room, screamed, and moved away.

The older brother turned around and saw his brother and his sister-in-law. They were pale and petrified. The older brother scolded them, "You two are such unfilial children."

The younger brother's wife defended herself, saying that she had tried to stop her husband, but he didn't listen to her. She then apolo-gized on his behalf, begging the older brother not to tell anyone about the sordid incident. Then she suggested that the gold teeth be returned to where they belonged.

But the older brother didn't do what was suggested. After failing to close the dead man's eyes and mouth, he neatly covered the corpse with the blanket. Then he turned around and reprimanded his sister-in-law, "You two have deceived me, so after I sell these gold teeth, do not talk about your share . . ."

Instinctually, he bent down, picked up the gold teeth, and put them in his pocket.

13

A Poor Family

Tô Hoài

It had become a habit for Mr. and Mrs. Duyện to quarrel over trivial matters. They raised their voices whenever they felt like it, for no particular reason. Their neighbors got so sick of their regular, overheated arguments that they eventually learned to ignore them. On this particular day, as usual, the couple was again fighting, loudly, over nothing.

Here is how it started.

Mr. Duyện lay down inside his house with his feet against a pillar and recited the opening lines from the epic poem *The Tale of Kiều*: "A hundred years in this life span on earth / talent and destiny are bound to feud." While he was reciting them with great vigor, the pillar began to shake with the movement of his feet.

His wife was sewing on the front porch and suddenly wanted to find her oldest daughter, Gái, probably to send her on an errand. She didn't see Gái around, so she called out, "Gái!" There was no response, so she called again loudly, "Gái! Where are you?" Still no response, so she shouted, "Gái! Where are you? Have you drowned in a pond somewhere?"

Her shouts ruined Mr. Duyện's concentration. "What a fuss you are making! Shut up!" he said irritably.

She did not shut up, and instead barked at him, "You have no right to forbid me to call our daughter." Then she complained, "You're good for nothing. Always lying down and singing."

Her complaint infuriated him. She had implied that he was worthless because he didn't work that day. Gosh! How ungrateful she was! He toiled all year long, so surely he could enjoy some leisure on a day when there was no work for him to do. He then scolded her for her impertinence, "Let me tell you, crippled woman, that if I stopped working for about ten days, this whole family would starve to death! Stop being . . ." He didn't know how to finish his sentence, so he became quiet.

"The more you work, the more you eat. I'm crippled, but I *do* work. Here, feel my neck," Mrs. Duyện said.

They indirectly had touched on a sensitive topic. Her right leg, since birth, had been a handicap. She couldn't walk straight and hobbled like a lame duck. Her disability and poor family background meant that she couldn't find a husband until she was thirty. Mr. Duyện was neither a local nor a son of a dignified family—he came to the village as a hired laborer and had a hump on his back. He couldn't walk straight either, and his hump resembled a wine gourd. When they first met, they decided to marry immediately. Then she gave birth to three children in the first few years after their wedding: Gái, Cẳng, and Chân. If their two youngest children had not died, there would be five kids altogether, but it was extremely hard for the Duyệns to feed even their three children. Oftentimes they quarreled because their children ate but didn't work. Normally, when their parents quarreled, Gái sobbed silently while Cẳng and Chân just stood by, watched, and listened with their hands over their buttocks.

Today Mr. and Mrs. Duyện had been quarreling while their children weren't home. But when their argument became more violent, the kids suddenly appeared out of nowhere. Gái carried Chân on her back. He was sleeping with his head leaning on her shoulder, mucus running from his nose and saliva from his mouth. Cẳng walked clumsily behind her and pretended to be a mandarin, berating his sister and spanking her arm with a rod made of leaves. But as soon as Cẳng stepped onto the front porch and heard his parents' loud voices, he saw Gái become silent and didn't know what to do. Only Chân was unaware—he was still sleeping. At that moment, Mr. Duyện spoke furiously and said something quite unpleasant to his wife. Just after he finished his sentence, his wife saw the kids walking into the house and screamed, "Come here and witness your father scolding me."

"Yes. I am cursing this crippled woman's father," Mr. Duyện replied.

Mrs. Duyện held her face with her hands and sobbed. She then said to the wall facing her, "Oh! Ancestors! We're married with children—some dead, some alive, but my husband has no respect for me. He calls my father names. Why am I so cursed? I have been frugal all my life in order to feed my children. . . ."

"It's your fault. You gave birth to them, so now you have to feed them," he rebuked.

"Listen to what he said, everybody! I didn't sleep with a dog," she said.

Mr. Duyện ran toward his wife and was about to beat her. "You bitch," he cursed.

She then lay on her back on the floor and started to act hysterical. "Go ahead and kill me. Kill me!" she challenged him.

Gái and Căng became frightened by their father's belligerence, so they held each other tightly and cried loudly. Chân woke up and cried too. Some village dogs started to bark, although they didn't know what was happening. Mr. Duyện became angrier, and the veins on his forehead and neck protruded. He stomped his feet and yelled, "I'll kill all of you. Then I'll stab myself. I'll get rid of all of you first, my burdens, and then your mother."

His "burdens" got frightened and ran away. Mrs. Duyện got up, raised her dress, and clumsily ran toward the gate. Her husband went into the kitchen, grabbed a chopping knife, and ran into the front yard, but no one was there. He threw the knife onto the ground and said, "If I catch any of you here, I'll kill you on the spot. Oh gosh! All of you make my life so miserable. My life wouldn't be like this without you."

Then he heard his wife say, "I neither ruin your life nor steal anything from you. Watch your tongue. God is watching."

The fact that she hid herself beyond the gate and talked back to him further enflamed his fury. The more he chased her, the faster she hobbled. He became frustrated, and his fingers started to shake. He wanted to break something to alleviate his anger, but there was nothing in the house for him to break. The bed, the desk, the pillar—they would hurt his hands because they were all made of hard wood. There was the knife, but he had already vented his anger on it.

Outside, his wife wouldn't keep her mouth shut. She kept calling Heaven and Earth to witness her plight, but her pleas went unheard. Her words were like a knife stabbing at his head. Suddenly he shouted, "You have a big mouth. I'll burn this house down."

"If you do, the neighbors will make you pay for their damages," she warned him.

"I will go to jail so that all of you can become beggars," he said.

His wife, standing outside the fence, saw her husband searching for a match to strike a fire and cried, "Please help me. This bastard wants to burn my house . . . He . . ."

Nobody came to rescue her. Everyone was still at work. Eventually, there was no fire because he couldn't find a match—the Duyệns hadn't been able to afford a small box of matches for at least two years. Their daughter, Gái, always had to walk to the village to ask for some fire when she cooked their daily meals. And the family went to bed just after the sun went down. Reassured that nothing bad would happen, Mrs. Duyện was quiet. But then her husband threatened, "You think I won't dare to burn it, do you? I'll go ask for some fire."

All of a sudden, the sky grew cloudy and gray. The winds began to blow violently and the air became cold, while great sheets of water began pouring out of the dark sky, followed by claps of thunder. It was the beginning of the summer, and it didn't usually rain. However, if there was rain, it was always a torrential downpour. The sky grew dark; water was everywhere. The rain hammered the banana leaves in the garden with a relentless drumming sound. The winds blew stronger and stronger. Eventually, the low-lying areas became flooded. After a while, the rain gradually stopped and the sun came out. Leaves were now lush; birds hopped around, chirping and singing livelily.

Everybody in the village ran outside. Men were wearing only their loincloths. Women put on their camisoles and straw hats. The children were naked. Everyone held a basket and rushed toward the rice paddies, gardens, and vegetable beds. After the rain, the puddles filled with air bubbles and worms began to crawl out of the wet earth. The colorful frogs and toads jumped out of the bushes and shrubs looking for the worms. The fat, older frogs moved slowly but with a stately presence. Big frogs, small frogs—each with shiny, mercurial skin, body parts clearly defined, and eyes that darted back and forth—hopped about quickly and ate voraciously. Then the villagers went out to catch them.

The entire Duyện family joined the crowd in hunting frogs. After the rain, Mrs. Duyện ran home and grabbed a basket. She realized that her husband and Gái already had taken the two baskets hung in the kitchen and left the house. Chân and Cẳng were secured in a crib like two puppies. Mr. Duyện had already forgotten the earlier row with his wife and now was thinking about the delicious roasted frogs that would be on the night's dinner table. Mrs. Duyện ran fast because she didn't want to waste the great opportunity to catch as many frogs as she could. She met her husband, and he was no longer mad at her. He also tried to catch frogs.

She then met Gái, who proudly showed her how many frogs she had caught. Gái had about half of the basket filled with frogs. She was very happy and smiled, showing her stained and decayed teeth. Then Gái went back to a nearby pond while her mother walked fast toward the area where the village shrine was located.

Gái tiptoed and scoured the shrubs. The grass was tall and made her itch. Whenever she caught a frog, she broke its legs and quickly threw it into the basket; then she smiled. She walked along the pond, amid wild, thorny pineapple shrubs. She heard frogs jumping into the pond.

The time to catch frogs ended, and everyone returned home. Mr. Duyện got home first, and then his wife. Chân and Cẳng cried in the crib, so she handed her basket to her husband and released the boys. As she comforted them, Mr. Duyện looked at the baskets of frogs. His face became expressionless, probably because he was imagining the delicious dinner ahead. Suddenly Mrs. Duyện asked, "Is Gái home yet? Why don't you go and look for her?"

Her voice was soft and sweet. Mr. Duyện couldn't believe that not long before, they had been having a vicious squabble. He stood up and walked outside, mumbling, "Where the hell is she?" Then he called, "Gái."

From inside, his wife said, "I saw her walk toward Mr. Tràng's pond earlier."

Mr. Duyện waded along Mr. Tràng's pond and walked toward the wild pineapple shrubs. He saw Gái, but she seemed to have fainted on the grass, holding her basket. Her face was pale, her arms and legs were curled up. She yawned a few times, and her eyes fluttered and then closed completely. Her legs and arms stretched out. She was dead.

Mr. Duyện, seeing his daughter die right before his eyes, screamed in panic. Although he was nervous, he noticed the mark of a long, large snake about the size of a big bamboo stick in the fresh mud nearby. He bent down and picked up his daughter. He suddenly felt sorry for the miserable life Gái had lived in his family. She was so bony and malnourished that he could see all of her ribs under her skin. Poor thing! She was dead. Tears trailed down from his eyes. He could still feel some warmth from her hands, but her legs were cold. He carried Gái's dead body on his back and hurried home.

14

The First Love Letter

Tô Hoài

By age eighteen, Mì's eyes had grown attractively deeper and darker. They angled upward and darted around coyly. How beautiful! Her lips were like rose petals, and whenever she smiled, her rosy cheeks became two lovely circles.

There was no doubt that Mì was the most beautiful girl in the village. All the men said so and fell in love with her. She was by no means stuck up, but it wasn't easy to win her heart because she was both pretty and literate. She penned letters for her illiterate neighbors and could read *The Tale of Hoàng Trừu* fluently.[1] It was rare to find a literate and talented woman in Nghĩa Village.

A man from another village once fell in love with Mì. One day, he handed her a letter. After reading it, she told her female friends, "He's illiterate, so he must have asked someone to compose the letter. But the writer stole many sentences from a novel that I've already read. Such a fool! Who does he think he is? I'm out of his league." Then she chirped, "Being illiterate is a travesty!"

---

1. A poem written in the traditional six- to eight-verse *lục bát* form that includes 1,584 lines about a talented, righteous Chinese prince named Hoàng Trừu who travels to eighteen foreign countries to find a wife.

Her mocking words about her admirer spread immediately throughout the village. Like everyone else, Cuông heard about it, especially because his cousin, Nghiên, was Mì's best friend. Once Nghiên read the entire letter to Cuông. He couldn't remember much of it, except for one thing—it was beautifully crafted.

Dear my wife,
The delicate rose petals. The dawn chorus. The billowing bamboo screen. The
melodious breeze. Don't you know about my hidden feelings for you?

The poetic language was moving, and sometimes Cuông mumbled the lines to himself because he, too, was in love with Mì. Cuông, who was nearing the end of his teenage years, was romantic and started to nurture passionate feelings of attraction. He saw Mì nearly every afternoon, although they didn't live in the same village. When the sky turned red at dusk signaling the end of a workday, everybody left his or her looms, and Cuông walked to his home's front gate and stood still. When he saw Mì's white silk ribbon fluttering in the wind from afar, he blushed; his arms and legs felt paralyzed. When Mì walked closer toward him, he quietly walked behind the gate and hid until she had passed completely. Then he bent down, craned his neck, and secretly watched her with a dull face. If he were to be caught, he would quickly stand up, his hands behind his back, his face lifted, pretending to be listening to the sound of a flute-kite flying high in the sky. This became his habit every afternoon, and nobody knew how long he had suffered unrequited love.

But that all changed after a series of *chèo* performances in Hượng Village.

"I was with Mì the night they performed *Lục Vân Tiên*," Nghiên said to Cuông.

"That night I snuck out and went to the communal house."

"I know. When Mì saw you pass by, she said to me, 'He's so strange!'"

Cuông was elated. He felt as if every bone in his body was rattling. Then he inquired, in a hurried tone, "Why did she say that?"

"I asked her that, and she explained, 'He stands outside every afternoon, and whenever he sees me, he walks back inside.'"

"That's not true. I never do that."

His denial contradicted his true feelings. His heart felt like a garden blooming with flowers because it seemed Mì did pay attention to him.

He was so overwhelmed; he didn't want to shut his eyes and couldn't sleep for a few nights. Every now and then, he smiled for no reason and thought that she must be in love with him, so all he needed to do was write her a letter. Unfortunately, he was illiterate, and he wouldn't know what to say if Mì read a letter he didn't write and then asked him questions about it.

He sighed and thought that he had to learn how to read and write *Quốc ngữ*.[2]

Cuông took a massive hen to sell at the seasonal Bưởi Market. Despite how much she ate, the hen laid an egg only every other day, rather than daily. The hen cackled loudly all the way to the market. After selling it, Cuông tried to avoid female vendors and stopped by a stall owned by an old, bleary-eyed man and paid six pennies for a book written for a six-year-old reader. He stuck the book inside his shirt so nobody could see it and strolled home.

That night, Cuông started to study *Quốc ngữ*. His fourth-grade nephew, Tế, became his teacher. Cuông paid Tế a penny for each tutoring session and the little boy was more than happy to help his uncle. Cuông began to learn the alphabet slowly. He soon persevered and was able to spell simple words. In the evenings, after working at the loom, Cuông carried an oil lamp to the front veranda where Tế was waiting for him. Cuông squatted on the floor, paid close attention to the words Tế pointed at with his finger, and read them aloud. After a while, he had memorized the words.

After Tế went to bed, Cuông would sit by the lamp and mumble the words, his head nodding up and down. After he had memorized everything without looking at the book, he opened his notebook and lay flat on the floor with his legs in the air. He bit his lips as he repeatedly wrote down the letters he had just learned, one line after another. He dipped the nib into the ink bottle and wrote neat, careful letters. It was an exhausting task, but he refused to give up. After completing one page, he would stand up, breathe a sigh of relief, close his notebook, and go to bed. Before he fell asleep, he always thought about the words he'd just learned and joyfully imagined the scene in which Nghiên would hand Mì his letter and how Mì would blink her eyes cheerfully as she opened it. Nothing could discourage him from learning.

---

2. A Vietnamese script introduced in the seventeenth century and used as the standard today.

Cuông studied diligently but told no one, including Nghiên and his friends. He didn't want people to gossip about him as it would only bring embarrassing attention to his illiteracy. He was afraid that all of his work would be futile if Mì knew about it. The winter was reaching its end, and Cuông needed to study harder and faster. He had almost reached his goal and was able to spell difficult words with his mouth twisted. Mì often appeared in his dreams, causing his hopeful heart to leap.

One evening in early spring, when a cozy and relaxing atmosphere was still lingering in every household, Cuông carried his books, pen, and a bottle of ink to the veranda. Without Tế, Cuông sat down timidly. He tilted his head and gazed into the lamp flame. He was dreaming about something vague. He crossed his legs, his back straight as if meditating, and sat for hours in silence. Then he took out a sheet of paper, straightened its edges, and slowly laid it flat on the floor. He dipped the nib into the purple ink and started writing. The metal nib shone next to the oil lamp as he clumsily moved it across every line on the white paper.

Cuông halted after each word and hesitantly scratched out the next. He continuously adjusted his hand. He was so absorbed in writing that his neck became stiff, his pupils strained, and his mouth twisted as he tried to make the letter *o* as round as possible. After he had written about four and a half lines, he dropped the pen and looked wistfully into the garden. It was already midnight. The moon poured a gentle, dim light over the bamboo and palm trees. Cuông bent down, lifted the sheet with his hands, and stared pensively at the messy writing scrawled between the light blue lines. When he mumbled what he'd written, his eyes brightened. With difficulty, he had solemnly crafted vowels so that they were works of beauty. It was a short letter, but it took him hours to compose. A letter for the girl he loved. It read:

Dear Mì,

I have been thinking of you for a long time without daring to tell you about it. I am writing you this letter. I hope the wind will take it to the clouds and then deliver it to you. Please reply when you receive it. I swear to love you forever.

Nguyễn Văn Cuông

The letter was a huge accomplishment for Cuông. He reread it and held it close to the lamp for the ink to dry quickly. Then he folded it, placed it in his notebook, and hid it under his pillow. It was five o'clock in the morning. The roosters had started to crow. The moon had completely vanished.

Cuông had started to learn *Quốc ngữ* at the end of the winter and hadn't finished it until after Tết. But this first love letter was never sent to Mì because on the first day of spring, she married a man from another village. Cuông only heard about her wedding when Nghiên told him, and it was already too late. He could blame no one because he simply had no one to blame.

He kept the folded love letter in his wallet for a few days, his sweat discoloring it. One evening, he lit the oil lamp and burned it. His eyes filled with regret.

The villagers soon learned about Cuông's ability to read and write fluently, but he remained dejected. He read *The Tale of Kiều* to alleviate his despair.

One day, he told Nghiên, "*The Tale of Kiều* is superb. Lots of sad lines, though."

"When Mì was single, she loved that epic." Nghiên smiled and said, "I should've been your matchmaker."

15

Bright Moon

Nam Cao

Điền owned four cane chairs, the only objects of value among all his furniture. He did not purchase them, though, as he never wanted to spend money. Since he moved into his home, he had spent money on furniture only once—for a bed made of grapefruit wood, sold to him by a penurious aunt who desperately needed the money to buy medicine for her husband. In any case, Điền had felt it was time he owned a bed. That March, his wife had given birth to a son, and so he was now the father of two children. All four members of his family shared the bed, which was fine during the winter, since body warmth kept everyone cozy. But during the hot days of summer, it surely couldn't be very clean, so he worried.

Điền was sometimes concerned with cleanliness since he, after all, was an educated man. He had been a teacher for three years at a private school where he obtained the chairs. Just last year, he was still employed to teach first grade, earning twenty piasters each month, but he suddenly became unemployed when the school decided to use its classrooms for other, noneducational purposes.

The principal, unable to collect the last month's tuition from students, owed Điền half a month's salary. But because they were good friends, the principal had decided to find a way to settle this debt with Điền. If he had been able to afford it, he would have paid Điền the ten piasters himself. The principal didn't want Điền to be affected by the unexpected mishap, so he smiled, a bit embarrassed, and said, "So, let's do this, Điền. If you don't mind, please take these cane chairs home. They are yours now. A noodle-stall owner offered seven dimes apiece, but it has already cost me one piaster to tighten the canes on two of them. It would be a waste to sell the chairs to him. I notice that your home still has no chairs . . ."

Điền forced himself to smile. He was not amused by the suggestion and didn't want the chairs at all. Some were unstable, some had deformed legs, and the paint had flaked off like the skin of a leper. They looked pathetic. Normally, it caused him considerable emotional pain to spend seven dimes to purchase a train ticket to return to his hometown, because he had to borrow the sum. Now he would have to spend his own money to have the chairs delivered to his home, but how could he reject the principal's offer? Điền did not want to hurt his boss's feelings—he would never do that because they were good friends. They had been humiliated enough by other people, and it would be especially unpleasant if they were to humiliate each other. While Điền was thinking of a way to turn down the offer, the principal continued, "You should take the boat. It won't cost you more than five dimes."

Five dimes plus five cents to rent a mosquito net would bring the total amount to fifty-five cents. If he paid the shipping fee for the four chairs, it would be the same amount he would have paid for a train ticket. He would have adequate space on the boat—he could use one chair to sit on, another to rest his legs on, and feel really comfortable, as though he were at home. It would be stupid to take the train and have to deal with the crowded cars. *Taking the boat is a good idea*, Điền thought. He wouldn't have to put up with people elbowing each other's chests to obtain a train ticket. He wouldn't have to sit on someone's lap or have someone sit on his. Moreover, he wouldn't have to smell the rancid sweat of other passengers and the awful odor of pig waste in the fourth-class cars.

It was as if the principal could read Điền's mind. "Don't bother yourself with the delivery of the chairs," he said. "A boy will tie the chairs together in twos and carry them to the boat for you. I'll pay another boy five pennies or up to one dime to deliver the chairs to your house."

Điền calculated in his head—everything would cost him no more than one piaster. Two dimes for four cane chairs! Even if they were shaky, it was still a very good deal. The four cane chairs, for which the

noodle-stall owner had offered seven dimes apiece, were thus trans-
ported by boat to Điền's home.

So Điền now owned four cane chairs. He didn't know how much they
normally would have cost, but he assumed that buying them brand
new would be expensive. Each chair would cost at least three to four
piasters. That would make the whole set worth almost twenty piasters.
In his village, no household possessed such expensive furniture, and his
wife, therefore, treasured the chairs greatly. It hurt her feelings when
their gauche guests, after complimenting the elegance and beauty of
the chairs, plopped down their buttocks, as big and heavy as clay water
containers, onto the chairs, making the canes sag deeply. They then
rested their dirty feet on the rungs, and reclined their buffalo-sized
backs in a way that caused the hoops to bend. How long could chairs
last with that sort of abuse? Even an iron chair would be damaged. And
these, after all, were only cane chairs.

One day, Điền's wife suggested to him, "As you know, these country
people are not very cultured. We need to protect our valuables. Why
don't we put the chairs away? They will be ruined soon if people sit on
them like that."

Điền laughed. He thought about women's stinginess—they bought
clothes to keep in the wardrobe and not to wear and chairs to store away
and not to sit on. He was about to say no, but after a minute of thinking, he agreed. His wife was always better than he was when it came to
managing household matters and expenses.

Now, without a job, Điền was no more than a dependent. His wife
had to give him money for everything, including five pennies for a hair-
cut. She carried all the family's burdens on her shoulders, so it was
only fair to let her have some authority inside the house. Otherwise,
she might complain that, when something needed to be repaired, Điền
never paid. From that day on, the four chairs hung from hooks attached
to a lean-to. They were used only when Điền and his wife entertained
respectful, courteous guests.

However, on moonlit nights, although no guest was there, Điền
would often take the four chairs to the front yard and call his wife and
children out. She held their youngest child on her lap and occupied
one chair, their daughter sat on another, and Điền took one for himself
and stretched his legs across another. They then sat and waited for the
moon to rise. If their son didn't cry and their daughter didn't need to
have her itches scratched, complete happiness would be achieved.

The breeze blew away all worries and bitter feelings. The moonbeams fell like cool, fresh water sprinkling over their faces, making their skin soft and silky and erasing everyone's scowls. His wife's forehead was no longer wrinkled with worries, and her face brightened. She looked as if she were ten years younger. In those moments, Điền thought about how charming and lovely she looked! He could hardly recognize the quarrelsome woman who scolded their children, the servant, the cat, and the dog—the woman who seemed to stir up chaos in their home every day. She bent down toward their son and looked affectionately at their daughter who smiled at her mother, and she smiled back. He watched his wife and children, and he felt elated as he looked up at the moon.

Điền loved the moon, which was not unusual, because he was an avid reader. It went without saying that one could appreciate the beauty of the moon only if one read literature and poetry. The moon was a golden sickle amid clusters of stars. The moon was a silver plate on a velvet, sky-blue carpet. The moon transferred dreams to earth. The moon was a stream of cool water for thirsty souls to dive into. Oh, the moon, the moon! It was the inspiration for generations of poets! Điền had no regrets. His parents had sold their rice paddy and garden so that he could obtain a formal education. They had expected him to become a state official and have a stable job. Thus they were embarrassed that he had almost achieved the goal but finally failed to fulfill their expectations. Because of his chronic health conditions, Điền was not offered a job at a state institution. People said that the money his parents had spent on his education was a wasted investment. But he believed that although his education didn't help to fill his stomach, it was useful in other ways. He could read literature and poetry, through which he understood the beauty of a breeze or the moon. He was displeased by stunted souls, like that of his wife. To her, the moon was nothing beyond the fact that it saved her two pennies worth of lamp oil. Peanut oil cost at least two piasters per liter now. When two countries were at war, the poor were also affected.[1] Every night, she kept their lamp on for only a short while, but it was long enough to cost her two cents worth of oil.

On moonlit nights, she could save those two cents—it wasn't much, but twenty cents equaled two dimes; twenty dimes equaled two piasters,

---

1. This reference is hypothetical, recalling the numerous conflicts suffered by the Vietnamese during the twentieth century.

and twenty piasters. . . . Oh gosh! If one kept calculating like that, it would be a never-ending process. But why did one always have to calculate? Those who did so made their lives miserable. Điền always blamed his wife for doing that without noticing that he also had that same habit. At that very moment, while enjoying the moon and forgetting the trivial worries of life, he was also calculating in his head. He noticed the vastness of the sky and the plentiful smattering of stars. He remembered a line in a poem by a Western poet who compared a sky full of stars to a field. If the sky were a field, then the field must be endless, but all Điền needed was a piece of land about the size of the field behind the back of his house. That would be enough to release him from daily financial concerns. He would let his wife take charge of the land so that he could pursue his own dream . . .

His dream was to be a literary man. Once upon a time, Điền had immersed himself in reading and writing. He was very eager to become a writer, and he vowed not to complain if he had to suffer the poverty and hardships that writers often suffered. He used to say to the friends who shared his thinking that he would reject a job offer that paid hundreds of piasters a month if he could find a position as a writer that paid him five piasters. . . . But although he wrote for many years without making a penny, he still had to put food on the table. His parents were poor. None of his younger siblings could go to school or enjoy a decent meal. Poverty led to several unpleasant tumultuous outcomes. His father left the family. His mother had to perform backbreaking labor to earn enough money to feed her two youngest children. As for the older children, some worked as wet nurses, some as water-buffalo herders; some carried banana flowers or sweet potatoes to sell at the market, earning barely enough to keep them from starving to death.

Back then, Điền had wondered if he was being selfish. What would a career as a writer do for him and his family anyway? His duty was to help his family. For the time being at least, he had to put aside his literary dreams in order to make money. So he began teaching grade school. His monthly income was twenty piasters, which was quite a large sum by his parents' standards, and they urged him to get married. His wife, who came from a relatively wealthy family, married Điền merely because he was educated. Then they had children. His large parental family could not rely on him for anything once he had his own small family. His thoughts were always occupied with concerns about money. His mind was full of worries. Sometimes, when he thought about his past dream, he sighed and consoled himself, *I will write again when I have money*. But he knew very well that he would not write again, because he never would have money.

And now here was another moonlit night. Điền took two chairs to the front yard. His wife had been busy all day, and the house servant had asked for a day off to attend a relative's death anniversary. His wife had to finish weaving cloth so that she could sell it the next day to pay off the interest on some of their debts. After she had finished weaving, she quickly left to collect the money. When she returned home, their youngest child had cried so much that his throat became raw. The oldest child was a mess. Her face and nose were covered with dirt. The house was in shambles, and the servant had not yet returned. How could his wife manage everything by herself? Her anger reached a boiling point, and she screamed loudly, stamping her feet violently on the floor. She spanked their daughter, scolded their son, threw the broom, kicked a bamboo basket, and whined endlessly. She then put their son to bed early. And after sobbing silently, their daughter grew tired and fell asleep.

Điền was sitting outside alone, trying to maintain his nonchalance, but his cheeks felt rough—they were getting thicker and numb. He felt desperate. His wife must love him a lot, but she knew that people needed food, water, and clothes when they were sick, and she tried to take care of those needs for her husband. She ate very little so that her husband could have enough food. She sold her clothes to get medicine for him, but she didn't know that her sacrifices failed to make him happy. Điền longed for romantic love and affectionate words. His wife's grimaces, terse language, and way of expressing love too simply, if not too roughly, saddened him. He felt something missing in his emotional life. Whom could he really love? If he remained in that family, amid all the irritating worries about money, his soul would soon be empty, and his poetic inspiration would be suffocated—along with the inspiration that he still hoped someday to recover.

In the sky, the moon was flirtatious, like a young girl who had just fallen in love. The breeze made the leaves move gently in a way that recalled a dancer's steps. The banana leaves shining in the moonlight quivered pleasantly. Điền thought of well-off women who bathed in scented water, wore blue silk, and lay on swinging benches, moving their lithe, sexy legs. . . .

Why did these romantic, sexually provocative thoughts enter his mind? He didn't know. Maybe he wanted to caress someone's scented hair and silky skin and hold an affectionate hand. Beautiful women were very adept at romantic love and could afford good food and nice clothes; they could care for their bodies—they didn't have to do any hard labor. The truth was that his wife was an uncultured, indelicate person, whom he considered to be undeserving of his attention. He had to leave, Điền realized suddenly, if there was any hope of his soul feeling refreshed. He would do any sort of work to feed himself. And he'd then be able to sit down and write confidently, produce something significant. His words must become polished, his ideas refined. His pen then would be capable of conveying romantic love fully. Art was the mythic moonlight that beautified even mundane, ugly things. . . .

The images of beautiful women lying leisurely on swings danced in his mind again. They would read his writings and feel delight. They would love him and send him beautifully inscribed, scented letters. His imagination expanded like the moonlight. He thought about romantic love with those women who spent their time only on makeup and romance. Suddenly, the moon lost its mystique. Điền looked down and felt embarrassed, as if he had been caught trespassing. He listened.

"What's wrong with you?" his wife asked acerbically.

"I have a stomachache," their daughter responded.

"Oh, no. God help me, please," his wife said. Then she upbraided the child, "You're never careful with what you put into your mouth. Go ahead and die. Why call for me?"

The child didn't dare cry loudly but just writhed quietly and moaned softly. Sometimes, she couldn't control it, and Điền would hear her sobbing, as if someone were vomiting. He remained seated outside with his face down. A bitter feeling came over his entire body. It began in his throat, then it traveled to his brain, and tears started to fall from his eyes.

His wife gently put their sleeping son into a hammock, and then she took a knife to the garden, dug up some ginger roots, washed them thoroughly and ground them. She squeezed half a lime into the ground ginger to make a medicine—a common remedy among destitute families for all kinds of illnesses. She filtered out the juice and gave it to their sick daughter, who became frightened the moment the smell of the ginger reached her nose. She bit her lips and refused to open her mouth. She lay on her back on her mother's lap. Her mother used one hand to support their daughter's head. With her other hand, she held a bowl of ginger juice close to the child's lips. The girl kept her lips tightly closed. Frustrated, her mother shouted, "Open your mouth!"

The girl began to cry. The woman finally poured the bowl of ginger juice down her child's throat. She writhed violently to resist. She coughed up the juice and screamed. She spit the ginger juice all over her mother's blouse. Their son, who'd been watching the scene, was startled. He too began to scream. Điền's wife, enraged, spanked their sick daughter's back and threw her onto the bed the way she would a cat.

"See if I care! Go ahead and die," she said.

"Please, Mommy," the girl cried and begged her mother. "I can't stand the bitter juice! I beg you. My mouth is burning."

"Shut up, or I'll slap your face," her mother shouted.

The girl did not shut up. Her mother became more aggressive and grasped her daughter. "Will you shut up now?"

The girl was frightened and finally became quieter, but her sobbing could still be heard.

Điền loved his children. The thought occurred to him suddenly: he couldn't abandon his family. He could not be happy if his children were suffering.

Oh! The moon was so beautiful! The moon was gentle, clear, and calm. It made dilapidated cottages look beautiful, even though their occupants suffered, cried, and complained about their miseries. They ground their teeth and cursed life. Life was full of suffering and mishaps. No, absolutely no! Điền could no longer be a dreamer. Realities were inescapable. They eradicated his romantic dreams, which could be realized only by people living lives of leisure. He wanted to avoid the ugliness of reality, but how could he? His wife was miserable, so were his children and parents, and even he himself. Many other people were in the same situation. Destitution marred the freshness and beauty of people's souls. Utterances of pain echoed strongly, but real art did not require deceptive moonlight. Art must encompass even the miseries produced by indigence and hardship, and this echoed violently in his heart. He didn't need to go anywhere. He didn't need to escape his reality. He could face the unpleasant realities, open his soul, and welcome the full gamut of life.

The next morning—amid his children's crying, his wife's scolding, the raucous sounds of someone claiming a debt in the village, and a neighbor's cursing after losing a chicken the night before—Điền sat down to write.

16

The Eyes

Nam Cao

A young man from the village pointed me to a small brick gate and said, "Right here. Mr. Hoàng lives here."

"Thank you." I tapped his shoulder and said, "I'll drop by your house later."

"Hold on," he interrupted when I was about to enter the gate. "Let me call Mr. Hoàng to chain the dog first. It's big and mean."

I watched the young man closely. I remembered my previous visits to Hoàng's home in Hà Nội. After ringing the house bell, I had always waited for Hoàng to grab the leather collar of his Western-bred dog, which was as huge as a calf. Only after he had ducked its head under a staircase did I have the courage to walk behind the creature and step into the living room.

I was very fearful of that aggressive German Shepherd. On one of my visits, I didn't find Hoàng restraining the dog as usual, and he told me sadly that the dog had died. Although I expressed my sympathy, I actually felt relief at the news. His dog had died during the famine.[1] (In the year 2000, our descendants probably still will be talking about that period of great scarcity, making listeners shudder.) The dog did not die

---

1. The famine of 1945 in northern Vietnam occurred during the Japanese occupation of French Indochina. It is estimated that nearly two million Vietnamese died of hunger.

because of Hoàng's inability to feed it enough beef every day. Hoàng was a writer but also a smart black market trader. When we visited him, we looked like skeletons holding unsellable manuscripts, but Hoàng always looked comfortably well off, and his dog didn't have to suffer a day without food. Although human corpses were ubiquitous in the town, the dog died probably because it either had eaten rotten human flesh or had inhaled too much of the stench of the dead. Poor creature!

Yet now, as I was visiting Hoàng again—this time the home where he was relocated to, which was hundreds of kilometers away from Hà Nội—I was being warned of another fierce dog. *How interesting!* I smiled and thought. The young villager, without knowing why I was smiling, grinned. As he shouted out Hoàng's name, I heard the sounds of worn-out wooden clogs on the feet of someone swiftly sweeping the brick yard. A little boy in a black beret and gray sweater answered the gate. His black eyes stared at me.

Ngữ, Hoàng's son, excitedly cried out, without remembering to greet me, "Daddy, it's Mr. Độ!" He then quickly went back into the house.

"What's going on? What's the matter?" Hoàng's voice was both deep and blusterous as he asked his son (he always used that outlandish tone whenever he talked to his child). The boy mumbled something unintelligible. Then I heard Mrs. Hoàng's voice: "Ngữ, chain the dog. Chain it immediately to the pillar over there."

Hoàng lumbered out because his body was so heavy. His arms were so enormous that the flesh under them protruded, making his arms appear abnormally short. In Hà Nội, his heavy physique had made him look steady and stately in his formal French suits. Now his fat body was very prominent under light blue clothes covered by a white sweater worn so tightly that he could hardly breathe. He remained behind the gate, extended one of his corpulent hands toward me, leaned his head back, and opened his mouth slightly—the gesture of someone in great surprise or joy. I suddenly noticed a change on his round, fleshy face: he had grown a horseshoe-shaped mustache that looked like a small brush.

Speechless for a while, he started to mumble from the back of his throat, "Oh, my gosh! Welcome! It's such an honor." He then turned his head and said to his wife, "It's Mr. Độ. He has traveled such a long distance to visit us."

She ran toward the gate while still fastening the last button of her *áo dài*, which was donned in a rush to greet me. She gave a warm welcome: "We've been looking forward to meeting you again. When I heard my son, I thought he must've mistaken you for someone else—for someone who lived just fifteen or twenty kilometers away. . . ."

After he shook my hand, Hoàng gently pushed me forward. His wife quickly ran into the house to arrange some chairs. Why did they welcome me with such unusual hospitality? I began to question the negative feelings about Hoàng that I had developed since the revolution, when Hoàng suddenly began to treat me almost as a stranger. I had tried to visit him a few times to see if he had changed his opinions about the crucial twists and turns in our nation's history, but he had never been home. His door had always been locked. His son had looked through a small hole in the door, first asking carefully for my name and then returning later to inform me of his father's absence.

As a result, I became skeptical after a few visits. On my last visit, I had heard Hoàng and his wife's voices even before I rang the doorbell, but his son insisted that his parents had left for their farm in the countryside the night before. Undeniably, Hoàng didn't want to see me. I didn't know why, but since then, I had stopped visiting.

Once we met in the street by accident. We coldly shook hands as a courtesy, said hello quickly, and then went our separate ways. I was becoming aware of Hoàng's idiosyncrasies, especially when he turned all of a sudden into a complete stranger, for reasons known only to himself. Sometimes, his attitude toward friends changed because a friend's literary work received praise from a critic who had previously criticized Hoàng's work. Sometimes the change required no real conflict. One could be very close to Hoàng while one was merely a regional author who only contributed fiction to Hà Nội magazines, but if one relocated to the capital and started to socialize with other writers, Hoàng would terminate the friendship. He probably knew that he had become anathema in the Hà Nội literary community.

Personally, I never understood why so many people despised him until he began to treat me as a stranger. I later gained a better understanding of Hoàng. When the Allies assisted the Vietnamese in disarming the Japanese, some prostitutes abandoned their Western dresses and put on Chinese clothes. Meanwhile, my friend Hoàng, having no one to lean on, founded a daily newspaper just to lambaste everyone. He ranted against many people at first, then even against his former friends, who were generally kind and had done him no harm, because the appearance of their names in the national liberation front newspapers upset him. Outraged, he referred to them disparagingly as impecunious proletarian writers whose lives suddenly changed for the better thanks to blessings earned from tending their ancestors' graves.[2] He accused them of selfishly depriving people of the opportunity for advancement in order to improve their own lives. I smirked, not because I felt uneasy with his harsh condemnations, but because I couldn't believe that some Vietnamese authors still used their writings to gain such ignoble ends.

But Hoàng would not change. I thought that our true friendship had long ended, so why was he so cheerful at this rendezvous with me? Had the passage of time actually allowed him to change? Or had our nation's heroic revolution reeducated him?

In all honesty, I was moved when he said, "There is not a single day that we don't mention your name. Once I was reading a neighbor's newspaper and saw your writing, and I assumed that you had been assigned to do propaganda work in this province. When an official visited our village, I asked him to deliver a letter to you. I relied on chance because I wasn't sure if my letter would ever reach you. Now we are able to meet again. You don't look like a strong man, so how could you walk for such a long distance? How could you find this village? When I first moved here, I would get lost if I went even twenty steps from my house. There are so many narrow pathways around here, and they all look the same to me. Sometimes I was only coming home from the field and I got lost. . . ."

Hoàng's current residence was a clean, spacious, traditional three-section house, with a big front porch, a brick yard, and flowering vine-covered walls. There was a pretty, green vegetable garden. Fortunately, his entire family lived together here under one roof. The actual owner of the house was a merchant from Hà Nội who had depended on Hoàng and his wife's finances and clients. Now was the appropriate time for him to reciprocate out of gratitude. The merchant had moved to his father's house next door and allowed Hoàng to use this house as he pleased.

"I don't know how our lives would be if we hadn't been able to use his house," Hoàng said. "I see many relocated people struggling miserably. Can you imagine this: a relocated older brother moving into his younger brother's home, but then forced to move out into a cottage in the garden when the older brother's wife gave birth?"

"Let me remind you," I replied, "that villagers here stick with their traditional customs to avoid bad luck. . . ."

---

2. Many Vietnamese people believe that if the graves of one's ancestors are well tended, their family will receive good fortune.

"I know," he responded in an angry and disapproving tone. "I know that, but who would care in that situation? That's not yet the whole story! Although the older brother is living a life of poverty, his younger brother not only shows him no compassion but also derides him, referring constantly to the comfort and extravagance of his older brother's previous life. For example, he'll say, 'When your business was going well, I told you to send me money to purchase land in the countryside, but you stubbornly said that you didn't need it because you wanted to buy houses in the city. Why don't you go back to your city houses?' So awful! You see . . . but only rarely do any of us experience such terrible times in our history. Who could resist a luxurious life when they were wealthy? How many people would toil like water buffalos, gladly live in a slum, and never dare to splurge on good food or clothes, saving money just to buy land and rice paddies as the younger brother did?"

Mrs. Hoàng joined the conversation. "Many people caused us to worry. Perhaps ninety people out of a hundred believed that the French wouldn't dare to go to war with us. I once naively believed that when we evacuated our home, after the government issued its decree just to scare them. Then all of a sudden, the war broke out. We could run, but how could we take our valuables with us? Fortunately, we were able to take some money and we had some goods stored at our suburban farm. With luck, we can survive for another year. Once everything is spent and gone, we'll suffer. I'm afraid that people will deride us. That's why we don't dare to eat a chicken now, although we can afford it, because people would find out and mock us later. They're very mean-spirited here, you know!"

"I have no idea how they still have time to be so nosy and inquisitive when they're supposed to be quite busy," Hoàng grinned and said. "If you slaughtered a chicken today, the whole village would know about it tomorrow. Although you've just arrived, I've seen some people trying to figure out who you are. I'm certain that the news of your visit today will spread throughout the village by tomorrow. They will talk about your name, your age, your physique, how many moles you have on your face, how many holes you have in your pants."

I smiled and explained to Hoàng, "They must be vigilant of all outsiders visiting the village because they are responsible members of the self-defense force."

"They are stupid and ridiculous. They believe that a woman who appears pregnant must be hiding a grenade in her pants! It takes them at least fifteen minutes to peruse a brief document, and they ask any passerby to present identification. They stop and question anyone exiting the village. When one returns, they question again. If you just left the village and realized that you had forgotten your hat at my house and came back to get it, they would stop you first before they let you reenter the village. Then, when you exited, they would interrogate you again. It seems to me that they take great pleasure in doing this."

He gave a muffled laugh, looked me over from head to toe, and continued. "You have lived in the countryside, and I'm sure you understand these people's peculiarities. Why don't you explain their silly behavior to me? I had lived only in Hà Nội before, so I know of these folks only through your short stories. Now that I'm living among them, I can't stand them."

Hoàng's disdain became more obvious as his lips pouted and his nose curled up, as if smelling a rotten corpse. He and his wife took turns ridiculing the rural people.

"The youngsters and women have become quite ludicrous," he said. "They're all stupid, rude, selfish, greedy, and stingy. There is no mutual kindness between father and children, or among siblings. These country folks can't even spell Vietnamese words correctly, but they love to discuss politics. Whenever they open their mouths, all you hear are propositions, petitions, criticisms, admonitions, and terms like *colonial fascism*, *reactionism*, *socialism*, *democracy*, and even *new democracy*! If a stranger gets apprehended, he shouldn't fathom escape. They will brainwash him with propaganda for hours. They think, no doubt, that people relocated from Hà Nội, like us, must hold regressive opinions and are backward. They wouldn't waste any opportunity to do their duty as propagandists. But how should they propagandize?"

Hoàng glowered and continued. "Let me tell you this story. You probably will think I'm making it up, but if there is any fabrication in it, may God strike me dead. Once I went to the town market. Although I had asked for directions carefully, I forgot them when I reached a fork in the road and didn't know which direction to take. A young, lanky man carrying bamboo on his shoulders walked by. I greeted him and asked for directions to the market. The guy stared at me as if I were an alien from Mars. This signaled that I first should present to him my identification paper. Then he responded, 'Go that way until you see a huge banyan tree, then take a right, go for a short distance, take a left, pass a field, then follow the path leading to Ngò Village, go around the village shrine, turn right, and the market is not too far from there.' I can't remember the exact details. All I knew was that his directions were convoluted and confusing. Then he told me, 'Wait right here until you see a peddler, and just follow him. Goodbye for now. I have to take this bamboo to the Upper Hamlet to stop the enemy's advanced mobilized unit. Our long war is divided into three stages: defense, active resistance, and counteroffensive. The defense stage means . . .'"

Mrs. Hoàng burst out laughing. I smiled, but I was not quite pleased.

Hoàng noticed this and swore again, "May God strike me dead if I'm making it up! At that moment, I was so surprised that I couldn't laugh. I didn't dare to anyway because the man could've done me harm. Since then, we have kept the gate locked and stayed inside."

I forced a smile. What I wanted to tell Hoàng was never said. He would never listen to me, because to him I was merely another insignificant propaganda official. Even if I were able to talk him into doing what I was doing—carrying a rucksack and traveling to different villages to gain a better understanding of the countryside and its people—it would be useless. All he could see in the incident that he recounted was that young man who was carrying bamboo joyfully, but he failed to realize the young man was trying to stop the enemy. The young man had explained the three stages like a parrot, and Hoàng saw only the man's uncouth behavior without perceiving the noble cause behind his dedication.

If Hoàng were to maintain that perspective about life, the more he traveled and observed, the more bitter and more upset he would become. I was aware of this. As a writer, I was merely an inexperienced novice in his eyes. That's why I dared not share my opinions with him.

I hesitated but made some conciliatory comments: "Lots of things are unusual. Country people remain a mystery to us. I have lived among them. I used to get upset because the majority of them were uneducated, fearful, cowardly, and submissive. I became very skeptical when people talked about 'the strength of the people.' Our country's population consists primarily of peasants who never would be able to carry out a revolution. The times when Lê Lợi and Quang Trung ruled are long gone and will never return.[3] However, I was flabbergasted when the counteroffensive occurred. Surprisingly, these peasants were the revolutionaries. I have joined them in their attacks on state office buildings. I have interacted with them on the South-Central Front. A lot of men with betel-blackened teeth and bulging eyes even mispronounced the

---

3. Lê Lợi: Emperor of Vietnam from 1428 to 1443. Quang Trung: Emperor of Vietnam from 1788 to 1792.

word *grenade*, calling it *grelate*, and sang the song 'Go Fight' like a tired chant, but when they fought, they were very brave and courageous. If you meet them, you'll be astonished. It is they who make the revolution, although a few months ago, they might have been too timid to react to the soldiers' flirtatious behavior toward their wives."

Hoàng smirked and argued, "But you can't deny that their behavior is silly. I've seen some national guards or even some soldiers playing with guns or grenades, which could easily take someone's life. Some don't even hold a gun properly or know how to use it. That's where our country stands. If they have never touched a gun in their lives, how can they shoot? But they can learn when they go into the war. Let them fight the French! But the most dangerous part is that they are appointed as officials. For example, the chairman of my district in Hà Nội was a pork-offal vendor on the street before the war, so how can you expect him to administer a district? The chairman of my village here, after looking at my wife's identification, saw her name as Nguyễn Thục Hiền. He insisted that she must have borrowed her identification from a male because all women must bear the middle name Thị."

His wife laughed so hard that she started to cough and tears came to her eyes. She wiped them away with a handkerchief, shook her head, and said, "If you lived here, you'd laugh every day. Ironically, the village chairman requested that my husband teach literacy classes or help with propaganda."

"I have nothing to do, and sometimes I get bored. But how could I work with those people? So, I have to accept being labeled as *reactionary*," Hoàng chimed in.

"Since you have so much free time, have you written anything interesting?" I asked, just to change the topic.

"Not yet, because I don't even have a proper desk. But eventually we need to write something for the next generation. If we have talent, we might even write something better than Vũ Trọng Phụng's *Dumb Luck*."

If Mr. Phụng were still alive, he might be surprised.

After an early dinner at about four o'clock, Hoàng invited me to accompany him and his wife to visit some friends who had also relocated there from the cities. There was a retired village guard, a former teacher who was fired because he had raped a student, and an old judge who used to deal with legal issues and bribery. Hoàng disliked them because they knew nothing about literature. They were only good at playing cards. Talking with them was boring, but if he didn't socialize with them, he would have no one to hang out with. As we were walking together slowly, he spoke quietly about the evil, the stupidity, and the absurdity of each person, while we waited for his wife.

She walked fast to catch up with us. Her cheeks had become rosy from being near the kitchen fire. She apologized and said, "I just wanted to take a look at the pot of simmering sweet potatoes, so that we'll have some to eat later. There are no real delicacies in this village. While you're here, I'll buy some large sugar cane stalks and soak them in grapefruit juice to scent them. They taste really good."

When we arrived at a large big brick gate covered with vines, Hoàng rang the bell. A little boy answered the gate and greeted him respectfully, "How may I help you, sir?"

"Is Mr. Phạm home?"

"He has gone to the teacher's house, sir."

"Really? I thought the teacher was here all morning."

"No, sir. He didn't come here this morning."

We turned back and followed a few zigzag paths to reach another vine-covered brick gate. A wet nurse holding a baby was standing at the gate.

"Good evening, sirs. Good evening, ma'am," she greeted us.

"Is the teacher home?"

"No, sir. He has gone to the village guard's house."

"I was told earlier that the village guard was here."

"No, sir. That isn't true."

Hoàng turned back. After a few steps, he said to his wife, "They must be playing cards again. Madame Yên Kỷ, I bet, isn't home either, is she? She is addicted to the game. They must be either here or at Mr. Phạm's home, and they have someone tending the gate."

To this, Mrs. Hoàng said nothing. He tapped my shoulder and said, "Isn't that sad? Those educated people are all like that, while the common folks . . . Well, you already know."

It was only by coincidence that Hoàng moved here and lived among these unscrupulous members of the educated class. Why didn't he become a soldier or participate in propaganda plays? Why didn't he join other cultural revolutionary groups to learn how students and officers were volunteering for the military, or how doctors were working in research institutions or military hospitals, or how his friends—other writers and artists—were engaging themselves in the lives of the common people? Those writers and artists gained inspiration for their art from their engagement with the masses.

I gave a slight smile. "Listening to you disappoints me. So do you think our revolution eventually will fail?"

"Yes, I do. I've lost hope. If you observe carefully, you'll see. However, I haven't lost *all* hope because I still have trust in Uncle Hồ. Both the August Revolution and the current war rely on him.[4] He is talented, but it will be extremely difficult for him to succeed, especially now. You see, the representative for the liberation of France, the fourth greatest nation, was Charles de Gaulle."

I mentioned a few names in the liberation of France who were even more important than Charles de Gaulle.

Hoàng shook his head and said, "Even they can't compare to Hồ Chí Minh, who has done many things *so* admirably. Even if our people are worthless, he can manage situations to help our country gain independence. For instance, the Preliminary Agreement of March 6, 1946 caused the Americans to realize that they couldn't deceive him. The French are nobody! If the French hadn't been urged on by the Americans, the French wouldn't have dared to violate the Preliminary Agreement. The French should have been satisfied with the concessions that they received and treasured them."

After eating the sweet potatoes and drinking several cups of tea, Hoàng and I lay down. It felt good to lie under a thick blanket beneath a mosquito net. Two twin beds were placed parallel with a narrow aisle between them. The net was bleached white. Just looking at them made me feel comfortable.

A pack of cigarettes and a box of matches next to an ashtray were placed at the head of the bed. I wore my street clothes to bed and was concerned that some bugs might jump from my shirt and infect the fresh-scented blanket. Oftentimes, I shared my own blanket with workers in a printing plant, and I could not guarantee I didn't have their bugs on my body.

Mrs. Hoàng arranged a few things in the house, closed the door, and brought a large oil lamp and a bottle to our beds. "Are you going to light the big lamp?" Hoàng asked.

"Yes, but I need to add some oil first," she said.

"Do you like *Romance of the Three Kingdoms*?" he asked me.

I admitted that I had not read the whole thing.

"What a pity! Among all Eastern and Western novels, I love *Romance of the Three Kingdoms* and *Romance of the Eastern Chou* most, but regardless,

---

4. The August Revolution of 1945 and the French War.

nobody can surpass the Chinese when it comes to the epic novel. Those two are my favorites. *Water Margin* is as good as *Three Kingdoms* and *Eastern Chou*.[5] Normally you read a novel only once. The second time you read it, you start to lose interest, but *Three Kingdoms* and *Eastern Chou* are the exceptions. I never get bored rereading those two."

"Do you have those two books?"

"I left *Eastern Chou* in Hà Nội because I couldn't bring it with me when I was relocated here. Very sad! Fortunately, I kept *Three Kingdoms* at my suburban farm, so I could bring it here with me. If not, I would die of boredom."

He used the ashtray and continued. "I asked if you read *Three Kingdoms* because my wife and I often read a few episodes before we sleep, but not tonight. If you want to chat, we can."

I, of course, insisted that Hoàng and his wife follow their routine. He seemed very happy and said, "We'll read, then. We'll listen together and fall asleep. You look tired and should get some sleep soon. Does the light bother you?"

I told him that I often slept in the printing plant, with the bright lights on and amid the loud noise from running machines. Here I would sleep well under the warm blanket, even if there was shooting nearby.

Hoàng's laughter sounded like a rooster's crow. "Sounds good." Then he told his wife to get the book.

Mrs. Hoàng ran to get the hardcover, leather-bound book.

"Do you want to read, or do you want me to?" she asked.

"You do it."

She put the lamp back at the head of the bed, took off her *áo dài*, and lay next to her son, who had lain down first.

"Where were we last night? Did we . . . ?" she asked.

"No need to worry about it. Reread the section where Cao Cao cajoles Dong Zhuo. Đỗ, do you think Cao Cao is talented?"

"He is, indeed," I answered perfunctorily.

"He's the smartest character in *Three Kingdoms*. How in the world did he get that smart?"

Mrs. Hoàng found the episode and began to read it aloud. Hoàng smoked while listening. He slapped his thighs whenever he heard a good passage and uttered, "So clever! So clever! Darn! Only Cao Cao could do that."

---

5. These are famous classic Chinese novels.

17

A Mistress's Son

Kim Lân

Tư lay in bed. His head felt heavy on the filthy cotton pillow. He stared at the floor without thinking about anything. His arms felt tired and heavy; every now and then, he tried to tap the bed to drive off the sadness and numbness running through his bones. He turned his body to avoid fatigue. He closed his eyes slowly and tried to listen to how his body was feeling. Hunger pains gnawed at his stomach. He appeared haggard. He felt irritable for no reason and wanted to grumble. Tư was so hungry that he fainted. He had not eaten anything for two days. His mother had given him a nickel that he spent the day he received it. He thought she would come back that afternoon, but she had been gone for two days. He had been struggling with hunger since then, and it was unbearable. Tư could do nothing but lie down or sit wearily in his home's tiny, narrow rooms. He had rummaged through all the trunks and clay jars inside and outside the house to see if there was any corn left, although he knew there wasn't. The searching helped alleviate his hunger.

Feeling thirsty, Tư propped himself up. He blinked quickly and closed his eyes to avoid the glare of the sun.

The harsh golden sunlight poured across the yard, filling the old, tiled house with its golden light and a strong smell. He took small sips of water and could feel the liquid flowing down his throat and into his body. For the past two days, he had been drinking water to survive.

Tư was the son of his father's third wife. His parents were married not via an arranged marriage, and not because of love, either. His father was thirty years older than his mother, and his father's first wife, whom he called Old Mom, let her husband marry his mother so that she could take care of the farming. As a woman from the countryside, his mother was familiar with farming. Old Mom treated his mother with kindness—simply because she wanted the job to get done. His father died, and then a year later, Old Mom died. After that, nobody in the family farmed. His half-brothers ran a business in the market, and Tư had to quit school and stay home. He and his mother became jobless. There were no more rice paddies, and they could not run a small business because they had no money.

His half-siblings became indifferent to them, treating them as if they were invisible. Although his mother was poor, she had self-respect and would never ask anyone for help. She became a seamstress to earn money. Oftentimes she couldn't find work, and then she and her son had nothing to eat. On those days, she often stayed out because she didn't want to witness her son's hunger. To help her with this burden, several times Tư had asked her for permission to work as an assistant at the tailor's or wooden clog shops, but they said that they couldn't hire him because their sales had been slow. They promised they would call him in August, so reluctantly, he had to live as a parasite.

Tư contemplated his life. He felt a deep resentment in his heart, especially toward his father for not having taken good care of him. He resented something nameless that had thrown him into such a dire situation. Tư smirked pathetically. A bitter thought came to his mind: as the son of a mistress, he was not responsible for attending to the ancestral altar, so he was an insignificant person. Tư felt uneasy and uncomfortable. His mind was filled with random thoughts. He casually lay down and closed his eyes, wanting to sleep so that negative thoughts wouldn't bother him. But he couldn't fall sleep with an empty stomach. Suddenly, he heard Mr. Cả's voice calling him from outside the gate. Tư sat up, saying, "Yes, sir," loudly, and ran outside to open the door.

Tư greeted Mr. Cả, his eldest half-brother, in a soft voice, but Mr. Cả said nothing and walked inside majestically. He was big and fat while Tư was so skinny. His face was short and round, and he always had a happy, carefree countenance. His skin was rosy and shiny, as if he applied oil to it. He prided himself on his authoritative appearance. He was the owner of a fabric shop, and wherever he went, he always put on nice, impressive clothes and carried a bulging briefcase filled with fabrics, gifts, or candy for his children.

He solemnly looked around the house, frowned, and reprimanded, "The house is too messy. In your free time, you should clean it up a bit."

He was just trying to sound important. In fact, he couldn't care less about the house. That was why, after he came back from the market in town, he played cards at Mrs. Quản Uyển's house, a gambling den, for two days. He took off his headdress and threw it on the table; then he lay flat on the couch with his face up. He looked into the rafters and sighed, exhausted. Then he said to himself, "Damn it! Such bad luck! I lost twenty piasters, and it was just a small game."

He yawned a few times and fell asleep.

Tư swept the house quietly and gently arranged the furniture. After he finished, he went to the kitchen and rested. It was late afternoon. The sunlight faded, receding almost across the entire yard. The sun sank down behind the house; trees cast their shadows on the roof. Occasionally, the foliage that the sunlight traversed quivered when there was a breeze. The water in the pond rippled and pushed floating scum toward a corner. On the bamboo bridge, a young woman was washing rice as the golden sunrays danced on the water's surface. A few gray thatched roofs that emerged from the banana bushes with leaves as shiny as silk emitted lazy smoke. The smoke quietly rose and drifted with the wind, leaving a gentle, elegant impression on the azure sky. The beautiful scene seemed to mock Tư. He sat down on the ground, his back leaning against the yellow wall darkened by smoke. He stared blankly at the gray smoke slowly rising into the air. He heard the sound of rice being washed on the pond's bridge. His mind was troubled as he thought about his neighbor's dinner. He looked sadly at his cold kitchen, imagining the three Kitchen Gods sitting quietly as if pitying themselves in whispers. Tears trailed down his face, flowing silently down his cheeks.

In the living room, Mr. Cả had just gotten up. He stretched his shoulders and twisted his body, his joints cracking. He yawned and called, "Tư."

"Yes, sir."

"You tend to disappear quickly when you have a chance."

Tư stood up wryly and staggered into the living room. Mr. Cả threw a dime on the table and softened his voice.

"Go buy a dime's worth of *phở*."

"Yes, sir."

"Take a bowl with you."

Tư slowly trudged along. Although his hand was holding a bowl of noodle soup, he felt exhausted. Steam rose from the broth. He craved the food. He looked at the tender white noodles in the broth, the thinly sliced beef arranged neatly on top along with onion, cilantro, and pepper. The aroma wafted into his nose. His stomach seemed to wake up; his belly grumbled. Saliva kept flowing from his mouth. He was craving a bowl like this.

Tư placed the bowl of noodle soup on the table for his brother and quietly went to the veranda.

Mr. Cả cursed, "Damn it! The *phở* tastes awful!"

Tư swallowed his saliva. So ironic! After Mr. Cả finished eating, he snatched up his briefcase and left, still bitter about his gambling losses the day before.

After Mr. Cả was gone, Tư didn't even bother to close the door. He intended to take the bowl to the basin to wash it but decided not to because he noticed the leftover broth at the bottom. Nobody would want it, of course, at any other time, but at this moment . . . Tư held the bowl of *phở* to his nose and smelled it; the aroma filled his nostrils. He tasted a mouthful and exclaimed, "Gosh! So delicious!"

He wished he had a bowl of cold rice to mix with the broth. As he thought about cold rice, he remembered one day, when he was hungry, just like today. Thân, his dearest friend, had paid him a visit and insisted that he come to Thân's house.

"Everybody is gone," Thân said. "Just me here today. We're best friends, so I'll be honest with you. Stay here and have cold rice with me."

That cold rice with pickled eggplant was so delicious! Tư still remembered it well, perhaps he would remember it for the rest of his life. He compared Mr. Cả to Thân and was furious. Tư scowled fiercely. He gritted his teeth and threw the bowl of *phở* into the yard. The sound of the broken bowl soothed his anger. He laughed, feeling unreasonable and regretful. Tư was exhausted. His whole body trembled. He lay down and fainted.

●

The afternoon had long passed. The scene darkened. Wind rustled the leaves. The dark foliage swayed against the dark sky. Thân used one hand to carry a parcel wrapped in newspaper and the other hand to push the door open. A screech broke the silence. He walked slowly and looked anxiously into the dark rooms.

"Why is the house so dark?" Thân muttered.

Then he became quiet, knowing that what he said was untactful. He walked leisurely into the living room and put the parcel on the table. His friend, Tư, was still lying on the couch, unaware that Thân had come for a visit.

Thân shook Tư and said, "Tư! Tư!"

Tư mumbled in a tired voice, "Is that you, Thân?"

"Yes. It's me. Were you sleeping?"

"No," he said softly and tiredly. "When you entered, I knew it. But . . . I'm . . . too tired."

Thân sadly looked at his friend in the dark and said in a soft voice, "I'm bringing you some boiled jackfruit seeds. Please eat them."

Tư was so moved. Tears ran down his cheeks. He said in a choked voice, "You're so kind to me."

"You don't need to say that."

The two friends sat quietly in the dark. Tư chewed the seeds in silence. He suddenly thought about his mother, so he lifted his head and said, "Please save half of these." Tư wanted to save some for his mother.

"Sure. There's plenty," Thân said gently.

Tư then thought about himself and his future. The dark future of the son of a mistress. He no longer felt dejected.

"What's going on?" Thân asked.

"Nothing," Tư said.

The two men uttered no more words.

18

Common-law Wife

Kim Lân

Only at dusk, when human faces were inconspicuous, did Tràng come back. On his way home, he ambled along a sinuous, narrow path that went through a village market set up by the new village residents. He was walking and smiling, his small eyes looking attentively into the twilight. His quivering, wide jaw made his ugly face look as if he were thinking of something both interesting and painful. He had a habit of walking and mumbling to himself at the same time. He gibbered and sighed about whatever was on his mind.

The village children, seeing his sturdy body striding down the market path, would rush out and surround him. They laughed and cried noisily.

"Ah, Tràng is back!"

"Tràng, will you pick me up?"

"Have you had some wine for the day, Tràng?"

"Tràng . . ."

Some grabbed him from behind, some from the front, tickling and pulling him. Some grasped his legs and didn't want to let him go. Tràng merely looked up and laughed. That was how the village of newly settled residents had once become lively every afternoon, but now the village children no longer greeted Tràng as usual when he came home. They sat gloomily and quietly at street corners. In the twilight, Tràng walked wearily. His old, brown shirt hung across his arm. His bald head stooped slightly forward. It seemed like his big, broad, bearlike shoulders were burdened with the worries and hardships of the day.

Starvation had come to the village. Influxes of families had arrived here from Nam Định and Thái Bình. They had wrapped sedge mats around their bodies and looked very pale, lying about everywhere in the marketplace. Corpses were as common as rice stubble after a harvest. Not a morning arrived when the villagers, on their way to the market, did not see three or four corpses lying in the street. The air was putrid due to the garbage and dead bodies.

Amid the darkness of hunger and starvation, one afternoon the villagers saw Tràng walking with a strange woman. Tràng looked merrier and more cheerful than ever; he chuckled and his eyes twinkled brightly. The strange woman walked behind him, about three or four steps back, carrying a small straw basket. Her head was bent down and half covered by a torn, tilted hat. She looked shy and demure. Tràng, lest the children tease him as usual, put on a serious look, shaking his head to signal that he wouldn't allow them to tease him that day.

The children did not dare approach; they just stood in place. Suddenly someone shouted, "Tràng!"

Tràng turned around, and the child continued, "You're a couple!"

"Naughty child!" Tràng laughed.

The woman seemed annoyed. She knitted her brows and arranged her shirt. The market at dusk was empty and desolate. Strong winds blew in from the field. The streets were buried in darkness because no houses had lights. Under the banyans and bombax trees, starving people were walking as quietly as ghosts. Crows uttered tragic calls.

The villagers wondered at the shadow of Tràng and the woman walking together. They went to their front doors and talked together, attempting to comprehend what they were seeing. Their dark, gaunt faces suddenly brightened as if something new and fresh were just coming into their dull, hungry lives. A villager sighed. Another asked, "Who's that woman? Could she come from Mrs. Tứ's hometown?"

"No. Even when Mr. Tứ was alive, none of his relatives came for a visit."

"Very strange, isn't it?"

They were silent for a while, but then another chuckled. "Could she be Tràng's wife? Maybe so, because she looks very shy."

"Gosh! Who wants to feed another mouth at this time? We don't even know if we can survive this famine."

Everyone grew quiet again. The woman, knowing that the villagers were talking about her, became even more demure, and her feet fumbled as she walked. Noticing this, Tràng felt quite good, and he strutted. The woman mumbled something. Tràng turned back and asked, "What?"

"Oh, nothing."

"Why do they keep looking at us?" he whined, feeling annoyed.

Behind a dark door, a head popped out. Someone called his name and said, "It's not too late yet. Why don't you come in for some tea?"

Tràng turned his head and politely refused. "Another time."

A bald-headed man winked his eye, looked at the woman, and asked Tràng, "Who is she?"

"Just a friend. Let's talk more next time."

Tràng returned to the path quickly, running after the woman as if he were embarrassed and had to hasten away. When she reached an ancient village shrine, he said loudly, "Go this way." They quietly turned onto a narrow path that cut between two tall bamboo clumps. It was quiet and comfortable there. He tried to say something romantic to her but did not know how. He clumsily fidgeted with his hands while walking with the woman. She said nothing and just looked anxiously at what was in front of her. The bamboo clumps gently rasped in the breeze, and dry leaves rustled under their feet.

For a while Tràng forgot his gloomy life, and even his fears of hunger. In his heart were only the special feelings that he had for the woman—something new and strange that he had never felt before was running through his body, as if someone were lovingly caressing his back.

"Are we close?" the woman asked.

"Almost."

"Anybody home?"

"Just me alone and Mom."

She smiled. "Um, it's either 'alone' or 'with Mom.' You're funny."

"You're right." He laughed.

Their conversation had become a bit friendly by then. He walked closer to her, thinking quietly for a while, held up a small bottle in his hand, and said, "Here is some oil for the lamp tonight."

"Such a luxury!"

"Not really. It cost me two dimes—kind of expensive, but that's okay."

"You shouldn't have spent that much money."

"You're my new wife, so some light for tonight is necessary. We can't just jump into bed together immediately, once the sun goes down." He grinned.

"You're naughty!"

She spanked his backside and scowled. He liked this and laughed. Some dogs were startled and ran into a bush, barking noisily. Tràng picked up a brick and threw it at them, shouting, "Stop barking."

"Not home yet?" she asked.

"No."

"Ummm."

She scowled again and gestured histrionically. Tràng tittered and bent down to lift the latch to open the gate.

"We're home now," he said.

She quietly followed him in. His empty house stood precariously amid a garden full of weeds. She looked around and sighed, her small breasts protruding. Tràng went inside, picked up a torn wattle and set it aside. Then he put away the pots and pans and the clothes that lay scattered on the bed and the floor. He turned back, looked at her, and said with a smile, "See how a house looks if it has no woman."

She smiled back. Tràng gently patted the bed and said, "Have a seat."

She sat down on the edge of the bed, and they both felt awkward. Tràng remained standing in the middle of the house for a few seconds and felt somewhat frightened. He didn't know why he had such feelings. He walked to the front yard and complained, "Why does Mom get home so late today?"

He ran into the street and waited for his mother but then returned and cast a furtive glance at the house. The woman still sat there on the bed, holding her straw basket, and looked puzzled.

Why does she look so sad? Tràng thought. He spat and then smiled. Looking at her sitting in the house, he couldn't believe that everything had happened so fast. Oh, was he now a married man? He hadn't expected everything to occur like this. He was just joking with her and suddenly they became spouses.

Sometimes he went to town with a rice-collection van.[1] Whenever he passed the storage house, he saw women sitting flirtatiously there. He assumed that they were hawking some fallen goods or waiting for someone to hire them to do chores. Once, while pulling an oxcart of rice up a hill, he sang to forget his fatigue, *If you want to eat rice with pork, come help me pull this cart.* He didn't intend flirtation, but the women

---

1. A van belonging to an organization that collected rice for the Japanese before the August Revolution of 1945.

pushed each other and joked among themselves, "He's calling for help. If you want to eat white rice, go help him."

"You don't have white rice and pork," one woman said sarcastically to Tràng. "Are you joking or being serious?" Tràng turned his head, wiped the sweat off his face, and laughed. "Serious, of course. If you want to help, come quick."

She stood up and helped Tràng pull the oxcart. She threw a glance at him and snickered. "I'll give you a hand. What am I afraid of?"

Tràng liked it very much. Since his birth, no woman had given him such a flirtatious smile. On that very day, after loading the cart, Tràng sat down at the market gate to quench his thirst. Then suddenly the same woman came and said, "You're a liar." He looked at her and did not understand what she meant. Actually, he didn't recognize her at that moment, as she looked so skinny in her ragged clothes. Only her eyes could be seen on her haggard, gray face, which looked like a hoe blade.

"You've promised this and that, but you swallowed your words," she said.

He remembered her and smiled. "If I didn't give you what I said last time, then I'll do it today. Why don't you sit down and chew some betel leaves?"

"I'll eat anything but betel leaves."

She stayed standing in place. Touching his pocket, he said, "Okay, eat whatever you want."

Her eyes brightened. "You are *boucoup* rich."[2] Then she asked, "Are you sure? I'll eat."

She sat down and ate. She ate four bowls of *bánh đúc* without saying a word and then used the chopsticks to wipe her mouth. "Very delicious! What if your wife complains that you bring no money home today?"

He laughed. "I have no wife. If you want to go home with me today, come help me load the cart."

Tràng was just joking with her, and she suddenly thought he was being serious. At first, he felt worried, thinking, *These days I can't even feed myself. How can I feed another mouth?* After a few seconds, he clicked his tongue, saying, "It'll be okay." That day he took her into town and bought her a small basket to hold her belongings. Then they went to have a nice meal and pushed the oxcart home together.

---

2. In the original version, Kim Lân wrote *"boucoup* [very] rich."

Suddenly Tràng stopped and listened. He heard someone cough out-side. An old woman was hobbling out of the bamboo clump and up to the gate. She was walking, muttering, and counting something. See-ing his mother, Tràng shouted like a little child and called back at the house, "Hey, Mom is here," and rushed out to greet her.

"Why do you come home so late today? I've been anxiously waiting for you."

Mrs. Tứ blinked her eyes and replied slowly, "What's going on?"

"Mom, just go in first, please."

Mrs. Tứ followed him in. When she reached the garden, she stopped and looked with astonishment. "So strange. Who's that woman? Why is she standing by my son's bed? Why did she call me Mom? She cannot be Mrs. Đục's daughter. Who is she?" The old woman blinked her eyes again, as she felt they were covered with rheum. She looked carefully at the stranger, trying to recognize her. Mrs. Tứ turned to her son and seemed not to understand what she saw.

Tràng cheerfully said, "Why don't you have a seat on the bed first, Mom?"

Mrs. Tứ walked in. The woman thought Tràng's mother had a hear-ing impairment, so she greeted her loudly. "Good evening, Mom."

"Um, who is this?"

Mrs. Tứ then sat on the bed hesitantly and Tràng reminded his mother, "Mom, my wife said hello." Hearing that, Mrs. Tứ was totally confused. He moved closer and said, "She comes here to be my wife. It's karma that brought us together. . . . It is fate. . . ."

Mrs. Tứ bent her head and was silent; she understood now. The poor old mother understood something from experience, and she felt sorry for her son's fate. "Gosh, people get married when everything goes well in their lives, but my son . . ." Tears ran down from her blurry eyes, and she wondered if they would have enough food to eat during the hard, dull days.

Mrs. Tứ sighed and looked closely at the young woman, who was bending her head and touching her torn shirt. Mrs. Tứ thought, *She must be so desperate and starving that she has to marry my son. As a mother, I am not able to care much for him. If they can survive these days, he can be a husband and settle down. If Heaven has decided so, let's accept our fate and stop worrying.*

She coughed and gently said to her new daughter-in-law, "I'm very glad that good karma has brought you together."

Tràng was relieved. He coughed and walked into the garden.

Mrs. Tứ continued, "We're penniless. You two should work hard, and Heaven may bless you with good fortune and prosperity. We never know. No family is poor or wealthy for three consecutive generations. Isn't that true? Work hard to earn money for your children."

As she looked out, darkness covered her eyes. In the distance, a white, bright river twisted and curved across the dark field. A wind carried in the smell of smoldering rice husks from houses that had to attend to dead bodies.[3] She breathed gently and sighed. She thought of her husband and her youngest daughter. She thought of her life, so fraught with hardships and sorrows. She wondered if her son's life would be any better than hers, now that he was married.

"Please sit down. Your legs must be tired," Mrs. Tứ said, feeling compassion and pity for her daughter-in-law.

The daughter-in-law stood still, stirring only a little bit. The old woman lowered her voice and kindly said, "It'd be good if we could afford a small, humble party. But we're so poor, and no one will blame us, especially in this situation. All I hope is that you two will get along well. This year, starvation is a real threat. I love both of you for moving in together, even at this time."

Mrs. Tứ choked and could speak no more. Tears ran down her face. Tràng had been observing and felt uneasy. He walked inside and struck a match to light an oil lamp. Seeing the light, Mrs. Tứ wiped her tears and looked up. "Oh, there's some light to make the house a little brighter. Oil is extremely pricey these days." She then stood up and walked to the other room to lie down. Tràng mumbled, "Crying for nothing."

From the other room, Mrs. Tứ said, "When you have a day off, get some jute and reknit the wattle to separate the rooms."

"Yes, Mom," Tràng replied politely.

He was about to tell the woman to change clothes and lie down, but seeing her sitting there in bewilderment, he didn't dare. He quietly sat down on a chair. Both felt awkward and didn't know what to say. The dim, yellow light from the corner warmed up the house, and its brightness stretched out to the walls. Outside, the wind blowing from the river sounded like people talking. In the quiet, the couple heard someone crying—it was loud and then soft, alternatively. The woman sighed.

"Are you sad?" Tràng asked.

"No."

---

3. Smoldering rice husk produces smoke to drive away the coldness of death.

"You and Mom talked too much, and I had to wait so long." She glanced at him; he moved closer. "It's getting late. Let's go to bed," he suggested.

The woman gently knocked his forehead, saying, "That's all you are waiting for. So naughty!"

He laughed and blew out the light. In the night, the crying became clearer and more noticeable.

The next morning, Tràng got up when the sun was already high. He felt happy, as if he were walking out of a beautiful dream. He couldn't believe that he now had a wife. He put his hands behind his back and walked to the front yard. The summer sunlight blurred his eyes. He kept blinking, but suddenly he noticed something new. The house and the garden looked clean and neat, everything in its place. His ragged, smelly clothes, which had been hanging in the corner for months, were drying outside. Two water barrels under the guava tree, which had always been empty, were full of water. The trash that used to be in the front of the entrance had been cleared.

In the garden, his mother was pulling weeds. His wife was sweeping the yard, and the broom made swishing sounds. Although what he saw was simple, he was completely moved. He suddenly realized that he loved his home more than ever. Now he had a family, and he could have children there. The house was their cozy shelter. His heart was infused with happiness and joy. He was living his life and was responsible for his wife and future children. He ran to the yard and wanted to do something to repair the house.

Mrs. Tứ, seeing her son, said to her daughter-in-law, "Oh, he's up. You go in and have something to eat, or you will be late."

"Yes, Mom."

The woman entered the kitchen. She looked so different that day—a real gentlewoman without a sharp tongue or tart words, as when Tràng had seen her in town. Did she change because of her new status? Mrs. Tứ also felt better than usual. Her old sunken face looked brighter today. She cleaned and straightened the house eagerly, and everybody seemed to be sharing the same thought: cleaning the house and putting things in order would probably change their lives and make them feel less needy.

The meal in a time of starvation looked miserable. In the middle of the torn mat, there lay only some sliced banana hearts and a dish of salt to eat with porridge, but everybody ate happily. Mrs. Tứ ate and talked to her daughter-in-law about her family and her work. She only talked about the happy things that might come in the near future.

"Tràng, when we have some money, we'll buy chickens. I believe that we can put up a chicken coop in that kitchen corner. It won't take long for the hens to produce a whole flock of chicks."

"Yes, Mom," Tràng said politely. Never before had they lived so harmoniously and contentedly. Their happy conversation ceased abruptly. The pot of porridge was soon emptied, after each had eaten half a bowl.

Mrs. Tứ put down her bowl, looked at the newlyweds happily, and said, "Wait for me here. I have something special." A short while later, she came back and said, "This is sweet mung bean soup. Quite delicious."

The daughter-in-law received a bowl from Mrs. Tứ's hands, and her eyes darkened. Tràng also took a bowl from his mother, who was still smiling and said, "It's maize bran, but very good.[4] Try it. Many people in our village can't even afford it."

Tràng picked up a pair of chopsticks and quickly put some in his mouth. He scowled. The taste of bran was so unpalatable that it stuck in his throat. From that moment forward, no one said a word. They swallowed in haste and avoided looking at each other. A sad, bitter feeling penetrated their minds.

An unceasing roll of quick drumbeats began to come from the village's communal house. The crows on the tall bombax trees in the market were frightened and flew up, circling in the sky like dark clouds. The daughter-in-law sighed quietly and asked softly, "Mom, what's that drumming noise?

"The tax-collection drum is sounding.[5] Some people are required to plant jute, and some are required to pay taxes. It's so hard to survive these days." Mrs. Tứ walked outside, afraid that they would see her tears.

The daughter-in-law felt confused. She mumbled, "Do we have to pay taxes here?" Silent for a while, she continued, "Up in Thái Nguyên and Bắc Giang, no one pays taxes. They even destroyed the Japanese rice-storage granaries and distributed rice to the hungry."

Tràng looked haggard. He frowned. The bran in his throat started to melt and tasted bitter. He began to think about the people who had

---

4. Maize bran, a byproduct of processing maize, was typically reserved for feeding pigs.
5. Taxes imposed by the Japanese occupation government.

destroyed the Japanese granaries. He asked quickly, while still chewing, "Were they the Việt Minh?"[6]

"Yes. How do you know?" his wife replied.

He didn't answer. His mind settled upon the scene of the hungry and the starved, flocking along the levies between the rice paddies to reach the granaries. In front of them was a large red flag.

Once, when he heard that the Việt Minh were pillaging rice, he didn't understand and became frightened, and he took his cart by a shortcut to another field. Now he understood that the Việt Minh were attacking granaries and giving rice to the hungry, and he felt vague regret. Drumming continued to call from the village's communal house. His mother and his wife had put down their chopsticks and stood up. He suddenly thought about the flocks of starving people and the fluttering red flag.[7]

---

6. Việt Minh: "A member of the Vietnamese political and military movement that challenged the Japanese and defeated the French between 1941–1954" (*The American Heritage Dictionary*).

7. The communist flag symbolizes hope and optimism.

Acknowledgments

The translators thank the authorized descendants of all the deceased authors whose fiction is included in this book for entrusting us with this wonderful task of translating their fathers' and/or grandfathers' literary works into English. We were able to obtain the copyright permissions thanks to the help of our friends Tạ Duy Anh, Văn Phụng Trường Sơn, and Võ Thị Xuân Hà. We gratefully acknowledge the support of Ms. Amy Farranto, acquisitions editor at Northern Illinois University Press, and Professor Kenton Clymer; they recognized the importance of this project and made it the best it can be. We are grateful to the two reviewers for their time and constructive feedback, and to our dedicated production editor and copyeditor, Jennifer Savran Kelly and Carolyn Pouncy, for their valuable suggestions and meticulous editing of the manuscript.

We thank Dr. Ngô Văn Giá for writing the commentary to help readers gain a profound understanding of *Light Out* and its sociohistorical context. Special appreciation goes to Fulbright University Vietnam for allowing Quan Manh Ha to use his professional development fund to assist faculty with production costs and reprint costs for this scholarly publication. And finally, our most heartfelt thanks go to our beloved families for their love and ineffable support.

CONTRIBUTORS

Khái Hưng (1896–1947) is the pseudonym of Trần Khánh Giư. He was born into a mandarin family in Hải Phòng. He studied at Albert Sarraut High School, the most famous school in Indochina, established in 1919, in Hà Nội. Later, he taught at Thăng Long Private School, where he met Nhất Linh. He joined the Self-Reliant Literary Group, founded by Nhất Linh in 1932, and later became one of the three founding members of the group. He was captured by the Việt Minh and was executed in 1947, at the age of fifty-one.

Kim Lân (1920–2007) received the National Prize in 2001 for his contribution to Vietnamese literature. Although his stories emphasize the marginal living conditions in rural Vietnam in the 1940s and early 1950s, they are optimistic in their portrayal of the simple beauty in the souls of Vietnamese peasants. "Common-law Wife" originally appeared in 1954. It is set during the famine that occurred in the northern provinces of Vietnam from October 1944 to May 1945 under the Japanese occupation, when an estimated two million people starved to death. After the August Revolution in 1945, he continued to write journalistic articles and fiction, and he was mostly inspired to write about the pastoral village culture in northern Vietnam. Besides the canonical story "Common-law Wife," he is known for another famous story titled "Village," which portrays rural Vietnamese people's patriotism and appeared in the *Arts and Letters Magazine* in 1948.

Nam Cao (1915–1951) is the pseudonym of Trần Hữu Tri. He was an acclaimed short-story writer and novelist. Throughout his writing career, Nam Cao was very aware of the responsibility of the realist writer: a writer must exercise both dignity and morality. Some of his famous works include "Chí Phèo" (1941), "Redundant Life" (1943), "The Eyes" (1948), and "Story on the Frontier" (1948). His story "Bright Moon" (1943) is his manifesto on the literary aesthetics of realism, preceded by Vietnamese Romanticism (1930–1945).

Ngô Văn Giá (1959–) is Professor Emeritus of literary studies and creative writing at Hà Nội University of Culture. He is a member of the Vietnam Writers' Association and a well-respected scholar of literature in Vietnam. His research interests include modern and contemporary Vietnamese literature, literary criticism and pedagogy, cultural studies, and journalistic writing. He is the co-editor of *Wild Mustard: New Voices from Vietnam* (Curbstone, 2017).

Ngô Tất Tố (1893–1954) is a famous Vietnamese writer from the first half of the twentieth century. He was also a respected Confucian scholar, journalist, and translator who greatly influenced Vietnamese literature during the colonial period. Proficient in both Han script and French, he participated in one of the last royal examinations. As a nationalist and a patriot, he produced polemical literary works and newspaper articles that exposed the corruption of Vietnam's semifeudal, semicolonial society, France's exploitation of the Vietnamese, and especially the plight of Vietnamese peasants under the French occupation. Ngô's ineffable contributions to modern Vietnamese literature posthumously earned him the Hồ Chí Minh Award of Literature and Arts in 1996.

Nguyễn Công Hoan (1903–1977) was born in Hưng Yên Province in northern Vietnam. He graduated from a teacher training college in 1926 and then taught grade school in Hải Dương, Lào Cai, and Nam Định. After the August Revolution of 1945 against the French, he held various important positions in the North, such as supervisor, editor-in-chief, and chairman of different state organizations. He was a pioneer of Vietnamese critical realism, and his writings, especially his short stories, often satirize the corrupt lifestyles and hypocrisies of the ruling class in the semifeudal, semicolonial Vietnamese society during the early twentieth century. His characters are common and unfortunate people who are victimized by the oppressive colonial system under the French occupation. His stories emphasize an absence of morality and compassion, the effects of materialism and humiliation, and the contrasts between the miserable life of poor peasants and the luxurious life of mandarins, local authorities, and landowners.

Nhất Linh (1906–1963) was born in Hải Dương Province in northern Vietnam and served as the co-founder of the Self-Reliant Literary Group. He had an ineffable influence on Vietnamese prose of the first half of the twentieth century. He studied science, the publication industry, and journalism in France from 1927 to 1930 and returned to Vietnam upon graduation. Nhất Linh—an anticommunist, anti-Việt Minh politician—advocated social reform and political change in Vietnam. After 1954, he moved to the South but soon realized that he could not support the former South Vietnamese government and its president Ngô Đình Diệm. Nhất Linh committed suicide in 1963, in Sài Gòn, leaving behind the message: *Let history render judgment on my life.* His death was mourned by thousands of students, intellectuals, and readers.

Thạch Lam (1909–1942) was a member of the Self-Reliant Literary Group (1932–1945), which was co-founded by his brothers Nhất Linh and Hoàng Đạo. The group promoted the New Poetry movement, individualism in literature, French-influenced romanticism, and modernism. Its members' writings primarily condemned feudalism and Confucian values that suffocated personal pursuits of happiness. After Thạch Lam was denied college admission in France, he worked as a journalist. He is best known for his clear narrative style and the subtlety of his characters' emotions. His fiction differs from that of other members of the group because he preferred to focus on the life of working-class people in countryside settings and did not romanticize reality. In addition, he avoided writing political fiction. Literature, to him, needed to condemn social ills and help people to live morally. During his childhood, he had lived in poverty. He died of tuberculosis at the age of thirty-three, survived by his wife and three children.

Tô Hoài (1920–2014) was born in Hà Nội, and his work was well received in several genres. He started his writing career after the August Revolution of 1945 against the French. His writing style is clear, simple, and oftentimes humorous and witty. Tô Hoài's inspiration primarily came from his close observations of life. The settings of his fiction are either suburban Hà Nội or the mountainous northwest. He earned several prestigious awards presented by the Vietnam Writers' Association, and many of his stories are widely taught in Vietnamese high schools today. His most widely read book is *The Diary of a Cricket*, a children's tale that has been translated into nearly forty languages. His literary virtuosity lies in his masterful versatility in the Vietnamese language and his meticulous delineation of regional settings and their residents.

Vũ Trọng Phụng (1912–1939) is a significant satirist from the early twentieth century. His writings often expose and criticize the ludicrous, corrupt, and decadent lifestyles and behavior of the Vietnamese people who attempted to adopt and practice Europeanization in their own lives. Recurring issues addressed in his fiction are concepts of progress, civilization, social reform, and modernity, which were introduced into colonized Vietnam by the French colonists. He is considered the Balzac of early twentieth-century Vietnam under the French colonial occupation, and his works are best categorized as satire or parody. He died of tuberculosis at the age of twenty-seven in Hà Nội. Some of his works have been translated into English and published in the United States, including *Dumb Luck*, *The Industry of Marrying Europeans*, and *Lục Xì: Prostitution and Venereal Disease in Colonial Hanoi*.

"The Teeth of an Upper-Class Family's Dog" ("Răng con chó của nhà tư sản," or "Răng con vật nhà tư bản"), by Nguyễn Công Hoan. First published in *Tạp chí Annam*, no. 23, 1931. Copyright © 2023 by the author's grandson Lê Trung Trực.

"Two Sisters" ("Hai chị em"), by Nhất Linh. First published in the short-story collection *Tối tăm*, 1936. Copyright © 2023 by the author's son Nguyễn Tường Thiết.

"An Insipid Life" ("Chết dở"), by Nhất Linh. First published in the short-story collection *Tối tăm*, 1936. Copyright © 2023 by the author's son Nguyễn Tường Thiết.

"A Poor Family" ("Nhà nghèo"), by Tô Hoài. First published in the short-story collection *Nhà nghèo*, 1944. Copyright © 2023 by Kim Đồng Publishing House.

"The First Love Letter" ("Lá thư tình đầu tiên"), by Tô Hoài. First published in 1942. Reprinted in *Tuyển tập Tô Hoài*, 1987. Copyright © 2023 by Kim Đồng Publishing House.

"A Mistress's Son" ("Đứa con người vợ lẽ"), by Kim Lân. First published in *Trung Bắc chủ nhật*, in 1942. Copyright © 2023 by the author's son Thành Chương.

"Common-law Wife" ("Vợ nhặt"), by Kim Lân. Written and revised in 1954 and 1955, and first published in the short-story collection *Con chó xấu xí*, 1962. Copyright © 2023 by the author's son Thành Chương.

www.ingramcontent.com/pod-product-compliance
Lightning Source LLC
Chambersburg PA
CBHW030824020726
47499CB00006B/2059